The boy's question startled Wood. "My—my old wife didn't like living in what she called the wilderness."

"That wouldn't be a problem with my mom." Jeremy gave Wood a knowing grin. "You know, I think she's beginning to like you. I heard her tell Aunt Gabby you have possibility. Maybe she's going to like the whole mail-order groom idea after all."

Mail-order groom? The words echoed like thunder in Wood's head. What was Jeremy talking about?

Fragments of conversation with Gabby replayed in Wood's memory. "Hannah needs a man," not "Hannah needs a hired hand." "You're perfect for each other," not "you'll work well together." Wood felt moisture begin to bead on his brow.

"Jeremy, you said once you knew the real reason I was here." At the boy's nod, he continued. "Will you tell me now?"

He gave Wood a puzzled look, then said matter-of-factly: "Sure. You're going to marry my mom."

ABOUT THE AUTHOR

Pamela Bauer was born and raised in the Midwest and still makes her home in a small community in Minnesota, with a cornfield in her backyard. She and her husband of twenty-seven years have two children and a dog who, Pam says, thinks he's human! Pam hails from a big family, and most of the books she's written in her ten-year career feature the family relationships she knows so much about. And *Mail Order Cowboy* is no exception—what with a meddlesome matchmaking aunt, a young son who wants a dad and one unknowing husband-to-be!

Books by Pamela Bauer

HARLEQUIN AMERICAN ROMANCE
668—THE PICK-UP MAN

HARLEQUIN SUPERROMANCE
236—HALFWAY TO HEAVEN
288—HIS AND HERS
330—WALKING ON SUNSHINE
378—THE HONEY TRAP
406—MEMORIES
481—SEVENTH HEAVEN
484—ON CLOUD NINE
487—SWINGING ON A STAR
548—THE MODEL BRIDE
605—I DO, I DO
670—MERRY'S CHRISTMAS

MAIL ORDER COWBOY

PAMELA BAUER

Harlequin Books

TORONTO • NEW YORK • LONDON
AMSTERDAM • PARIS • SYDNEY • HAMBURG
STOCKHOLM • ATHENS • TOKYO • MILAN
MADRID • WARSAW • BUDAPEST • AUCKLAND

This book is dedicated to Cheri Haack and the other
145,000 women farmers who every spring "lay it all on
the line" so that the rest of us can put food on the table.

Thanks, Cheri, for the inspiration and for taking the time
to talk farming with this city slicker.

ISBN 0-373-16718-0

MAIL ORDER COWBOY

Copyright © 1998 by Pamela Muelhbauer.

Prologue

As James Woodson Harris sat astride his horse with his hands tied behind his back, his life passed before his eyes. In a split second he witnessed a jumbled sequence of images in a condensed history of his life.

He saw himself falling off the paddock fence when he was only three, his teacher slapping his knuckles with her metal ruler in the one room school-house when he was seven, his mother wiping his brow as he suffered with rheumatic fever at nine, his father lying in a casket in the parlor when he was fourteen, Jenny walking toward him on their wedding day, the stagecoach taking her away six months later.

Thunder rumbling in the distance brought the images to an abrupt end. Wood looked up at the sky and willed the dark clouds to part and deliver a bolt of lightning to the small gathering of men. It was probably the only thing that could save him now. That or a sudden appearance by the sheriff. Actually, he wasn't sure if the lawman's presence would change anything, for it was an out-of-control, angry group of men who milled about the oak tree.

A noose dangled in front of Wood's face and he heard

a stony voice order, "Get that damned thing on so we can get out of here before it storms."

Jeering echoes of the sentiment ricocheted through the small crowd. Someone took great pleasure in pointing out the fact that Wood's skin was the same sickly shade of green as the sky.

Wood gagged as the rope encircled his neck, momentarily cutting off his breath in a preview of what was to come. Panic rose within him. "You're making a mistake," he tried to protest, but there was barely enough air for breathing. There was none for speaking.

He felt a glove sting his cheek. "Shut your filthy mouth. Hangin's too good for you. If I had my way I'd stretch you out like a piece of leather and let the vultures eat your flesh, peck by peck."

The horse beneath Wood shifted restlessly, and more thunder rumbled. Angry cries for vengeance filled the air. Hopelessness engulfed Wood as rapidly as the dark clouds had swallowed up blue sky.

"Wait!" A raspy voice rose above the chorus. "I need to give him the sand of salvation. Let me through."

Wood tried to get a glimpse of the person who spoke, but all he could see was a small, hunched-over, dusty figure of a woman whose head sported a large hat with a brim so wide it hid her face. If it weren't for her tattered skirt, he might have mistaken her for a man.

"I said let me through," she repeated irritably. "I need to give him his last rites."

The man who had slipped the noose around Wood's neck snickered. "He deserves no rites."

To Wood's surprise, however, the crowd parted as if this haggard woman were Moses at the Red Sea. The hangman spat in disgust. "I suppose it's only fitting that the last person to touch you should be an old crone who spreads vile odors."

"Vile?" The woman made a sound of indignation as she

pushed back the brim on her hat and stared up at the hangman. "You're the one who's vile. I bring sweet salvation." She smiled a toothless grin that put to rest any suspicions that the lines in her face could be from the sun.

When she turned her attention to Wood, a wave of uneasiness washed over him. The grim smile disappeared, and her eyes pierced him with an eerie awareness. A pungent aroma assaulted his nostrils.

"Someone give me a boost up," she spat out, in an order that went unheeded.

She repeated the command several times before a scruffy-looking youngster, who couldn't have been more than sixteen, stepped forward. The young man grimaced at the stench emanating from the old lady's decrepit body, but did as she directed. He lifted her so that she was eye-to-eye with Wood, her bony frame only inches from his muscular torso.

In all of his thirty-four years Wood had never seen a woman with so many wrinkles on her face. Every inch of exposed flesh appeared to be creased by time, which was why he was surprised to discover her touch was as gentle as a summer breeze in evening.

She smoothed gnarled fingers across his forehead, down his cheeks and over his jaw, mumbling in a language unknown to Wood. Disparaging comments filtered through the crowd, and the hangman warned her to hurry. When she wrapped her arms around Wood's waist, he didn't flinch. In an odd way her touch comforted him, and he wondered why she should concern herself with a stranger about to hang for two murders. He soon realized that she wasn't trying to console him, but was tying a string around his midsection.

"All right, all right. That's enough," a gruff voice interrupted her chanting. "You're done." The hangman ordered the lad to put her down, but she protested, claiming she hadn't finished what she'd come to do.

She pried Wood's fingers open, saying, "Hold tight to your salvation." She poured sand into his palm, then closed his fist once more. "Whatever you do, don't open your hand," she warned close to his ear.

Another clap of thunder split the air, and suddenly a great gust of wind shook the tree. The horse whinnied and Wood knew the time had come. He had seen his life pass before his eyes. Next would come the flash of light.

"Let's get it over with!" The leader of the vigilantes cried out as the storm clouds roiled overhead.

The old woman disappeared into the angry mob, and Wood heard the slap on the horse's hindquarters. In a split second the noose tightened about his neck as the horse moved out from beneath him.

"I'm not guilty!" he wanted to cry out, but the rope choked back his words. At the realization of what was about to happen, he called out in despair, "Hannah!"

Then there was a flash of light so bright he thought his body would surely explode in its brilliance.

He heard nothing. No explosion, no voices, no angels calling him to the heavens. Again, life flashed before his eyes, but this time he recognized none of it. It was as if he were in someone else's body, seeing events and places foreign to him. He closed his eyes and waited for the pain that was sure to follow, but he felt nothing, just an odd sensation tingling through his limbs.

Then he realized his hands were free. He reached for the noose choking him, only to discover it was no longer there. With a thud he felt himself hit the ground, and then there was blackness. There could be only one explanation.

He had to be dead.

His last conscious thought was that he would never see Hannah again.

Chapter One

Present Day

After several hours of trying to balance the figures in the ledger, Hannah Davis finally gave up and closed the book with a decisive thud. Staring at the numbers wasn't going to change a thing. She was still borrowing from Peter to pay Paul.

Once again she was playing her hand and hoping to win. Only in this game Mother Nature held the wild cards. It was the same gamble all farmers took when they planted their crops in the spring. Hannah laid it all on the line, betting the weather wouldn't force her to fold.

It was what she liked least about farming—having to depend upon something so totally out of her control. And in Minnesota the growing season was short, meaning the gamble was a big one.

She scrunched up her scratch paper and tossed it at the trash can in the corner. It missed its target. "Damn."

"Numbers must be pretty bad if you're cussing this early in the day."

At the sound of her great-aunt's scratchy voice, Hannah got up to retrieve the paper from the floor.

"It's not any worse than any other year. I need a little luck with the weather."

"What you need is a man." Gabby waggled a finger at her niece.

"I need a lot of things, but a man is not one of them," Hannah retorted, although she knew it would do no good to argue with the gray-haired woman hovering at her side. As dear as she was, Gabby was set in her ways. Actually, *cemented* would be a better word.

"I don't know why you're so stubborn when it comes to men."

"Yes, you do." Hannah retorted, shoving the ledger into a drawer. "Men don't stay."

"Not all men leave. Your grandfather was married to your grandmother for thirty-seven years."

"Poor grandmother."

Gabby clicked her tongue. "The reason the two of you clashed so often was because you're a lot like him—you're stubborn, but in a good way."

"Gee, thanks for the compliment." Sarcasm laced her voice.

Affection softened the edge on Gabby's words. "I know it's important to you to prove to the world that you can make a go of the farm without a man's help, but it wouldn't hurt to have a man around the place—and I'm not talking about a part-timer like Barry."

Hannah briefly closed her eyes. What was the use in arguing with a woman who had lived all her life in the shadow of her older brother…a man who had thought he was an authority on what a woman could and couldn't do? No, Hannah couldn't blame Gabby for being her grandfather's sister.

"Well, we don't have a man, so we're going to have to get by without one," she stated flatly.

"For now, maybe." Although Gabby had been retired for ten years from her position as head librarian at the county library, she often sounded as if she were still behind the checkout counter collecting fines on overdue books.

That was the voice she used now, when she said, "If you're going to town, you'd better wash that spot off your shirt."

Hannah dabbed at the dark smudge. "I bet it's grease. I changed a belt on the combine this morning."

Gabby clicked her tongue again. "I thought Barry was supposed to do all that mechanical stuff."

"He is, but you know how busy he's been, what with taking Caroline to those expectant-parent classes. Besides, I can take care of the machinery."

"That's not the point. You shouldn't have to do it. Your grandfather—"

"Grandfather is the reason I'm in the financial bind I'm in," Hannah finished for her. "And you and I both know that it's because he had old-fashioned ideas that a woman couldn't run a farm without a man's help."

"You've proved him wrong." Gabby's voice held admiration. "If he were alive today, he'd be proud of you."

"I wouldn't be running the farm if he were still alive," Hannah said soberly.

"But you are in charge and you're doing a wonderful job. And if it weren't for the debts..."

"We'll manage the debt," Hannah told her confidently.

"But you shouldn't have to. If you would just reconsider his suggestion."

"Don't you mean his order?"

Gabby sighed. "You're running out of time. Next month you turn thirty. The money will be gone..." She let the words dangle temptingly.

"I don't care about the money." It wasn't exactly true. Hannah did care about her inheritance, but the one thing she would not do was marry to get it. Which was exactly what her eccentric grandfather decreed was necessary. Just because he didn't trust a woman to run his farm, he had put a provision in his will making it necessary for her to marry before her thirtieth birthday or lose the farm. So far Hannah had been able to borrow enough money to keep going, but one more poor harvest could spell financial disaster.

Needing to put the subject of her grandfather and his will behind her, she lifted the hem of the lace curtain covering the window. A bank of clouds lingered on the western horizon. "Is it supposed to rain?"

"The gal on channel seven said there's only a twenty percent chance for showers late this afternoon."

"It looks like Filmore County could be in that twenty percent." Hannah gazed pensively out the window for several more seconds before letting the curtain fall. "I wonder if I should skip going to town."

"But what about your appointment at the beauty shop?"

Hannah glanced at the clock on the wall. "I could reschedule it for tomorrow."

Disappointment caused Gabby's mouth to droop. "You should go. You've been complaining that your hair is too long. And I bet Marlis is counting on you coming in today."

"I don't think she'll mind if I reschedule."

"But what about the chicken bedding? Didn't you promise Jeremy you'd pick it up?"

If Hannah didn't know better, she'd think her aunt wanted her out of the house. The thought of her niece not going to town was putting additional furrows in her already-wrinkled brow. The question was Why?

Hannah eyed her curiously. Gabby looked pretty well groomed for a weekday. A fresh coat of lipstick outlined her mouth, and the faint aroma of lilacs drifted through the kitchen. Instead of slippers, she wore shoes and nylon stockings. Maybe the bloom in her aunt's cheeks wasn't from the heat, which was unusually oppressive for September. Could it be her aunt was expecting a guest?

If she was, why hadn't she told Hannah? Unless it was someone she wanted to keep secret. Like a man.

The idea was almost too incredible for Hannah to contemplate. Gabby had been single all her life. It was true that old Bernie Lamphart had had a crush on her ever since they'd been teens. The whole town knew about that, and they also knew Gabby had no time for the retired grocer. She had no interest in men.

Or did she? Hannah wondered.

Lately Gabby had insisted she be the one to bring in the mail. Hannah had attributed her anxiety to sweepstakes fever. She knew her aunt entered every contest she could get her hands on, with the hope of becoming the next millionaire. Now Hannah wondered if maybe it wasn't a personal letter Gabby anticipated. Was she corresponding with a man...a man who was coming to visit her today?

"Are you expecting company?" Hannah asked, getting straight to the point.

Gabby looked flustered by the question. "Er, Mabel said she might bring by some of her freshly canned tomatoes."

It was a lie. Hannah could tell by the way her aunt's eyes avoided hers. "Oh. Is that why you baked the strudel?"

"Umm-hmm," she said, turning her back to Hannah. She pretended to smooth crumbs from the countertop.

Hannah found it rather amusing that her usually chatty aunt was at a loss for words. Maybe Bernie had finally worn down Gabby's resistance. She thought about possible candidates for her aunt's suitor. Understanding how awkward it would be to be seventy-five and never to have had a boyfriend, Hannah decided to give the woman some privacy.

"I think maybe I will go to town," she decided aloud. "You're right. My hair is too long."

The relief on Gabby's face was obvious. "What time should I expect you back?"

"Probably not before four-thirty or five. I need to stop at the implement dealer and order a couple of parts for the gleaner."

"It'll do you good to get your hair done. You want to look your best—just in case..."

"Just in case what?" Hannah asked.

"Why in case you run into someone special," she said with a naiveté Hannah found amusing.

She knew her aunt was an incurable romantic. Maybe it came from her being single all of her life. Hannah could have told her that romance was overrated, but what good would it have done? If Gabby wanted to fantasize about love, who was Hannah to deny her?

It was the image of Gabby standing on the porch, her cheeks glowing, that Hannah took with her as she drove to town. Getting a haircut was only one of the reasons for visiting Marlis at the Cut and Curl. The other was to get information. If there was anything happening between two people in Filmore County, Marlis Thatcher would know about it.

Hannah smiled to herself as she drove the pickup down the dusty road. Did Gabby really think she could keep this mystery man a secret?

IT WAS PAST THREE O'CLOCK and there was still no sign of him.

Gabby paced between the kitchen table and the window, pausing only to lift the corner of the curtain and glance outside. When the grandfather clock in the living room chimed on the half hour, she went back upstairs to her room and pulled a small metal box from the closet.

After getting a tiny key from the zippered compartment inside her purse, she took the box over to her bed. Like a secret agent uncovering clandestine information, she unlocked the lid and extracted an envelope.

Inside was a letter which she unfolded and read.

Dear Ms. Davis,

I write this letter in response to your ad in the personals. Like you, I've never done anything like this before, but I figure it's worth a shot, since I too am lonely. I am a hard-working man who neither smokes nor drinks. That doesn't mean I don't like to have a good time. I do. I'm as comfortable dancing the polka as I am baling hay. Most important of all, I am an honest man. Although I've moved around quite a bit, I've reached a time in my life when I'm ready to settle down in one place. I was glad to hear you're looking for a husband because I'm looking for a wife. Could it be we're looking for each other? I guess the only way to find out is for us to meet. If you tell me the time and place, I'll be there. One thing I can assure you is that I'm not afraid of hard work.

I've enclosed my picture. If I meet with your approval, I'll come just as soon as you let me know you're ready for me.

Sincerely, Alfred J. Dumler.

It was a drastic measure—advertising for a mail-order groom—but the situation called for drastic measures. If her niece wasn't going to make one last effort to save the farm, then Gabby had to take matters into her own hands.

She stared at the three-by-five photograph of a sturdy-looking man sitting on a tractor. It had been taken from such a distance that it was difficult to see the man's face clearly. Nor did it help that the picture had been creased in the mail. When Gabby had called to talk to him on the phone, he had sounded eager to come and visit the farm. So why wasn't he here? Had he changed his mind? Was her plan going to fizzle?

She looked again at her watch. Maybe the bus was running behind schedule. That would explain it. She reached for the telephone directory only to realize that she needed to turn on a light to see. Not only had the sun disappeared, but daylight was rapidly vanishing as well. It wasn't even four o'clock, yet it was as dark as dusk.

Gabby glanced out the dormer window and saw that the gray clouds that had loomed on the horizon a short while ago had pushed their way across the sky. Doing the pushing was a dark bank of storm clouds that had Gabby forgetting about phoning the bus company. She scurried about to close the windows.

Just as a gust of wind caught the back screen door and sent it banging against the outside of the house, Gabby heard a young boy's voice calling "Mom!"

Gabby hurried downstairs and ushered ten-year-old Jeremy inside. "Your mother's in town, Jeremy. Get in here before the rain starts," she instructed, catching the banging screen door.

"But I can't find Outlaw!"

"He's probably out in the barn with the cats." Gabby pushed Jeremy into the kitchen and bolted the back door shut, just as a bolt of lightning hit the sky.

"He didn't come to meet me at the bus stop," Jeremy told her, slinging his backpack over a kitchen chair. He ran to an open kitchen window and whistled. "Outlaw! Here, boy!"

When the first drops of rain hit the windowpane, Gabby ordered Jeremy to close it. As the skies dumped sheets of water all around them, she clasped her hands together and prayed, "Oh, please, not hail. We're almost ready to harvest."

Jeremy's face wore the same look of concern. "So far so good," he told her a few minutes later, his nose pressed against the pane. When another bolt of lightning split the sky, Gabby pulled him away.

"You know what your mother said about being near the window when there's lightning," she warned.

Jeremy backed away slowly. "That's weird," he said as he continued to stare outside but at a safe distance from the glass. "There's all sorts of lightning, but there's no thunder."

"We can't hear it because we're inside."

"But look at all that lightning! What if Outlaw got struck!"

Gabby drew Jeremy into the circle of her arms. "That dog's too smart to be outside in the rain. I'm sure he's in one of the sheds," she said in a soothing tone.

"I hope so. It would be awful to be stuck outside in this stuff."

Gabby was worried, too, but not about Outlaw. She could picture a man carrying a suitcase getting drenched by the rain. She could only hope the bus had been delayed.

For several minutes they watched in silence as the rain and lightning continued.

As soon as it stopped, Jeremy made a bee-line for the door.

"Where are you going?" Gabby called after him.

"To find Outlaw."

Gabby thought about going with him, but worried that Alfred Dumler might try to call. It was probably better that she wait at the house.

That didn't prevent her from anxiously pacing back and forth between kitchen window and back door, squinting as she stared out at the drive leading to the county road. A call to the bus company confirmed her suspicions—the bus was running behind schedule. However, it had already passed through Stanleyville, which meant Mr. Dumler would have arrived by now were he coming.

Gabby hung up the phone with a sigh. Maybe it wasn't going to be easy after all. If she couldn't find a husband for Hannah in the personal ads, where would she look next?

JEREMY HAD BEEN through the barn, the two pole sheds, even the chicken coop, but there was no sign of Outlaw.

He had searched nearly every inch of the homestead without any luck. There was only one place left to look.

The Nelson forty, which was next to the highway.

Fear forced its way into his chest causing his heartbeat to accelerate. Jeremy rode his bike down the dirt road with urgency. He didn't want to believe that Outlaw could be lying on the asphalt hurt—or worse yet, dead.

He said a quick prayer and pedaled faster.

He was halfway down the dirt road when he heard the faint sound of barking. The closer he got to the highway, the stronger the barking became. A smile spread across Jeremy's face. It was Outlaw. He'd recognize that bark anywhere.

Jeremy jumped off his bike. "Outlaw. Here, boy!" He whistled through his teeth, but the dog didn't come to him, though he continued to bark.

Again Jeremy called to him. Finally, the part collie, part St. Bernard came running out of a small grove of trees. He stopped about midway, barked, then turned around and ran back to the trees.

Jeremy followed him, running through tall grass. It was an area of the farm that hadn't been cleared for planting and was called the Nelson forty because it was forty acres of land his great-grandfather had purchased from a man named Nelson. It was too hilly for irrigation, so thick brush and gnarly old trees—many of them dead—were left to grow wild. Jeremy had wanted to build a tree house in one of the old oaks, but his mother had nixed the idea. His grandfather had said it was because it was the only place on the farm ever to be hit by lightning—a memory firmly planted in his mother's mind.

Outlaw continued to bark and jump around excitedly. As Jeremy drew closer, he saw that the oak tree he would have used for a tree house had been struck by lightning. A huge limb had been ripped away from the trunk, leaving the tree split in two.

Then later he saw why Outlaw was barking. A man lay on the ground beneath the oak.

The branch that had been torn off rested directly above his head. The man's position made it look as if he had fallen off the tree when the limb had split away. His arms were raised over his head, his legs spread apart, almost as if he were making a snow angel, Jeremy thought. Cautiously, he moved closer to him.

"Mister, are you all right?"

There was no sound except for Outlaw's barking.

"Outlaw, shut up!" After a couple of whines of protest, the dog finally quit barking.

Jeremy knelt down beside the man and leaned over him. His clothes were dusty and awfully wrinkled. Everything was brown—his shirt, his vest, even his jeans, which were tucked inside black boots that came nearly to his knees. His dark hair was littered with debris—mainly straw and leaves—and dirt streaked his sunburned face.

"How do you suppose he got so dirty?" Jeremy asked Outlaw in a near whisper.

The dog whimpered and sniffed the inert man.

"Stop that," Jeremy scolded him, throwing his arm in the front of the dog and effectively pushing him out of the way. "Don't get so close to him. Mister, can you hear me?" Again Jeremy spoke, but the man showed no reaction. Not the thick, dark brows framing closed eyes, nor the slightly crooked nose, nor the thick bushy mustache, trimming lips that looked dry and cracked from the sun.

"Do you think he's dead?" Jeremy asked Outlaw in a small voice.

Outlaw barked.

"He's not," Jeremy protested. "Or at least I don't think he is." He really didn't know for sure, but he didn't want to contemplate the possibility that there was a dead man beside him. It was too spooky.

Still, he needed to know for sure. "Go ahead, boy. Say

hello to him.'' This time Jeremy urged the dog forward.
The collie sniffed around the man's form, but didn't lick
his face—which is what Jeremy hoped he would do.

"I guess if you won't touch him, I'm going to have to,"
Jeremy told Outlaw with a grimace.

The question was, where? There were only three places
with exposed flesh—his face, his neck and his hands.
Somehow it didn't seem right to mess with his face. And
his neck…well, that had an ugly bruise on it in the shape
of an upside down *V*. He couldn't touch a sore on another
person's body. That left only his hands.

Both were curled tightly into fists. Warily, Jeremy
reached for the left one. His fingers hung in the air over
the knuckles for several seconds before they finally made
contact. As his skin met the stranger's, a tingling sensation
prickled Jeremy's fingertips, traveling up his arm and
throughout his body. Startled by the sensation, he jumped
backward.

"He must have been struck by lightning. He's giving off
shocks!'' Jeremy told Outlaw who had withdrawn as far
away as his master. Jeremy glanced once more at the broken tree, then hopped on his bike and pedaled as fast as he
could back to the house, Outlaw racing alongside of him.
By the time they reached the porch, they were both winded.

"Gabby, there's a dead man in the Nelson forty! He must
have been hit by lightning cuz he's dead, and when I
touched him it felt like electricity was running through my
whole body!'' Jeremy said in a rush, his eyes wide, his face
flushed.

Gabby felt her heart race. "Jeremy, slow down and re-
peat yourself. You're talking too fast. Now tell me what's
wrong,'' she instructed, not wanting to believe she could
have heard him correctly.

"I told you. There's a dead man in the Nelson forty!''
He recounted how he had found the man while looking for
Outlaw.

Gabby felt her knees go weak. "Oh, my," she cried out, then sank down onto the wooden porch swing. "Oh, this can't be. It just can't be. He can't be dead!"

"He looks dead," Jeremy assured her.

Gabby pulled a lace-trimmed handkerchief from her pocket and dabbed at her brow. A dead man in the Nelson forty was bad enough, but a dead man who had answered an ad and was coming to visit Hannah was horrible. A live mail-order groom was going to be difficult enough to explain to Hannah, but a dead one? Gabby fanned her cheeks with her handkerchief. "I need a glass of water. Go quickly!" she panted.

Jeremy did as he was instructed. Gabby took a sip, then splattered a few drops on her wrists. After regaining her composure, she stood and said, "We'd better take a look at him."

"It's a long walk," Jeremy warned her.

"I'll make it." Normally Gabby wouldn't even consider walking to the Nelson forty, but she needed to get to Alfred Dumler—if it was Alfred Dumler—before Hannah returned. She followed Jeremy out the back door and down the dirt road.

Through the tall grass they trekked, Jeremy with the exuberance of a child running ahead of her. By the time Gabby caught up with him in the Nelson forty, he was slowly spinning around.

Short of breath, Gabby asked, "How much farther is it?"

"He's not here!" Jeremy circled the oak in disbelief. "He was right here beneath this big branch." His foot kicked at the limb that had fallen off the tree.

Gabby felt an enormous sense of relief. At least Alfred Dumler wasn't dead. It might not have even been the mail-order groom Jeremy saw. "Maybe it was someone taking a nap...you know, a hitchhiker."

"He looked dead."

"Thank goodness he wasn't." Gabby put her arm around

her nephew's shoulder. "Come. Let's go get the mail, then we'll go back to the house, and I'll make you some lemonade."

They walked back down the road until they came to the big gray mailbox resting on a wooden post. Gabby reached inside and pulled out the stack of envelopes. Before she had a chance to look at them, Jeremy shouted, "Look. There he is!"

Gabby looked up and saw a strange man, who was obviously disoriented. He staggered as he walked, moving first in one direction, then another. Even from a distance Gabby could see that he looked like a transient. Before she could warn Jeremy not to go after him, he and Outlaw were already running in his direction. Gabby had no choice but to follow.

The man stopped moving when he saw the pair of them coming toward him. Gabby tried to connect the scruffy-looking man with the clean-cut farmer in the photograph in her lock box. She was about to dismiss the possibility that it could be Alfred Dumler when the man called out, "Hannah?"

"Gabby, he knows my mom's name!" Jeremy said in a fearful voice.

Gabby's heart beat in her throat. Slowly she approached the man. "What are you doing here?"

"I'm looking for Hannah...." Before he could say another word, the stranger passed out in a heap at their feet.

"Oh, my!" Gabby declared in horror, dropping the small pile of mail. "It *is* him!"

Chapter Two

Jeremy automatically stooped to pick up the mail, which the wind was threatening to scatter in several different directions. "You know him?" He looked at his aunt quizzically as he handed her what he thought was all of the mail. Unnoticed by either of them was a thin white envelope that had lodged itself between two stalks of corn.

"I might." She wrung her hands together as she stared at his unshaven face. "I'm not sure. It's hard to tell if he's the man in the picture."

"What picture?"

Gabby didn't answer. "He did ask for your mother, didn't he?"

"Yeah, but—"

"Then it must be him."

"Who?"

"Alfred Dumler. Although he's not at all what I expected." She studied the unconscious man, pressing a finger to her lips as she contemplated what she should do now that he had actually arrived.

"How come he's dressed so weird?" Jeremy wanted to know.

It was a question Gabby wanted answered, too. Although the photo of Mr. Dumler had been creased, making it difficult to see his face, she could tell that he was a clean-cut young man. It was one of the reasons she had agreed to his visit. He had *looked* trustworthy. Now that he was here, she could see she may have made a serious error in judgment.

His clothes were wrinkled, his hair unruly and his jaw unshaven. And he was dirty. Why, he looked like a bum! How dare he mislead her into thinking he was suitable husband material! Gabby would have liked to boot his dirty butt right back on the bus and send him back to Nebraska.

Two things stopped her. One was the fact that he was obviously not able to get back on the bus, and the other was her stubbornness. She refused to believe that she could have been wrong about her choice for Hannah's mail-order groom.

Gabby studied his sunburned face. He did have a straight nose—well, almost straight—which in Gabby's opinion meant he was a good decision maker. That small bump halfway down indicated he worked hard. As a nose reader, Gabby was the best, and this guy's proboscis told her he had good qualities. The tattered clothes could simply mean he had been down on his luck.

The longer Gabby stared at the man's face, the less offensive it became. In fact, she began to find it attractive—despite the grime and the beard stubble. It had a mustache, a good, strong chin and a mouth that even in repose said "I get my way." Gabby figured he probably wouldn't put up with any crap from anyone. Not even Hannah, who Gabby knew liked to give men crap.

"Maybe we should call 911," Jeremy suggested, but Gabby quickly dismissed the idea. She didn't need anyone in town finding out what she had done. She hadn't even told Hannah, who would raise a holy fit if the residents of Stanleyville knew about the plan before she did.

"We should get him some water," Gabby said anxiously. "If he's been walking in the sun, he's probably suffering from heat exhaustion."

"I think he was hit by lightning," Jeremy contended.

Gabby shook her head. "Uh-uh. Look at his clothes. If he had been caught in the storm they'd be all wet."

"Not if he stood under a tree." Jeremy lowered his voice as he said, "He's got marks on his throat."

It was then that Gabby saw the deep red bruise ringing his neck. Could Jeremy be right? "Run back to the house and get some water," she ordered the boy.

While he was gone, Gabby was careful not to get too close to the man. Even if he was Alfred Dumler, a man whose references she had checked carefully, she knew it would be wise to keep a safe distance. After all, she was alone.

She grimaced as she thought of what Hannah would say if she were to see him now. It was going to be hard enough to convince her she needed a groom, but this one? Gabby shuddered. What on earth could have happened to Mr. Dumler?

It was with a sigh of relief that she watched Jeremy come riding toward her on his bike, Outlaw at his side.

"Here. I put ice in it." He handed Gabby a red plastic water bottle with a built-in straw.

Gabby pulled her handkerchief from her pocket and bent down over the man. She poured a little water onto the handkerchief and dabbed gently at his sunburned face. Next, she drizzled water across his cracked lips. "Jeremy, boy, I think he's coming to."

WOOD OPENED HIS EYES expecting to find a mob of angry men swarming him. Instead, an elderly woman and a young boy stood over him, looking at him with the same strange curiosity he knew must be on his face.

"What happened?" he asked, his voice barely above a whisper.

"You fainted," the old woman answered. "Too much sun, I guess."

Behind the wire-framed glasses, blue eyes revealed a

gentle spirit. Was she the one who had saved him from the lynch mob? Her voice sounded familiar, similar to the old woman who had ministered to him just before he had hung, yet she was obviously not the crone. Still, when she brushed gnarled fingers over his brow, he had the sensation that she had done so before.

He raised himself on his elbows and tried to survey the land around him, but a sharp pain in his neck had him squeezing his eyes shut. Carefully, he turned, looking for any signs of rifle-toting men on horseback, but he saw none. Only fields of tall corn...and these two oddly dressed people.

"Did you save my life?" he asked, wincing. His throat felt as if he had swallowed a torch.

The old woman and the young boy exchanged glances. "Jeremy found you in the Nelson forty. We thought maybe you had heatstroke...you know, from walking with your suitcase and all. By the way, where is your suitcase?"

Heatstroke? Suitcase? Why would he have been walking when he had a horse? Didn't she realize that her neighbors had tried to hang him?

"You look confused. Don't worry. That's what too much sun does to a person."

"It's hot," Wood rasped.

She chuckled. "No one expects Minnesota to be this hot in September. I remember back in 1940 when it hit ninety-two degrees on the fourteenth of September. It was my cousin Eileen's wedding." She shook her head wistfully. "She chose September thinking it would be cool."

Had she said *1940*? He frowned. She must have said *1840*, which would mean her family had been among the original settlers in this area.

Again he surveyed his surroundings. What had happened to the Nelson Homestead? The log house where he had stayed, the corral where they kept their horses, the open prairie for grazing? They were nowhere in sight.

His hands weren't tied, and there was no rope around his neck. Wood thought the horse had slipped out from beneath him and that he had tumbled to the ground. Maybe he hadn't fallen to the ground but ridden away on the horse. Yet how could that have happened unless someone had slipped the noose from his neck and untied his hands?

"Did you get hit by lightning?" the boy asked.

Wood wondered if that's what had happened to him. Could it be that a bolt of lightning had saved his life? The last thing he could recall was a bright flash of light.

"I reckon I might have been," Wood answered cautiously. "The truth is, I can't remember."

"You are Alfred Dumler, aren't you?" the gray-haired woman asked.

Wood wanted to tell them that his name was James Woodson Harris, but thought better of it. He wasn't sure who these people were, but it would do him no good to reveal his name—especially not if he was still wanted for murder. They obviously knew the Nelsons—she said they had found him in the Nelson forty. What "the forty" was he had no idea, but he wasn't going to inquire, either. It was because of George Nelson that he had nearly been hanged.

The thought of how close he had come to death caused him to shudder. No, he couldn't let anyone know that he was Wood Harris, the man falsely accused of killing this old woman's neighbors. Before he could answer her question, she shot him another one.

"Maybe you should tell us why you're in our cornfield?"

"I don't know how I got here, ma'am," he answered honestly.

"What *do* you remember?" she asked.

"I was looking for Hannah. She's—" he paused, rawness in his throat again making it difficult to speak.

The old lady smiled. "I know who Hannah is. It's okay,

Alfred. You don't need to explain. We've been expecting you."

"You have?"

"Sure. Everything's a little confused, that's all. You poor man," the old woman crooned in sympathy. She offered him the plastic water bottle. "Here. Take a sip. It'll do you good."

He took the bottle from her, staring at it for several moments before tipping it upward. It was unlike any container he had seen. When he saw water trickle through the narrow tube protruding from its top, he held it over his open mouth. The liquid did little to ease the burning in his throat.

"Is that better?" she asked solicitously.

He nodded, then sank back, feeling as weak as a foal.

"Maybe we should call for help," the boy said.

"No," Wood croaked, not wanting to run into any men from the vigilante group that had tried to lynch him. "No help."

"We need to get you out of this sun," the old lady stated. "If you think you're able to walk, we'll take you back to the house."

"Whose house?" Suspicion tightened his whole body.

"Ours. It's not far up the road. Do you think you can make it?"

Wood squinted as he glanced all around and saw nothing but cornstalks.

"Is this your corn?" He looked at the old woman inquisitively.

It was the boy who answered. "Yup. We got soybeans, too."

"Soybeans?"

"Don'tcha know what they are?" The boy looked at him askance.

Wood could only shake his head in ignorance.

"You've probably just forgotten that, too. Come, let's

get you out of the sun," Gabby said to Wood, then waved an arm at the boy saying, "Jeremy, help him up."

Wood could see that the lad was reluctant to touch him. "I expect I can do it myself." He rose slowly, wobbling as he stood.

The woman steadied him with a hand on his arm. "Don't try to talk. There'll be plenty of time for that later." To the boy she said, "Jeremy, take his other arm. By the way, I'm Gabby Davis and this is Jeremy. I'm the one who gave you directions the other night when you called."

Wood had no idea what she was talking about. It was obvious she had him confused with this Dumler guy, but he didn't dare correct her. Better that she mistake him for another man than recognize him as an accused murderer. Until he knew why he was in the middle of a cornfield instead of hanging from a tree on George Nelson's ranch, he needed to be wary of everyone. All that mattered was that he was alive and would stay that way no matter what name he had to use.

"I wonder if you got off at the bus stop in Stanleyville, rather than the one at the junction of County Roads 13 and 47," Gabby remarked as they walked.

"Bus stop?" He shook his head in confusion. Why did she talk about things of which he had no knowledge?

It was possible that she was a bit simpleminded, considering her clothing. Wood was no authority on fashion, but one thing he knew for certain—women didn't show their legs beneath their skirts. This woman had hemmed her dress to just below her knees. Not only did she expose flesh on her legs, but her arms were bare, too, and on her feet were the strangest looking shoes he had ever seen. Her toes stuck out a hole in the front.

From the way the boy was dressed, Wood could tell he belonged with her. His clothes looked as if they had been passed down from an older brother, baggy and loose, and like Gabby, he wore a shirt with no sleeves. Even stranger

was that on one section of the shirt was a big check mark
with the words Just Do It.

Do what? Wood wondered.

As they walked, Wood kept an eye out for any signs of
the angry mob who wanted him dead. There were none.
Not a sound of turmoil anywhere. Just a sea of corn. He
wondered how many people worked this farm, that they
could plant so many seeds. The thought that the man who
had slipped the noose around his neck could own the land
filled him with apprehension.

"Who planted all of this, ma'am?" he whispered, gesturing with his arm to the cultivated fields around him.

"Barry helped Hannah with most of it," Gabby answered. "He's a young man who works part-time in the
spring and fall."

"Hannah's here?" Wood could hardly believe his ears.
When he had left Missouri, he had been confident he would
find his younger sister and bring her home. But after several
weeks of searching, his hope had dwindled.

Little did he know that his search would nearly cost him
his life. George Nelson had said there had been a young
woman named Hannah traveling with an outlaw suspected
of being a member of the Jesse James gang. Only a few
days ago they had stolen two horses from his ranch. Wood
had gone back to get firsthand information from George
Nelson and his wife. Only by the time he arrived, the
farmer and his wife were dead. Nothing Wood had said in
his own defense could convince the posse he hadn't killed
the couple.

He had been tried and found guilty without ever going
to court. As he had sat on his horse he had prayed for a
miracle. Now it seemed one had occurred. Not only was he
still alive, but it appeared that his sister had not ridden off
with the outlaws.

"Ma'am, where is Hannah?" he asked anxiously.

"She's in town, but she should be back shortly," the old woman answered.

"She lives here?"

Gabby frowned. "The sun really has gotten to you, hasn't it? She's the reason you came here. You haven't forgotten that, have you?"

He shook his head. Wood could hardly believe his luck. First he had escaped the lynch mob; now he had found Hannah.

As they rounded a row of pines, they came upon one of the biggest houses he had ever seen. It was two stories tall with a huge verandah on three sides. It reminded him of the grand houses he had seen in St. Louis and was nothing like the log cabin he had stayed in at the Nelsons'.

If Hannah were renting a room here, did that mean she had split from her outlaw boyfriend? Or she was waiting here for him while he pulled a bank job. He hoped it was the former, but judging by what the leader of the lynch mob had said, it could very easily be the latter. The Jesse James gang had robbed the bank of Northfield, which wasn't all that far from Stanleyville. Two of the gang had been killed during the robbery, but so had two of the towns-folk, which was why the vigilante group had been so ready to lynch him. When George and Mary Nelson were found dead at their homestead, Wood had become the victim of guilt by association. After all, he had stayed with them the previous night and had been asking questions about the James gang.

Right now, however, he didn't feel much like asking questions. Not that it mattered. Gabby and Jeremy didn't make much sense when they talked, anyway. What was important was that for the first time in weeks, Wood could cling to the hope that he had finally found his sister.

"Let's take him to the bunkhouse," Gabby directed Jeremy.

"There aren't any sheets on the beds," Jeremy reminded her.

"We can fix that."

At this point Wood didn't care about linens. With every step he weakened, and the world around him began to spin out of control.

"Get the door."

"Yuck! There's spider webs all over."

"Watch his head."

"It stinks in here."

"We'll open the windows."

Their words floated all around Wood. He was tired. He felt sick. He needed sleep. Whatever had happened to him during the lynching, it had drained every ounce of his strength.

"You need to rest," Gabby said helping him to a cot.

He closed his eyes and took a deep breath, trying to make sense of the last twenty-four hours. He couldn't. Nothing that had happened since that noose had been slung around his neck made any sense. Maybe he was dead. Startled, he opened his eyes.

"I'm not dead, am I?"

Gabby laughed. "Oh, good heavens, no. You're just a little confused, Alfred, but you're going to be just fine."

Again she called him Alfred. If she knew he was Hannah's brother, why did she think he was this Alfred person? He rubbed his temples. If he could only figure out if she knew about the lynching. It wasn't in his nature to be dishonest, but telling her his true identity was a risk he couldn't take. At least until he figured out how he'd landed in a strange cornfield. Right now he felt weak and helpless. His eyelids were heavy, his body boneless. As much as he wanted to get out of the bunk and ride far away from Minnesota, he knew he needed to get his strength back if he were to talk his sister into going home with him.

"I have to talk to Hannah soon," he murmured.

"You will," Gabby assured him. She patted his hand as if he were a small child needing comfort. "But first you must sleep. I'll get you some linens for the cot."

"This will suit me just fine, ma'am." He stretched out on the bare mattress.

"Very well. After you rest, you can wash up and then you can meet Hannah."

"You won't tell her I'm here just yet, will you?" He lifted his head in supplication. "I don't want her to see me like this. In my weakened state."

"Don't worry, Alfred, I won't mention that you're here just yet." Then she turned to Jeremy and said, "That goes for you, too, young man. Not a word to your mother until I say so. Understand?"

Jeremy nodded.

Then Gabby turned back to Wood. "Everything will work out just fine. It might take a little time, but Hannah will come around. You'll see."

Wood eased his head back on the cot. "I have to convince her I have her best interests at heart."

"Yes, that's exactly what you need to do," Gabby agreed.

"She's not going to get rid of me." Wood tried to sound confident, but his voice was weak.

"No, I don't believe she will," Gabby responded smugly as Wood closed his eyes. She turned to Jeremy and said, "He's asleep. We'll get him a basin so he can wash when he wakes up. You know, I think once he shaves he'll be rather handsome."

"Mom's not going to think so," Jeremy warned her. "She's going to have a fit when she sees him. She doesn't want anyone using this place."

"We agreed we're not going to tell her he's here until he's feeling better." Gabby steered Jeremy toward the door.

"Who is he, anyway?"

Gabby chewed on her lower lip, contemplating how

much she should tell her nephew. "Can you keep a secret?"

"Sure."

"You know how your great-grandfather left your mother all that money that she can't touch unless she marries?"

"You mean the prison money?"

Gabby clicked her tongue. "Marriage isn't a prison, and I wish your mother wouldn't refer to it as that. Anyway, your mother's thirtieth birthday is coming soon, which means she'll lose her inheritance if something isn't done."

Jeremy wrinkled his nose. "I don't get it. What's he got to do with that?"

"I arranged for him to come and marry your mother," Gabby said directly.

Jeremy's eyes widened. "No way! Mom won't marry him!"

"Not looking the way he does now, but once she gets to know him and sees what a good help he can be around the farm, she might." She gave him her gravest look.

"But she doesn't even know him!"

"Your great-great-grandfather married someone he didn't know. He had a mail-order bride. Sent for her through an ad in the newspaper and it lasted nearly forty years. Sometimes those marriages work the best." She could see she hadn't convinced him. "Jeremy, you don't want to lose the farm, do you?"

"No, but Mom says she'll find a way to keep it."

"Not if she has another bad harvest. Can we take that risk?"

He looked again at the sleeping man and wrinkled his nose. "He looks awfully weird."

"Appearances can be deceptive," she said as much to herself as to Jeremy. "You're willing to give him a chance, aren't you?"

He was silent for several seconds before finally saying,

"I am. But Mom's going to be really mad when she finds out."

"Is there a reason the windows are open in the bunk-house?" Hannah asked, the moment she stepped into the kitchen. Ever since her grandfather's death, the bunkhouse had been empty. She saw no reason to use the building that at one time had been home to the extra farm hands. She could no longer afford live-in help. Besides, there were memories in that building she would just as soon forget.

"I'm airing it out." Gabby turned her back to her niece, busying herself at the stove where she had several pots on the burners.

"I thought we were in agreement that it wouldn't be used."

Just then Jeremy burst into the kitchen. "Hey, Mom. Did you get the bedding for the chickens?"

"Yes, it's in the back of the pickup," Hannah answered. "What did you do after school today?" she asked as he reached for a handful of grapes.

Jeremy looked at his great-aunt before he answered. "I helped Gabby."

"Do what?"

He shrugged. "Stuff."

Hannah didn't miss the guarded glances that passed between Gabby and Jeremy. "Like what stuff?"

Gabby avoided answering by saying, "Oooh. I like what Marlis did with your hair! Turn around and let me see the back."

Hannah did as she was told. "She layered it. She said it would have more bounce." She chuckled softly. "As if I need bouncy hair."

"It looks nice, Mom."

Hannah eyed her son suspiciously. In all of his ten years he had yet to comment on her hairstyle.

"I'm glad you didn't cut it short," Gabby added.

"Marlis wouldn't. She said most women spend hours

getting curls like mine and she wasn't going to watch them go to waste on the floor." Hannah ran her fingers through the blond layers.

"We'd better eat. The food's ready!" Gabby announced, fluttering about with her hot pads flapping in the air.

Hannah helped Gabby carry the serving dishes to the table. "Are you feeling okay? You look a little flushed."

She heaved a sigh before she said, "I think I did too much walking today."

"Walking?"

Gabby took her place at the head of the table. "I went with Jeremy to help him find Outlaw."

"He was out during the storm, and I thought he might have been hurt," Jeremy explained, turning his attention to the soup in front of him.

Hannah looked at Gabby. "What storm?"

"It was only a brief shower," her aunt insisted.

"It sure had a lot of lightning," Jeremy exclaimed. "You know that big oak out in the Nelson forty? It got hit by lightning and split right down the middle."

"What were you doing out at the Nelson forty anyway?"

"I told you. Looking for Outlaw." Jeremy reached for a slice of bread.

Hannah looked at Gabby. "No wonder you're feeling the heat. You shouldn't have walked all the way out there."

"I was worried," she said, lowering her eyes.

Hannah looked at her quizzically. "And then you came back here and cleaned out the bunkhouse?"

"We didn't exactly clean it. We swept it out and opened the windows," Gabby told her. She exchanged another guarded glance with Jeremy.

Hannah didn't know what the looks passing between her aunt and her son meant, but she had a hunch they shared a secret and it had something to do with the bunkhouse.

She set down her fork with a clang. "All right. What's going on?"

Both shot her looks that were as innocent as a baby's. "Nothing," they echoed in unison.

"Jeremy, do you want to have a sleep-over? Is that why you had Gabby help you clean it?"

Gabby giggled nervously. "She caught us red-handed, Jeremy. We better 'fess up."

Jeremy didn't look as if he wanted to confess anything.

"I told Jeremy to ask you if it would be okay to use the bunkhouse for guests, but he was worried that you'd be upset. You know why." She gave Hannah a knowing look.

"You get a really sad look on your face whenever you go by there." Jeremy added.

Hannah knew what he said was true. Just walking by the bunkhouse created a dull ache in her heart. What Jeremy didn't realize was that the old building held memories she wanted to forget. It was there that she had met Jeremy's father, a young man who had come to help her grandfather on the farm. He had given her the best summer of her life, promised her the moon, then left without even saying goodbye. He and all the other men in her life who followed him had proved one thing—men don't stay. But she couldn't tell that to Jeremy.

"Have you two forgotten that there's no bathroom in the bunkhouse?"

Jeremy's eyes met Gabby's. "Oh-oh. I guess that means if a person sleeps out there, he'll just have to come inside to go to the bathroom."

"No," Hannah said firmly. "If we have any guests, they'll sleep in the house. I don't want anyone using the bunkhouse."

That ended the discussion, and the rest of the dinner talk centered on harvest preparations. Gabby had just brought the apple strudel to the table when Outlaw began to bark.

"What's with Outlaw?" Hannah asked.

"I'll go check." Jeremy's chair scraped the floor as he stood, but Hannah stopped him.

"Finish your dinner. I'll look."

When Hannah gazed out the screen door, the sun was setting, creating shadows and limiting her range of vision. What she could see, however, was Outlaw's tail wagging like crazy beside a large oak tree.

"He must have a squirrel cornered." Hannah's statement produced audible sighs from her aunt and son.

"Jeremy, why don't you bring him inside," Gabby suggested nervously.

Jeremy went to the screen door and ordered the dog to come in, but he ignored the commands. "I'll go get him. He's being stubborn again."

A few minutes later he returned with Outlaw. Two red spots brightened Jeremy's cheeks, his eyes were wide. "Gabby, we've got a problem!"

"What's wrong?" Hannah demanded.

"He's gone!" Jeremy squeaked.

"Gone?" Gabby repeated, dropping her knife and folk on her plate.

"Who's gone?" Hannah wanted to know, but neither Gabby nor her son answered. Both went scampering out the door, Outlaw trailing on their heels. "Is there someone in the bunkhouse?" Hannah asked, as she followed.

Into the wooden building they marched. Hannah saw the basin of water on the nightstand. "All right, what's going on? Who was in here?"

"A sick man." Gabby wrung her handkerchief in her hands. "And now he's wandering around out there, delirious. He had too much sun." She moaned. "Jeremy, do you think Outlaw scared him away?"

"He liked him," Jeremy said.

"Him who?" Hannah demanded in frustration.

Suddenly Outlaw stopped barking, and a man's voice echoed in the still, evening air. "Hannah! Hannah!"

"He's not gone!" Jeremy declared wide-eyed and headed for the door.

Gabby followed him saying, "He shouldn't be out of bed, not in his condition."

"Would someone please tell me what is going on here?" Hannah said in frustration as once more she was forced to follow the two of them. "Why is there a man calling my name?" She detained Gabby with a hand on her arm. "Gabby, is he a friend of yours?"

Before she could answer, Jeremy shouted, "There he is. By the barn!"

All Hannah could see in the setting sun was the silhouette of a man. As she followed Gabby and Jeremy, she heard the man call out to her.

"Hannah? Is that you?"

Perplexed, Hannah looked at Gabby. "Do I know this man?"

"Not yet," Gabby answered.

Suddenly he came staggering toward her. Fear caused Hannah's nerves to tingle as he came closer and she saw how dirty he was.

"The good Lord must have answered my prayers. I prayed for an angel to save me and here you are." His eyes raked her from head to toe. "You're pretty, too. I'd better say a prayer of thanks to the Almighty." He looked as if he wanted to wrap his arms around her, but before he could reach out and touch her he fell in a heap at her feet.

"See, I told you he's not well," Gabby fretted, stooping down to place an ear to his chest. After several seconds she looked up at the two who stood with mouths agape.

"He's breathing."

"Are you telling me that *this* is the reason why you cleaned up the bunkhouse? So that this...this...derelict could have a place to sleep?" Hannah's mouth dropped open in disbelief.

"He's not a derelict," Gabby responded.

"Jeremy, run back to the house and call Red Murphy,"

Hannah ordered her son. "Tell him there's a drunk passed out on our lawn."

"No! You can't do that!" Gabby protested. "He's not drunk. He's suffering from heat exhaustion. That's all. See how sunburned his face is."

Hannah grimaced. "All I see is dirt. He's a grub!"

"He's not that bad." Gabby tugged on his lapels, trying to straighten the wrinkles from the fabric. It was useless. The garment still looked like it came out of a rag bag.

"Look at him," Hannah said derisively. "His clothes are filthy, he hasn't shaved…" she trailed off in frustration, failing to understand how her aunt could have allowed this man onto their farm. "Gabby, who is this man, and why is he using our bunkhouse?"

Gabby shifted from foot to foot, then looked around nervously. Finally, she said in a shaky little voice, "His name is Alfred and he's our guest. I invited him to stay with us." She hadn't lied—not really. She simply didn't bother to explain that Alfred was Hannah's future husband.

Chapter Three

Uneasiness churned Hannah's stomach. She didn't want to believe that this man could possibly be Gabby's suitor. It was one thing for her aunt to date stodgy old Bernie Lamphart, quite another for it to be a man half her age who looked like something the cat dragged in.

Hannah asked the dreaded question. "Why have you invited him to stay with us?"

She didn't get a direct answer.

"I know he looks as if he's a little down on his luck right now, but he's quite respectable. I've checked his references," Gabby stated primly, as if she were seated behind a desk at the library.

"References for what?"

"For his character. Just because I haven't had much experience with men doesn't mean I'm stupid!"

Experience with men? Hannah swallowed with difficulty. "He *is* your boyfriend!"

"No, he's not my boyfriend." Gabby made a disgruntled sound that questioned how she could even entertain such an idea. "He's young enough to be my grandson!"

Hannah exhaled in relief. "Then who is he and why is he here?"

"His name is Alfred Dumler. He's from Nebraska. He's here because— Well, it's like this...." she hemmed and hawed then finally said, "I was reading the want ads in the farm journal and—"

Hannah's hand flew to her chest. "You didn't answer one of those ads put in by people who are looking for work, did you?"

"Not exactly," Gabby replied, giving the unconscious man a quick, apprehensive glance.

Not exactly? "Gabby, please tell me you didn't find this man in the want ads." When her aunt didn't reply, Hannah groaned. "Oh, my gosh! You did, didn't you?"

"You don't need to get upset. It's all right. I told you—I've checked his references."

Hannah tried not to panic. She wet her lips and calmly asked, "Did you hire him?"

"I wouldn't do that—not without asking you first," she said contritely.

Relief rushed through Hannah, and she pushed the bouncy curls back from her forehead. "Thank goodness. That means he can leave."

"No, he can't leave!" Gabby objected. "I asked him to come here."

It was with a great effort that Hannah controlled her temper. "We've talked about this before, Gabby, and you know we can't afford to hire anyone other than Barry and certainly not someone we have to board."

"He could turn out to be just what we need around here," her aunt argued. "Alfred knows a lot about farming. I've checked him out. I even did a credit report."

"Obviously not a very thorough one," Hannah retorted, looking at him disdainfully.

"I admit, he looks a bit strange, but it's only because he's not well. In the picture I have of him in my room he's all neat and clean. I can get it for you, if you want."

"I don't care how he looks in a picture," Hannah said impatiently. "It's the way he looks now."

"He looks like someone in need of care, and I don't

think we should be standing here doing nothing," Gabby said in a maternal tone. "We should help him get back to bed." She turned to Jeremy and said, "You take his feet and your mom and I will lift his shoulders."

Jeremy nodded.

"Wait a minute." Hannah folded her arms across her chest. "Where do you think you're taking him?"

"To the bunkhouse. But if you'd rather he stay in the guest room at the house...." Gabby suggested innocently.

"No, I don't want him in the guest room at the house! I don't want him anywhere on this property." Hannah could feel the color rush to her cheeks.

"But, Mom, he's sick!" Jeremy protested.

Censure sharpened Gabby's features. "We can't just turn him away."

"Oh, yes we can," Hannah contradicted her.

Gabby, in her sternest librarian's voice, said, "Hannah Marie Davis, your mother would roll over in her grave if she knew you were thinking about refusing help to someone in need. Not to mention I invited him here."

Hannah could have screamed in frustration. What had possessed her aunt to do something so irresponsible? It was true that Gabby had been prone to quirky behavior at times, but until now, none of her whimsies had ever landed them with an unwanted man on their doorstep.

She looked down at the unkempt stranger and felt a twinge of compassion. He did look rather pathetic. She already had a dozen stray cats wandering about the place....

She supposed she could let him stay—at least until he was well enough to travel back to Nebraska. "Oh, all right," she grumbled.

With a sigh, she stooped down and lifted the man's shoulders, leaving Jeremy and Gabby to wrestle with the rest of him. "All I can say is thank goodness he doesn't smell," Hannah muttered as the three of them hobbled their way back to the bunkhouse. His clothes were the coarsest cotton she had ever felt, and she wondered if he'd found them at a homeless shelter.

As soon as they had managed to get the stranger onto one of the wrought-iron beds, she dusted off her hands, saying, "He'd probably weigh twenty pounds less if he washed his clothes."

Gabby ignored her comment because Wood stirred. "Look. He's coming round again. He's probably hungry." She looked pointedly at Hannah.

"You want *me* to get him something?"

"There are plenty of mashed potatoes left." Gabby looked at her expectantly. "And tea is always therapeutic. Oh, and it probably would be a good idea to take his temperature. There's a thermometer in the medicine chest."

"Maybe you should just make a list," Hannah drawled sarcastically, then did as her aunt requested.

Alone with Wood, Gabby and Jeremy watched him toss and turn. "You think he's having a bad dream or something?" Jeremy asked.

Gabby pressed a hand to his forehead. "He's awfully warm. Maybe he has a fever."

At her touch Wood's eyes fluttered open. "Where am I?"

"You're on the Davis farm," Gabby answered him. "Remember us? I'm Gabby and this is Jeremy."

Wood raised himself on one elbow and looked around. "I'm not at the Nelsons' then."

Gabby gave him a puzzling look. "The Nelsons sold out twenty-five years ago."

Wood's eyes narrowed. "Are you sure?"

Sensing his confusion, Gabby repeated, "This is the Davis farm. You came here to meet Hannah, remember?"

At the mention of his sister's name, Wood sighed. "She's really here then?"

"Yes. She just went to get you something to eat. Are you feeling all right?"

"I'm a little dizzy," he admitted, falling back down and closing his eyes.

"I think you may have a fever. Maybe I should call the doctor."

At that his eyes shot open. "No! No doctor."

Just then Hannah called through the screen door for Jeremy's help. While Jeremy carried the tray with a cup of tea and a bowl of mashed potatoes over to Gabby, Hannah remained in the background.

"Do you feel up to eating?" Gabby asked Wood, who winced as he tried to push himself up into a sitting position.

He sank back down against the pillow and told Gabby, "I can't do it. I feel as if my body's made of straw."

Concern lined her face. "I'll help you. You just open up and I'll spoon it in."

"I like to tend to my own needs, ma'am, but I'd be obliged if you'd do just that." He opened his mouth, and she shoved the potatoes inside.

When he winced she asked, "You don't like them?"

"They taste good, ma'am, it's just that it hurts to swallow."

Gabby gave him a sip of the tea. "Here. Drink this. It'll make your throat feel better."

Wood did as he was told. Gabby fed him a couple more scoops of the potatoes before his eyes drifted shut. "Alfred?" she repeated his name several times, but he didn't answer.

"Do you think he's all right?" Jeremy asked in an anxious whisper.

"Gabby, how sick is this guy?" Hannah came closer to the bed.

"He said he doesn't need a doctor," Gabby answered.

"Well, he looks awful."

"Did you bring the thermometer?" Gabby asked.

Hannah nodded and handed her a narrow plastic case.

"He's waking up, again," Jeremy announced.

"I'd better take his temperature," Gabby removed the thermometer from its case and shook it.

"Dry." Wood's voice was barely above a whisper.

"Mom, he needs a drink of water," Jeremy remarked.

Hannah reached for the plastic tumbler. She watched long-lashed eyes slowly awaken. They were dark brown, full of slumber plus uncertainty. When they met Hannah's, they widened and she felt something tumble in her stomach. She had never seen anyone with such startling eyes. This guy did for brown eyes what Paul Newman did for baby blues. Hannah didn't understand how a man covered with dirt and looking like something that had been sleeping under the highway overpass could send a tremor of excitement through her.

Yet he did. Hannah figured it was more like fear than excitement. Neither feeling was welcome. She needed no man to stir any emotions in her, especially not one who looked like a bum.

"I need to talk to—" Wood began, only to fade away as his strength ebbed once more.

"Take a drink of water, Mr. Dumler," Hannah ordered, lifting the cup to his lips.

He sat forward, then took a sip. Those dark brown eyes regarded her with a cautious scrutiny. "Hannah...." He fell back against the pillow, squeezing his eyes shut in pain.

"That's the second time he's asked for me," Hannah whispered to Gabby, who shrugged innocently. Uneasiness had Hannah taking a step backward.

Again Wood cried out her name, "Hannah."

It was such a tormented sound, she couldn't help but feel sorry for the man. Whatever troubled him, he was in no state to deal with it this evening.

"Look, Mr. Dumler, try to rest. We can talk tomorrow," she told him, the helplessness in his face evoking all sorts of conflicting emotions in her. Curiosity, pity, annoyance...and to her dismay, sympathy. She didn't want to feel anything toward this man, yet she felt the tug on her emotions as if he were reaching out and touching her.

When he did reach out and grab her by the wrist, Hannah's heart skipped a beat. His fingers were hot as they clutched her flesh, and soon she felt that heat travel to the rest of her body. He tried to use her for an anchor so that he could pull himself up, but it was useless. He didn't have the strength. She pulled free, disturbed by the contact.

Hannah rubbed her skin where his fingers had been. It tingled—not from the pressure of his grasp, but from something else. His eyes met hers and she couldn't look away.

"You have to help me," he said in a low, husky voice that sent a tremor through her. But even more disturbing than his voice were his eyes. They pinned her with an intensity that held the promise of intimacy. The thought was an uncomfortable one. This man was a stranger and had no right to look at her as if there was some connection between them.

"You're not well, Mr. Dumler." She tried to look away from those compelling brown eyes, but found she couldn't.

"Wood," he murmured.

"Wood?" Hannah again looked to Gabby for an explanation, but she simply shrugged in ignorance. "What is it you need wood for, Mr. Dumler?"

He shook his head. "It's my name—Wood."

"Maybe it's what his friends call him," Gabby said softly.

Hannah didn't want to become any more familiar with him than she already was. "You want me to call you Wood instead of Alfred?"

He nodded. "What should I call you? Angel?" A ghost of a smile creased his lips causing Hannah's insides to tingle in an odd way. "I thought you were a dream, but you're real, aren't you?"

Hannah took a step away from the bed. She didn't want this helpless man looking at her as if she were his own personal nightingale. "I think I should go back to the house," she told Gabby. "You can nurse him or do whatever...."

"I'll see if he has a temperature," Gabby told her.

Wood groaned when she slipped the thermometer between his lips.

"Maybe we should take him to the hospital," Hannah suggested, thinking that at least they would get him off the farm.

Again there was a groan of protest from Wood.

"I told you he doesn't want to go to the doctor," Gabby said in a near whisper. "I think we should wait and see how he is in the morning." She studied her watch. "He's falling asleep." Within a few seconds she was carefully removing the thermometer.

"It's normal," she announced, once again shaking the mercury down.

"Then why is he so hot?" Again Hannah rubbed her own wrist, still feeling the impact of his touch.

"I told you. He was hit by lightning," Jeremy insisted. "When I touched him that first time I got a shock."

So did Hannah, but not the electrical kind. Her shock was more of a sexual awareness of the man—which was ridiculous. There was no way she could be attracted to someone so coarse.

Wood stirred, causing his arm to flop over the edge of the bed. Hannah automatically put it back at his side. As she did, she caught a glimpse of reddened skin beneath the cuff. She pushed back the stiff cotton and gasped. Rope burns circled his wrist. A look at his other hand confirmed her suspicions—his wrists had been tied together.

Jeremy noticed the marks as well. "See. I bet those were caused by the lightning—just like the ones on his neck."

Hannah's heart began to pound. "He has marks on his neck?"

Jeremy nodded. "They're under his collar."

Carefully, Hannah eased back a corner of his shirt and saw the inverted vee ringing his neck. "That's not from lightning," she told Jeremy.

"Then what is it?" Gabby asked.

"Jeremy, run up to the house and call Red Murphy and tell him to come over here right away," Hannah instructed, backing away from the bed.

"Why? What's wrong?" Gabby demanded.

"Just do as I say," Hannah ordered her son, who hadn't moved.

"But why, Mom?" Jeremy wanted to know. "Is he a criminal or something?"

"No, he's not a criminal," Gabby protested loudly. "He's a guest." She turned to confront Hannah. "Why won't you believe me when I say he's a good man?"

Hannah steered her aunt to a corner of the room, away from Jeremy's curious stare. "Those are rope burns on his neck," she told the older woman in a low voice. "Your Mr. Dumler must have tried to commit suicide."

Gabby gasped. "That can't be! He's a nice young man. I've talked to him on the phone and I've checked his references."

"Then why does he have marks on his neck as if he tried to hang himself? And the ones on his wrist are probably from having to be restrained. Your hired help could very well be an escapee from a mental hospital!"

"He's not! I told you, I checked him out before I invited him here. I even talked to the farmer he worked for in Nebraska. If you want, I can give you his phone number and you can call him and hear for yourself that Alfred's a good man." Indignation flashed in her eyes. "Why won't you believe me?"

Hannah could see she had offended her aunt. Her cheeks were flushed and she was fidgeting like a wind-up doll. "Gabby, it's not that I don't believe you."

"Then what is it?" The older woman pursed her lips

momentarily, then said, "This is 1998. They don't tie mental patients to the bed with rope. They have restraints. I think maybe Jeremy is right. Those marks could be from lightning."

Hannah didn't agree. "And if they're not?"

"He's not a mental patient," Gabby insisted. "There's nothing wrong with this man except that he was either struck by lightning or suffering from heat exhaustion. And that's only because he was on his way to see us."

"I'd feel better if Red came by," Hannah told her.

"For what? So he can take him to the jail and interrogate the poor man? Hannah, you can't call Red," Gabby pleaded. "When everyone hears that I found Alfred in a farm journal I'll be the laughing stock of Filmore County."

"Oh, Gabby," Hannah moaned. "No one needs to know about this."

The old lady gasped indignantly. "Of course they'll know. In a town the size of Stanleyville, there are no secrets."

Hannah knew what she said was true. Very little happened in any part of the county that wasn't discussed at mid-morning coffee break in the cafés in town.

"I'm uneasy about him staying here, Gabby," Hannah said honestly.

"You don't need to be. He's a good man." She continued to plead his case. "Look, even Outlaw likes him." Hannah glanced at Wood and saw that Jeremy's dog had jumped up on the bunk and had parked his body next to the stranger's.

"That's because he's finally found someone who's as dirty as he is," Hannah said dryly.

"You know Outlaw's a good judge of character."

Hannah chuckled sardonically. The truth was, the dog did seem to have an uncanny sixth sense when it came to people. He growled at the people Hannah didn't trust and licked the hands of those she did.

"What harm would it be to let the man sleep out here tonight? He's too weak to even make it up to the house," Gabby pointed out.

Hannah returned to his bedside and stared down at the stranger. Asleep he looked as innocent as Jeremy. She could feel her heartstrings being tugged. What was it about the man that made her want to ignore her common sense? It didn't help that Jeremy and Gabby were looking at her as if they had brought a stray puppy in from the cold and were waiting for her to say it was okay to keep him. Even Outlaw had a plea for understanding in his eyes.

"I really don't think he'd hurt us," Gabby said.

"It's not *us* I'm worried about. What if he hurts himself?"

Gabby pondered the possibility for several moments before saying, "We could always tie his hands to the bedposts."

Jeremy heard Gabby's suggestion and asked, "Why are you going to tie him up?"

Normally Hannah wouldn't have even considered such a suggestion. "In his confused state, he might do something that's dangerous," she explained for her son's benefit.

"Like what?" Jeremy wanted to know.

Hannah shrugged. "Fall and hurt himself. You said he's already passed out three times. What if he hits his head? It's probably not a bad idea, Gabby. Jeremy, run up to the house and bring me one of those old sheets I use to cover the furniture when we paint."

Jeremy did as he was told, returning with a tattered, paint-splattered white sheet, which Hannah tore into four long strips. Carefully, so as not to irritate the already reddened wrists, she fastened a piece of cotton to each of his hands, then tied them to the metal bed posts.

"Take off his boots," she ordered Jeremy.

"Are you going to tie his feet, too?" Gabby wanted to know.

"Yes, and if he's not making any sense in the morning, I'm calling Red. Understand?"

Both Jeremy and Gabby nodded.

Hannah finished fastening the cloth to the bedposts, then stood back and studied the picture before her. Spread out with his hands over his head and his feet apart was a man who looked as if he didn't have a friend in the world.

"He doesn't look very comfortable," Jeremy remarked.

"It's either this way or have Red come get him," Hannah stated firmly.

"He's probably just going to sleep all night, anyway," Gabby told Jeremy as they left Wood alone in the bunk-house.

Hannah hoped her aunt was right.

WOOD AWOKE WITH A START, gasping for breath. "I'm not dead," he said frantically, looking around at the unfamiliar surroundings. A shaft of light poured through the window, the air quiet except for the birds chirping outside. It was peaceful, not chaotic as the lynching had been.

At the memory of his brush with death, he briefly closed his eyes, wanting to erase the experience from his mind. He had hoped that a good night's sleep would clear his head and give him some answers as to how he came to be rescued by a dotty old lady, a crazy kid and a drooling dog—a dog that took up more than half of the narrow cot. But so far there were no explanations. Maybe if a guy survived a hanging he was forever crazy.

As he went to get up, he discovered both his ankles and his hands were tied to the bed. He exhaled a deep sigh. Maybe he hadn't been saved by the old lady after all.

He struggled briefly to free himself, then gave up trying. The old lady must have received word that he had been accused of murder. Why else would she have tied him to the bedposts? It made him wonder whether a noose would be dangling around his neck before the day was over.

"Hey, mister. Are you awake?"

It was a child's voice that had Wood glancing at the door. The drooling dog leaped from the cot and raced to the screen door where the boy who had been with the old lady yesterday stood peering in at him.

"You're Jeremy, right?" Wood called out to him.

"Uh-huh." The boy entered carrying a canvas sack slung over his shoulder. As the dog jumped up to greet him, he dropped the sack and lavished the animal with affection. "If you're all right, I better go. I'm not supposed to be here, but I wanted to make sure you didn't die or anything." Jeremy kept a cautious distance from the bed.

"Nope, I'm still breathing, though I'd breathe much better if I wasn't tied up," Wood told him. "Want to help me with these knots?"

"Mom said she'd undo them this morning if you're feeling okay."

"Is she the one who tied me up?"

He nodded. "She didn't want you getting hurt."

"And that's the only reason she did it?"

"Yup. *Are* you feeling okay?"

"I think so," Wood answered, relieved that the boy apparently hadn't heard about his near lynching. "I'll know once I get up and walk around, which I hope will be soon, because I need to use the privy."

The kid gave him a blank stare.

"You know, that place you go in the morning to relieve yourself," Wood explained.

"You mean the bathroom?"

"Bathroom? Is that what you call it here?" Wood didn't understand why anyone would confuse a bath room with a privy, but he wasn't going to bother to explain to this kid the difference. Judging by the conversations they had had yesterday, he figured the lad was a little slow in the head, anyway.

"There isn't one in here," Jeremy answered. "You have to come to the house."

"Maybe you want to untie me and show me where it is?"

Although Jeremy had expressed concern for his well-being, he wasn't about to go against his mother's orders. He took a step backward. "I can't. I have to go or I'll be late for school and then my mom will get mad." He retraced his steps to the door. "I'm glad you're feeling better."

"Wait!" Wood called out to his departing figure. The boy paused in the door. "Yesterday your grandma said Hannah was at your house. Is she still there?"

The boy gave him an odd look and said, "Gabby's not my grandma. She's my great-aunt. Well, actually, she's some kind of great-aunt. My mom's grandpa was her brother."

"So you live with your mom and your aunt and..." he prodded.

"And no one else."

"What about Hannah?"

The puzzled look stayed on Jeremy's face. "I already told you she lives here." He tilted his head, one eye narrowing as he asked, "Are you sure you're feeling okay?"

"Yup."

"That's good because otherwise Mom is going to call Red Murphy—he's the sheriff."

Wood stiffened. "Why would she want to do that?"

"Because of those marks around here." He gestured to his neck. "Gabby and I told her they were from the lightning, but I don't think she believed us. She doesn't know why you're really here."

"And you do?"

He nodded, wide-eyed. "Gabby told me she sent for you." A loud honking noise echoed on the still morning air. "Oops! I gotta go. There's the bus!" He rushed out the door, leaving a frustrated Wood to wonder what the hell he was talking about. *The bus?*

It occurred to him that he hadn't asked Jeremy about his father. The old lady had said someone called Barry helped with planting, still it was an awful lot of corn for one man to plant. Maybe both women were married, and their husbands weren't home because they were out with the vigilante group searching for him. Yet he said there was just the three of them—and Hannah.

That possibility was enough to cause Wood to hasten his attempts at freeing himself. But no amount of struggling and squirming would loosen the knots at his wrists. If it was indeed a woman who had tied him up, she had done a man's job of it. He had no choice but to wait for his jailer to appear.

He wondered if she was the pretty blonde who had fussed over him last night, holding the cup of water to his dry mouth. She had smelled like orange blossoms, which was odd since there were no orange trees in Minnesota. He had thought she looked like an angel with her wild blond curls framing her head like a halo. Was she the one who had saved his life? Now that would be a twist of fate—to almost hang only to be saved by the prettiest lady he had ever seen.

He wished his memory wasn't so cloudy. All he knew was that his close call with death had weakened him to such a state that not only had he lost his strength, but bits of memory, too. Now a good night's sleep had restored his strength, if not his memory. Physically, he was ready to get back on his horse and ride as far away from Minnesota as possible. After he found Hannah, that is.

Thoughts of his sister had him watching the door and waiting. The only way he would get to see Hannah was if Jeremy's mother would allow it.

After what seemed to be an eternity to Wood, she finally appeared in the door. Just like Jeremy, her steps were tentative as she crossed the room. As she drew near, he once again caught the scent of orange blossoms. Dressed in trousers and a man's shirt, she was every bit as pretty this morning as he remembered her to be.

"So my angel returns," he drawled, wondering why she felt the need to dress like a man instead of a woman. "You're not a dream after all."

"I'm not your angel." She didn't come close to the bed, but kept her distance.

"You don't need to be afraid of me, ma'am," Wood called out when she eyed him suspiciously.

"I'm not."

"Good. Then maybe you'll undo these fancy knots you tied and let me go find Hannah. I need to talk to her."

She stood silently assessing him, as if he were a bolt of fabric in the dry goods store that she couldn't quite make up her mind about.

"At least take pity on the fact that I haven't relieved myself since sometime yesterday. If I don't get off this bed soon I'm going to embarrass myself. You wouldn't want to see a grown man wet himself, would you?" Wood's grin did little to persuade her.

Apparently his physical needs were of little concern to her. She didn't move toward him. Instead she folded her arms across her chest and said, "I guess we weren't introduced last night, were we, Mr. Dumler? I'm the Hannah you're looking for. Now what is it you want to say to me?"

"*You're* Hannah?"

"Yes. You look disappointed."

He was about to tell her the reason why—that the Hannah he had expected to find was his sister. But then realized that it probably wouldn't be wise to give these people any clue to his real identity. The three of them had mistaken him for a Mr. Dumler, and he was content to let them think that's who he was. By now his name would be plastered all over "Wanted" posters in the area. Once these women went to town, they'd know that he had nearly been hung for murder.

"I'm not disappointed," Wood assured her. "Perhaps a little surprised, that's all." He could see that she didn't believe him.

"I'm sorry if I'm not what you expected, but I didn't answer your ad," she said in a defensive tone. "Gabby did and she's the one who's responsible for any assumptions you've made."

Ad? What was the woman talking about? And what assumptions was he supposed to have made? If she wasn't aware of his true identity, then why was she looking at him as if he were a fly in her apple pie?

"And haven't you made some assumptions about me, Hannah?" he asked.

To his surprise, she looked him straight in the eye and said, "Look, I'm going to be honest with you, Mr. Dumler."

"Wood," he automatically corrected.

"Wood, I didn't invite you here. My aunt did."

"Do you want me to leave?"

He thought a hint of red colored her cheeks, but he couldn't be sure. "Not until you're well enough to make it back to wherever it is you came from."

Wood knew that she didn't want him to stay a minute longer than was necessary. It was there in her eyes. He chuckled to himself. What she didn't realize was that he shared her sentiment. He wanted to leave. As beautiful as she was and no matter how tempting it would be to enlist this Hannah's help in locating his sister, he'd be foolish to spend one minute longer than was necessary at the Davis farm.

"I understand perfectly," he told her.

"Good. So how are you feeling this morning?" she asked politely, as if she hadn't just told him he wasn't welcome in her home.

"I feel pretty damn good for a man who's been tied to this bed all night." He didn't mean for the words to sound so sarcastic, but he had never been a woman's prisoner before and he found the experience rather unsettling. But then everything about the Davis family unnerved him. They dressed oddly, they talked funny and they couldn't quite decide whether to treat him as a friend or enemy. Right now Hannah Davis was looking at him like the latter.

"I had to restrain you last night," she said coolly. "So you wouldn't hurt yourself."

"And why would you think I would do that?"

"You were behaving rather strangely, wandering around the yard talking incoherently. Gabby and Jeremy said you've been behaving oddly ever since they found you stretched out in the cornfield. We weren't sure what you might do," she told him. She rubbed her hands across her folded arms. "If it had been up to me, I would have sent for the sheriff, but you're here at Gabby's invitation, and she assures me you're sane."

"You think I'm crazy?"

She took another step backward. "I don't know you, Mr. Dumler."

Her eyes met his, and Wood saw fear in them. He wanted to say something that would persuade her he wasn't going to hurt anyone, especially not her. "I am not crazy," he told her, although he wasn't quite convinced of it himself. "And I am not dangerous. I won't cause any trouble for you or your family."

She held his gaze for several seconds before looking away nervously. "Gabby assures me she's checked your references thoroughly. She seems to think you're trustworthy."

"But you don't, do you, Hannah?"

"I'm not seventy-five, Mr. Dumler...."

"Wood," again he corrected her.

"And I'm not in the habit of letting complete strangers into my house."

"If you'll untie my hands, this stranger will leave your house. I don't make a habit of staying where I'm not wanted."

He could see she was still a bit apprehensive about untying him, but finally she moved closer to the bed. Tentatively, her fingers reached for the frayed ends of cloth, carefully avoiding any contact with his flesh. As she struggled with a knot that didn't want to be undone, Wood saw straight white teeth tug on her lower lip. The longer she worked at the knot, the more he studied her face.

She knew he was staring at her. She'd sneak a quick peek at him, then quickly return her attention to the knot, a delicate pink spreading across her cheeks. For someone with such a sharp tongue, she had a very kissable mouth. Soft. Full. Wood had to look away for he could feel his body reacting to her nearness.

Not that it helped. Even with his eyes on the ceiling he was very much aware of her presence. The scent of orange blossoms wouldn't let him forget that she was close enough to touch.

"There." She breathed a sigh of relief as the knot finally came undone. "Can you get the rest?"

"I don't think even a sane man could untie one of your knots with only one hand," Wood answered.

"I get the job done," she said proudly. She had to stretch to reach his other hand, the action pulling her shirt free of her trousers so that Wood caught a glimpse of bare flesh. Automatically his body responded and he tried to focus on something—anything to take his mind off of her.

It was then that Wood noticed the leather band on her wrist. In the middle was a small gray square with numbers.

"Is that some sort of time piece?" he asked.

"It's a digital watch," she replied flatly, then straightened and gave him a look that said in no uncertain terms was she going to help him with his ankles.

Digital watch? Something was definitely odd with these folks. In all of the time he had been in Minnesota he had never heard anyone use such foreign words or dress so unconventionally. He needed to get away from the Davis farm. He freed his feet, then flexed his muscles, before pulling on his boots.

"Are you all right?" Hannah asked when he dropped his head in his hands.

He nodded. "My head's sore." Confused would have been a better word, but he didn't want to give Hannah Davis any fuel for the fire. "Jeremy said your privy's near the house?"

"Our what?"

"Privy." He remembered that Jeremy had told him they called it something else in this part of the country. "The bathroom."

"You'll have to come up to the house," she told him, her face revealing just how distasteful that thought was.

Wood was getting tired of her displeasure. "This might surprise you, but I don't want to be here, either. Just show me where the privy is, give me my hat and I'll be gone."

"I don't know where your hat is."

"I reckon I can get along without it," he said unhappily. "I don't suppose anyone found my horse?"

Her brow wrinkled. "You brought a horse? I thought Gabby said you came on the bus?"

What was the bus? Wood could only guess that it must be some kind of wagon. "I had a horse, but I'm not sure what happened to it."

Again, wariness had her stepping backward. She motioned for him to follow her outside. As Wood stepped into the bright sun, he squinted. When his eyes finally adjusted to the light, he stopped in his tracks. Across from the bunkhouse were four round metal buildings.

"What are those?"

"Grain bins," she replied in a tone that said he had to be the dumbest man on earth if he needed to ask that question.

"They're metal."

"Yeah. So?"

As she led him past the bins his footsteps slowed at the sight of the oddest looking contraption he had ever seen. It was red with two small wheels at one end and two large wheels at the other.

When he stopped to stare, she said, "What's the matter? You act as if you've never seen an old tractor before?"

A tractor? Grain bins? Bus? Wood did a complete circle, looking in every direction, trying to find something familiar in the landscape. There was nothing. It was as if he had fallen off his horse and landed in a foreign country.

"This is Minnesota, isn't it?" he asked.

"Yes."

From the look on her face Wood knew he needed to be careful or she would call the sheriff. "I thought so," he said as calmly as he could, although he was feeling anything but calm.

He wished he knew what the hell was going on. Maybe he was crazy. Where was his sister, Hannah? And how was he ever going to find her when he didn't even know where he was or how he got here?

Nothing made sense. A digital watch that flashed numbers, a canteen that was bright red, clothes unlike any he had ever seen before. It was as if he had awoke in another era.

The thought caused his heart to pound. Yesterday Gabby had said "back in 1940." Could it be that he was in the twentieth century? He shook his head. No, he *was* crazy if he thought that.

"Alfred! Are you well enough to be up and around?"

Gabby had come out of the house and stood in front of him, critically assessing his condition.

"He's fine," Hannah answered for him, which Wood thought was rather odd. But then everything on the Davis farm seemed odd.

Gabby shuffled over to Wood's side. "I'm the one who should be taking care of you."

"He needs to use the bathroom, Gabby," Hannah pointed out, hinting that the old lady should move out of their way so they could get up the steps of the house.

"Of course he does," Gabby crooned. "Hannah, you go in and start breakfast. I'll see that Wood is taken care of." She insinuated herself in between Wood and Hannah, wrapping her bony fingers around Wood's arm.

Hannah didn't object. In fact, Wood thought she looked relieved to be able to turn him over to her aunt. She climbed the stairs and disappeared into the house without another word.

As soon as she was gone, Wood asked Gabby, "Can you tell me what date it is, ma'am?"

"Why sure. It's September the eleventh."

So he had lost a few days. The question was, had he lost years, too. "I don't mean any disrespect, ma'am, but may I ask what year you were born?"

"Why, 1923," she answered cheerfully.

Wood felt as if all the air was being sucked out of his lungs. 1923! He hadn't misheard her when she'd said her cousin's wedding was in 1940. Hannah had said Gabby was 75. It couldn't be...Or could it?

He had thought that when he'd awakened in the Davis's cornfield he had lost a couple of hours of his life. Now he knew that simply wasn't true. Instead of a hundred and twenty minutes passing, he had skipped a hundred and twenty years...or a hundred and twenty-two to be exact.

It was 1998.

Chapter Four

"You didn't tell Hannah why you're here, did you?" Gabby asked anxiously.

Stunned from his discovery, Wood didn't answer. He couldn't. He was still trying to comprehend how he could have passed through a hundred and twenty-two years and not be dead. It had to be a dream, yet this old woman clutching his arm was as solid as the ground beneath his feet.

"Did you tell Hannah why you're here?" she repeated.

"No, ma'am."

She exhaled in relief. "Good. You see, Hannah doesn't know I placed the ad. She thinks you put one in because you were looking for work."

It only took a few moments for Wood to realize that Gabby was still under the false assumption that he was someone named Alfred Dumler. She had no idea that he was an 1876 man who by some strange phenomenon was now in the twentieth century.

He thought about telling her the truth, yet how could he? How could he explain something he himself didn't understand? Hannah Davis already suspected he was crazy. He had little doubt she would call the sheriff and have him dragged off to an insane asylum if he uttered one word about traveling through time. Not that he would blame her.

Hell, it had happened to *him* and he still wondered if maybe he wasn't crazy.

"Are you sure you're feeling all right? You're looking a little pale," Gabby remarked, giving him a thorough appraisal.

Pale? He felt as if he'd been thrown from a horse. Disoriented. Sore. Lost. No, he was definitely not feeling all right. "I reckon I'm feeling as well as can be expected, ma'am."

"You need some food in your stomach. We'll go inside and get you something to eat, but first I need to know that you're not going to tell Hannah why you're really here." She thrust her arm through his and pulled him close. "Will you do me this favor?"

Wood's voice was tentative. "You don't want me to tell Hannah that you were the one who was looking for a man, and not the other way around?"

She nodded vigorously. "Right. You see, I did it as a surprise for her. I figured once you got here and she got to know you she would…" she smiled shyly, "well, things would happen and you know."

Wood assumed she meant Hannah would approve of him as a hired hand. Obviously, Gabby had arranged for hired help without Hannah's knowledge. He could be that man for now—providing the real Alfred Dumler didn't turn up.

"You're not mad at me for pretending to be Hannah, are you?"

"No." Why should he be? Since he wasn't Alfred Dumler, it truly didn't matter to him what the old lady had done, although he didn't think she had a malicious bone in her frail body. She had been nothing but kind to him.

"Then you still want to go through with it?" she asked hopefully.

What he wanted was to go back to his old life. To his sister. To his job at the bank in Missouri. To the life he knew. He didn't want to be in 1998 where everything was as strange as a two-headed calf.

Yet he couldn't tell Gabby that. At least not yet. Until he could figure out how he could get back to 1876, he really had no choice but to let her assume he was this Alfred person. With nowhere to go, no place to stay and not a single friend, he was at the mercy of the Davis women.

"I appreciate your hospitality, ma'am, but Hannah doesn't want me to stay," Wood warned her.

Gabby flapped her hand in midair. "It's only because she's stubborn and thinks we can get along without a man around here. That's why I was the one who wrote the ad. I knew she'd never do it. You do understand, don't you, Wood?"

He nodded. "I'll do what I can to help you."

"Good. Now you need to get inside. We'll discuss our plan later." She winked at him then led him up the porch steps. "The bathroom's on the second floor, so you're going to have to do some stairs. Do you think you're strong enough?"

"It shouldn't be a problem, ma'am." Wood moved in front of her so he could open the screen door.

"It's really sweet of you to call me ma'am, but it's not necessary. Why don't you call me Gabby?"

"All right. Gabby it is."

She smiled gratefully at him as she sashayed by. "Here's the kitchen," she announced.

Wood took one step inside the house and stopped suddenly. If he had any doubts that it wasn't 1998, they were gone now. The room was not like any he had seen. Nearly everything was white—the cupboards, the walls, the ceiling—even the floor. The only splashes of color were the blue curtains on the windows.

"As you can see, everything's been updated," Gabby told him.

"What's updated?" he asked, wondering what the date had to do with anything.

"The microwave is new." She pointed to a square white box with a black front. "And so is the dishwasher."

Wood had no idea what a microwave was nor did he see any dishwasher. The only other person in the kitchen was Hannah, who stood in front of a large white metal box that appeared to be a stove. When she turned a knob, blue flames glowed in a circular pattern. She pulled a cast iron fry pan from the wall and set it on a grate in the fire.

When she noticed Wood staring at her, she asked, "Is something wrong?"

"I've never seen a stove like that," he remarked, although it wasn't the stove that had his attention, but Hannah's backside. Tight-fitting trousers clung to her derriere revealing curves women normally kept hidden beneath their skirts. If all the women in 1998 dressed so provocatively, he wondered how the men kept their concentration on the task at hand.

Hannah gave him a look that told him she knew exactly what he had been staring at and that she didn't appreciate it. She moved to a large metal closet with two doors, one above the other. "I suppose you haven't seen a refrigerator like this, either." With a yank of her fingers, the lower door opened.

Wood moved closer and peered over her shoulder. "You have light in that thing?"

"It's not *that* old," she snapped.

Wood watched her reach for a bowl of eggs, rearranging several jars in the process.

All he could see was the back of her head, her blond curls wiggling like broken springs as she foraged for food. He was having trouble deciding what was more fascinating—the modern refrigerator or Hannah.

She was unlike any woman he had ever known—and not just because she wore trousers. There was something in the way she carried herself that announced to the world she was not going to sit back and wait for anything to happen. Determination sparkled in those blue eyes, eyes that refused to be intimidated by his scrutiny.

As she closed the refrigerator door she asked, "Is there something you want?"

Wood realized there was. He wanted to get to know Hannah Davis. Of course that wouldn't be wise since he was not planning on staying a minute longer in 1998 than it took him to figure out how to get back to 1876.

"He probably wants something to drink," Gabby interjected, tying an apron around her waist. "Go ahead and help yourself, Wood. Take one of those small cans of orange juice off the top shelf."

Wood opened the refrigerator door and stuck his hand inside. "It's really cold in here, even with the light."

"Hannah's grandfather believed some of the older appliances were built better than the newer ones," Gabby told him. "He was probably right. It doesn't have all the fancy features the new ones have, but it is dependable."

Curiosity had Wood pulling open a drawer at the bottom of the refrigerator. Inside was a head of cabbage and some carrots. "Where's the ice?"

Hannah shot him another wary glance. "You want ice in your juice?"

Gabby shushed her niece and said, "It's on top."

He nodded, closed the lower door, then opened the upper one. Not only was there no light inside the top compartment, there was very little ice. Packages occupied most of the space, some square, some round. Corn, beans…in boxes? And what were Hot Pockets? He could feel two sets of eyes on him as he gawked at the contents and quietly closed the door.

"You can have ice if you want, Wood," Gabby insisted. "Pull out a cube tray."

A cube tray? "No, I don't need any ice, ma'am," he said, slowly closing the door.

As he turned he noticed a calendar hanging on the wall. Without thinking, he walked over to it and lifted the pages. Every one of them had 1998 on the top right-hand corner.

"It really is 1998, isn't it," he mused aloud.

"Time flies, doesn't it?"

He turned at the sound of Gabby's voice and noticed that both women were staring at him.

"Yes, ma'am," he answered, wondering what she would say if he told them a hundred and twenty-two years had flown without his knowledge.

Gabby gave Hannah a gentle nudge. "Why don't you show Wood where he can wash up, and I'll make the pancakes and eggs."

"I will, but first— If you'll excuse us, Wood. I need to talk to my aunt for a minute." She pulled the older woman by the arm out the door.

"What's the matter?" Gabby asked when they were in the hallway.

"What's the matter?" Hannah repeated in an urgent whisper. "Something's not right with that man. Did you see the look on his face when he was staring at the calendar? I know you don't want to believe it, but I think he could very well be a patient at a mental hospital."

"He's not!" Gabby denied in a scratchy whisper.

"He's odd, Gabby. He told me he had a horse but he doesn't know what happened to it."

"So he has a bit of amnesia."

"It's more than that. I can't let him stay here. He's going to have to go," Hannah declared authoritatively.

"But you haven't given him a fair chance. Maybe if you'd get to know him, you'd like him," she said with a naiveté that had Hannah rolling her eyes. "We can't just turn him out. He's not well," Gabby fretted, concern lining her already wrinkled brow. "He should at least stay for one more day. You know, to make sure he's recovered."

"It's going to take a lot longer than one day to cure what's ailing him—like men in white coats and heavy narcotics," Hannah drawled sarcastically. "You saw the fuss he made over the refrigerator. Didn't you think it was odd the way he stared at the food in the freezer?"

"He's probably never seen such an old refrigerator," Gabby rationalized. "It is rather odd looking."

"He's the one who's odd...the way he's been looking at everything in the kitchen with that dumb look on his face."

"Don't you think it's a handsome face?" Gabby asked.

"No!" Hannah denied quickly, although it really wasn't quite true. He did have a certain look about him that some women might find attractive—*if* he were clean and *if* he wasn't crazy. And his eyes...something about them made her extremely aware of the fact that she was a woman and he a man.

"You're getting awfully worked up over this," Gabby observed calmly as Hannah continued to pace.

She was worked up and with good cause. She had a strange man sitting in her kitchen expecting to be hired on as a farm hand—a man unlike any she had ever met before. Never had any man both frightened and intrigued her at the same time.

"I don't want him working here, Gabby. You're going to have to tell him he has to leave. If you can't do it, I will," she warned.

Her aunt placed a bony hand on her arm. "Can't we give him a couple of days? Barry could show him around the farm, and you could get to know him better."

"I don't want to get to know him any better," Hannah snapped.

Gabby frowned. "Oh. That's not good...that's not good at all." She raised a fist to lips that quivered.

When she looked as if she might start to cry, Hannah placed her hands on her aunt's frail arms. "Can you honestly tell me that the man sitting in our kitchen is the kind of man you thought would come for the job?"

"He's not, but..." she trailed off uneasily.

"That's my point. You didn't know from the ad that he would be like...like *that*. We've seen him, he's not what we want, so he has to go," Hannah stated simply, although it was obvious she hadn't convinced her aunt.

"It doesn't seem fair that he gave up his previous job and spent money to come here only to have us send him away without giving him a chance. He has such good references."

Hannah sighed and rolled her eyes. Hadn't her aunt heard a word she had said?

"I don't think you should judge him by his appearance," Gabby advised her. "If your grandfather were alive, he'd give the man a chance to prove himself. You know he would. He was as fair a man as there ever was."

"Maybe when it came to men."

"Yes, but he wouldn't have shut his door on anyone who needed a helping hand."

Hannah peered over Gabby's shoulder into the kitchen. She saw Wood sitting at the table looking like a confused puppy dog, wearing a shirt that looked like it had come out of someone's trash. The image tugged on her heart strings. Would it hurt to let him stay another night?

"All right," she finally conceded. "He can stay for one—maybe two—more days. But if I don't see some sign that there's a dependable farm hand in that body by then, he's going to have to leave."

Gabby nodded and hurried back to the kitchen. Hannah followed reluctantly.

Wood saw the triumphant twinkle in Gabby's eyes when the two women returned and knew that the old lady had won. Hannah didn't look as if she wanted to show Wood anything but the door, but she didn't argue with her aunt who suggested she take him upstairs to the bathroom.

"Maybe you should go get your suitcase," she said to Wood.

It was Gabby who answered for him. "He doesn't have one. It probably was put on the wrong bus. For all we know it could be in Wisconsin by now."

Hannah looked at Wood. "Is that what happened?"

"I suspect Gabby's correct," he answered, not missing the eye signals the old lady sent him. He could only guess at what a suitcase was, but it was obviously something he didn't have, since he had survived the hanging with only the clothing on his back.

"It'll show up sooner or later," Gabby said optimistically.

He heard Hannah mumble under her breath, "If he ever had one."

"And what makes you think I didn't have one?" Wood countered.

Hannah looked as if she were about to tell him exactly why when Gabby waved a wooden spoon in between the two of them. "Didn't I say he needs to get cleaned up now or breakfast will be ready? It'll be no good cold! Now go on. Scoot. The both of you."

Wood followed Hannah's brisk footsteps out of the kitchen and down a narrow hallway. As they climbed a flight of stairs, he couldn't help but notice her derriere. The fabric clung as if it were painted on her skin, her cheeks moving from side to side with each step she took. It was enough of a distraction to cause Wood to stumble.

She had no idea the effect her swaying derriere was having on him until they reached the top of the stairs. Then she shot him a hostile glance.

She led him to a room that was in total darkness until she flipped a switch on the wall. Wood stood in the doorway, staring at the ceiling. The source of the light was a round globe that was similar to the one he had seen in the refrigerator. Everything else in the room was strange looking.

Hannah opened a cabinet and pulled out towels and a bar of soap. She set them on the cabinet's marble top which had a large indentation in the shape of a seashell.

She put her hand on a metal bar protruding over the seashell shaped basin. "This is going to make a grinding sound when you turn it on." She demonstrated with a flip of her wrist, and a stream of water flowed out of the pipe accompanied by a sound that was not unlike that of a foghorn.

"It's noisy but it works." She stopped the water with another flip of the bar. "The shower's here or you can take a bath."

Wood stared in awe at the advances in plumbing that had occurred during one hundred and twenty-two years. Hannah didn't notice his bewilderment, for she was busy pushing a metal knob that protruded from the back of a white porcelain stool.

"You'll have to excuse my son. He seldom remembers to flush after he goes," she said with reddened cheeks.

Wood's mouth dropped open as the water disappeared down a hole in the bottom of the floor. *This* was a 1998 privy?

"If you'll excuse me," she said, fidgeting as she waited for him to step aside and let her out of the room, "I'll leave and you can…" she trailed off.

He tried to move to the side so she could step around him, but as he did bumped his shoulder on a hook protruding from the wall. He grimaced as a piercing pain traveled down his arm.

"What's wrong?" Hannah demanded.

He clutched his shoulder, rubbing it gently. "My muscles are sore. I suspect from being tied to the bed last night," he added, although he knew it was more likely the fall from his horse that had made his limbs ache or the beating he had suffered at the hands of the lynchmen.

A light pink flushed her cheeks, and he felt a twinge of guilt.

"Forgive me for teasing you, ma'am. I expect the soreness has more to do with falling off my horse than with your shackles," he finally admitted, causing her lips to purse.

She opened a drawer, pulled out a small white tube and handed it to him. "This should help. Rub it into the sore area. Think you can manage that?"

"I expect I can."

"Good." She moved over to the mirror on the wall and pulled at one of the corners. "This is one of those mirrors that allows you to see the back view as well."

Wood stepped in front of the glass and saw for the first time why Hannah had looked at him with such uneasiness. Dark stubble hid his jaw, dirt smudged his cheeks, and his hair looked as if he had been sleeping in a haystack. No wonder they had told him to wash up.

As he tilted his head to one side he caught sight of the bruise on his neck. Although the noose hadn't killed him, it had left an angry, red mark on his throat. Jeremy said Hannah had seen it, which would account for the fear in her eyes—and his being tied to the bed.

"I fell off my horse and got tangled up in some rope," he tried to explain.

"This horse that you can't find?"

He nodded.

She didn't believe his story. It was there in her eyes. "I'd better go see if I can find you some clean clothes." Her voice quavered ever so slightly as she walked toward the door.

It bothered Wood that she was frightened of him. Never in his life—at least his previous one—had he given a woman any reason to suspect he would harm her. He believed it was a man's role to protect women, which is why he had nearly died for his sister.

"You don't need to be afraid of me, Hannah," he said to her as she stepped through the doorway.

She turned to look back at him. "I'm not."

"No?"

"I just don't trust you."

"You can trust me."

She chuckled sarcastically. "Yeah, right. You show up on my farm in some sort of a stupor looking as if you've been on a three-day drunk and you expect me to trust you?"

"I haven't been drinking," he told her, although he could see she didn't believe him. "Do you smell any liquor on me?" He moved closer to her and this time she stood her ground, refusing to be intimidated by him.

"Look, Mr. Dumler—"

"Wood," he interrupted.

"All right, Wood," she said impatiently. "Since Gabby invited you here, I'll give you the benefit of the doubt for now. But if you give me one reason to doubt that you are an honest farm hand, I'll show you that door so darn fast your head will swim."

"That won't be necessary," he told her, liking the way her eyes flashed with emotion. Wood thought that for such a small thing, she had a lot of guts. He had a feeling that Hannah Davis could be one passionate woman should she choose to be.

"Then we understand each other," she said coolly and left.

"Oh, I expect we do," Wood said on a sigh, then took a survey of the room once more, shaking his head. "This is one fancy chamber pot." Over and over he "flushed" as Hannah called it. It's what he was doing when she returned.

"Is something wrong?" she asked, eyeing him suspiciously.

"No. Everything's good."

Doubt creased her brow. "I found you some clothes. They might be a little small, but at least they're clean." She set the garments on the cabinet's marble top, as well as a narrow brush, a tiny tube with the word toothpaste on it and a pink *T*-shaped object. "The razor might not be sharp enough to cut through that beard of yours."

Wood deduced that the pink object was a razor. His hand moved to his jaw. "It's all right. I don't mind this."

From her expression he could see that she *did* mind. "I'll go downstairs and help Gabby. We'll see you when you've cleaned up." She pulled the door shut as she left.

"Cleaned up?" She made it sound as if he were an old pair of boots that needed to be polished and shined.

He looked again at his reflection in the mirror and shuddered. Even *he* didn't like the image staring him in the face. Where was the respected banker who had spent the last ten years earning the trust and confidence of the citizens of Missouri? He knew he could wash away the dirt and heal his wounds, but the question was, would he ever become that man again?

As he held up dark blue trousers, he knew he would do whatever was necessary to get back to 1876. Just as he had risked everything to find his sister, he would take whatever chance necessary to return to his old life. Even if it meant he returned to the scene of the lynching.

It was a sobering thought—going back to a place where folks wanted to see you dead. It was enough to make him shudder. He had escaped being unjustly hanged, how could he risk going back?

Because he had no choice. His sister Hannah was there. And she needed him. He had spent most of his life protecting her. He wasn't about to stop now just because he was in another century. He would travel anywhere—even across time—to find Hannah.

However, it wasn't his sister but the image of another Hannah who occupied his thoughts as he washed away the dirt and the grime. There had been tenderness in her eyes when she had given him a drink of water. And another emotion when she had untied his hands. An awareness of him. Despite her determination to pretend that she was indifferent toward him, he hadn't missed the way she had trembled when her flesh had accidentally brushed his.

Until he found a way back to 1876, he would do whatever he could to prove one thing to Hannah Davis. That he was not a man to fear.

"SEE, HE'S NOT SO BAD after all, is he?" Gabby told Hannah as she set a placemat on the kitchen table.

"He's not babbling today, if that's what you mean," Hannah answered, not wanting to admit that she was thinking along the same lines. Maybe it was because she always had been a softie when it came to wounded animals. And this man definitely needed some TLC. Only she wasn't going to be the one to give it to him.

"He only looks strange because of his clothes."

"It's not just his clothes, Gabby. Do you know I caught him playing with the toilet? He just stood there flushing it, over and over."

"Maybe it wasn't working properly," Gabby suggested. "We've never had a plumber out to fix anything. Nearly every faucet in the house drips." When Hannah opened her mouth to rebut, Gabby clicked her tongue. "You're not being very fair to him. He might be a very good worker."

"Gabby, how many times do I have to tell you we don't need a man on this farm?" Hannah's voice rose with emotion.

"I hope that doesn't mean I should go home?" a deep voice called out through the screen door.

Barry Wold, the implement mechanic who helped out with planting in the spring and the harvest in the fall, stood on the porch looking in.

"No, you we need. Come on in, Barry," Hannah instructed with a wave of her hand.

"What's up? I thought you two would have eaten breakfast by now," the young man commented as he hung his hat on a rack near the door.

"We have a guest," Gabby answered.

"Gabby has a guest," Hannah corrected. "That's why she's cooking. What about you, Barry? Did Caroline feed you enough this morning or would you like a couple of eggs?"

"No more food for me, but I will take some coffee before I go grease those augers." He pulled out a chair and sat down at the table. He tossed the county's weekly newspaper onto the table. "So I take it you two have been arguing about hiring permanent help again."

"Gabby's taken the matter into her own hands," Hannah told him. "We have someone here who wants the job."

"You don't sound very happy about it," he observed.

"I'm not. I think it's a bad idea." Her sentiments were echoed in the way she slammed the plate and silverware on the table.

"We need help," Gabby repeated with a hint of frustration in her voice. "Barry can't be expected to do all the work, especially not with the new baby coming and all."

Hannah looked at the younger man. "Is it going to be too much for you?"

"Actually, I've been meaning to talk to you about my work here," Barry said, tugging on an ear nervously.

Hannah could only stare at him in nervous anticipation of what he was about to say.

"Caroline and I are thinking of buying our own place."

Hannah felt as if the bottom had fallen out of her stomach. Barry was the extra hand she needed to get through harvest each year. Without his help, she wasn't sure she'd get the job done.

"I'll be here for harvest, but come next spring, I want to be planting my own acreage," he told her. "I'm sorry, Hannah. I know how much you count on me to help you."

Hannah tried to smile, but didn't succeed. "I understand."

"Even if we do get a place, you know you can always count on me if you're in a bind."

Hannah swallowed back the lump in her throat. She knew that if Barry had his own crops, there would be no time for him to help her. "That won't be necessary, Barry. We'll find someone to take your place. It's just not going to be this particular someone."

"Why? What's wrong with him?" he asked.

Before Hannah could answer, Gabby told Barry about Wood. "He has lots of farming experience," she ended. "I'm sure he'll be a big help during harvest."

"So where is this mystery man?" Barry asked.

"I thought he'd be down by now. Maybe you should go check on him," Gabby said to Hannah.

"I'm sure he'll be down in a few minutes." Hannah remained at the table.

Gabby wiped her hands on her apron saying, "Well, if you're not going to go, I will. He might have passed out again."

Hannah shoved back her chair. "All right, I'll do it." She rolled her eyes at Barry before leaving the room. She took her time on the stairs, dreading having to see the man again. The bathroom door was shut when she arrived. She took a deep breath, then knocked.

"Wood, breakfast is ready. Are you coming down?"

There was no answer.

She knocked again. "Wood. It's Hannah. Are you okay?"

Still, there was no reply.

Hannah began to wonder if something had happened to him. Maybe he had collapsed in the shower. She remembered how they had found him passed out on the ground last night.

She opened the door and was greeted by a wall of hot air. At least there was no body stretched out on the tile. Then she glanced at the tub. The shower curtain was pulled. "Wood?" Still, no response.

Cautiously, she pulled back the edge of the shower curtain. A small shriek escaped her lips at the sight of Wood immersed to his chest in a tub full of water.

His eyes were shut, his head sagging against the wall. Hannah didn't know if he was sleeping or unconscious. She tried to focus her attention on his head and not the rest of his naked body which was in full view. "Wood!"

Suddenly his eyes flew open. When they saw Hannah, they were just as startled as hers. He grabbed the washcloth and covered as much of himself as it was possible to hide with an eight-inch square of cloth.

Not that it mattered, for Hannah had whipped the shower curtain shut with so much force it whooshed. She crossed the tiny bathroom floor as fast as her feet would carry her. From the doorway she called out, "Breakfast is ready."

"Yes, ma'am."

By the time she returned to the kitchen she was certain that her cheeks were still flaming. However, no one looked at her any differently than they had when she had left. Gabby simply inquired about Wood.

"Is he coming down?"

"In a few minutes." Hannah steadied her trembling hands by shoving them into her jeans pockets.

"Well, at least he's okay," Gabby placed a lid over the stack of pancakes.

"Yup. He's fine."

Hannah sat down at the table and gave her attention to Barry, but no matter how hard she tried, she couldn't forget the sight of Wood naked in the water. It had been a shock to her system, seeing a stranger in all his glory, his knees bent so that his long legs could fit in the tub, the whiteness of his body a sharp contrast to the sunburned skin on his face and hands. With one quick glance, she had seen more of him than she wanted to see of any man.

She forced the memory from her mind and vowed she would act as though she hadn't seen him at such a private moment. However, a few minutes later when he entered the kitchen, her entire body warmed.

Although he now wore a chambray shirt and a pair of faded twill work pants, she couldn't forget that only minutes ago he had been naked. She didn't want to stare at him, but she couldn't help be a bit bewildered by the transformation he had made. She could hardly believe what a difference a bath and a razor made in his appearance. Gone was the stubble that had darkened his jaw, leaving a neat mustache. Shampoo had put some life back into hair that had clung to his skull as if it had been painted on his head. Hannah could see why Gabby had been impressed by a photograph of the neat and clean Wood. He was a handsome man.

But it was his eyes that captured her attention. There was something compelling in their dark sparkle, something besides the fact that they shared a secret with her, one which he found amusing but she found embarrassing. Despite her attempt to not allow him to intimidate her, she was the first one to look away.

"Why, look at you!" Gabby gushed enthusiastically. "Now you look like the man I expected. Come and meet Barry." She ushered him over to the table where he sat down across from the younger man.

Gabby introduced the two men who both sized each

other up with a critical eye. Hannah thought that next to Wood Dumler, Barry looked like a Boy Scout. Even after a bath and a shave Wood still looked rough around the edges.

"I hear you've come looking for a job," Barry said amiably as Gabby set a stack of pancakes in front of Wood.

"Gabby thinks there's enough work to warrant having another pair of hands around this place," he answered.

"We can always use that, but I have to admit, Hannah does a pretty good job of running the place on her own." Barry gave Hannah a smile of admiration.

"I expect she does," Wood agreed. "She looks like a capable woman."

Hannah's head jerked in his direction. Capable? What was that supposed to mean? That she was sturdy looking? "You two don't need to talk as if I'm not here," she snapped.

"The boys could use coffee," Gabby pointed out to Hannah, who welcomed the opportunity to get up from the table. Just because she had seen Wood Dumler in the all together didn't mean she should act as if he were a man whose opinion mattered.

Because it didn't. He was a stranger and one she didn't plan to hire. It didn't matter what he thought about her as a farmer or as a woman, and she needed to remind herself of that fact.

She retrieved the glass carafe from the coffeemaker, aware that Wood's eyes followed her movement. As she leaned over his shoulder to fill his cup, she could smell the fresh scent of soap, and again the memory of him in the bathtub flashed in her mind.

"Thank you, ma'am," Wood said softly, his eyes meeting hers.

She quickly looked away and moved over to Barry who appeared to be intrigued by Wood.

"So what made you want to come all the way from Nebraska to work in Minnesota?"

Wood exchanged glances with Gabby who answered for him, "He wanted to try something different, didn't you, Wood?"

Wood nodded.

Barry pressed onward. "You ever harvest corns and soybeans?"

"I've never worked a farm this big," Wood replied.

"And you won't be working this one until you're well." Gabby set a bottle of syrup in front of Wood's plate. It was apparent by the way she fluttered around Wood that she had become his champion. "Are you feeling any stronger?"

"I expect I will be once I eat these cakes."

"Help yourself to butter and syrup, Wood," Gabby instructed.

Wood set his fork down and reached for the plastic bottle. He studied it for several seconds before Gabby said, "That's a pop top. You just push up."

Long fingers fumbled with the top and finally managed to open the bottle. He poured a liberal serving over the pancakes.

Hannah couldn't help but notice the size of his hands. They were large, but they weren't callused nor did they appear to be hardened from doing physical labor. They looked more like the hands of a surgeon than a farm hand.

"You forgot to give Wood a knife," Gabby observed and went over to the drawer to get him one.

Hannah tried to make eye contact with her aunt, wanting to discourage her from giving Wood the utensil. Gabby, however, seemed oblivious to Hannah's efforts. She plunked a stainless steel knife down next to Wood's place with a satisfied, "There you go."

Wood didn't miss the apprehensive look Hannah cast in

her aunt's direction. Hannah Davis didn't trust him. Nor did her hired hand. That much was certain.

Wood didn't know what he could say to earn their trust, or if it even mattered. If he could figure out how to time travel back to 1876, he wouldn't need to pretend to be this Alfred person. If not, he'd have to rely on Gabby to help him play the part.

"Maybe you want to come out with me this morning," Barry suggested. "I could use some help sweeping out the bins, and you could get an idea of how things work around this place."

"He needs to rest this morning," Gabby responded before he could. "And if he's feeling better this afternoon, I'm going to take him to town to get a few things."

"You aren't supposed to drive until you get your new glasses," Hannah reminded her.

"I can see fine." Gabby dismissed her concern with a flap of her hand.

"Not distance," Hannah retorted.

"No one has to take me." Wood spoke up. He looked at Hannah and said, "If you let me take one of your horses, I expect I can get to town on my own."

Hannah exchanged looks with Barry and Gabby. It was Gabby who finally said, "No one rides a horse to town in these parts, Wood. Hannah probably wouldn't mind if you borrowed the old pickup in the garage."

"Only if you have a valid driver's license," Hannah added.

Wood felt three pairs of eyes on him. What in the world were they talking about?

When he didn't say anything, Hannah repeated, "Do you have a driver's license, Wood?"

He knew there was no point in pretending he did. "No. It's not necessary where I come from."

The way the three of them were staring at him Wood would have thought he had an extra eye on his head. Was there some law in Minnesota that required farmers to have a license to drive their horses?

Gabby broke the uneasy silence. "You really don't need a license here on the farm, either. No one's going to check."

Hannah disagreed. "Wait a minute. I'm not going to let an unlicensed driver on any of my equipment."

"You've been taking that stuff out since you were a kid," Gabby reminded her.

"Yes, but I had an adult with me most of the time. Driving a beat-up old pickup is one thing. The combine is another. It's too expensive to leave in the hands of someone who's not experienced."

Wood felt as if he had fallen into a sink hole. He was beginning to think the smartest thing to do would be to admit that he wasn't Alfred Dumler and that he hadn't come for a job. Then he looked at Hannah and thought about the insane asylum. He kept silent.

"My wife's cousin runs a driving school over in Harmony. He could probably take lessons there," Barry suggested.

"There you go. That problem is solved," Gabby said cheerfully.

Hannah did not look as if she liked the solution one bit. She pushed back her chair and stood. "We need to get to work." She looked at Barry, who finished his coffee, then rose to his feet.

Wood watched Hannah walk over to a pegged rack on the wall, reach for a cap and slip it over her blond curls. "We'll be back around noon," she told Gabby. To Wood she said, "You have this morning to get your act together."

Then she stomped out the back door leaving Wood to wonder what it meant to get an act together. Did she think he was a stage performer?

"Don't worry about it, Wood." Gabby patted his hand

reassuringly. "She'll show you how to run the equipment. Once she gets to know you, everything will be just fine."

Wood nodded in agreement, although he should have said the only way things would be *just fine* would be if he could figure out a way to get back to 1876. Right now he wanted no part of running any equipment—whatever it might be.

He needed to go back to his old life. He hadn't died by the noose, and he sure as hell didn't want his old life to be dead. It didn't matter how pretty Hannah Davis was. He wasn't going to live the rest of his life as a twentieth-century farmer.

Chapter Five

"Are you sure you're feeling all right?" Gabby asked Wood as she cleared away the breakfast dishes. "Yoo-hoo, Wood?" She waved a hand in front of his face.

Wood looked at her. "What is it, Gabby?"

"You've been staring at that clock on the wall for so long now I thought you might have fallen asleep with your eyes open."

Wood knew what she said was true. He had been staring at the clock, waiting for each movement of the large hand. He found it amazing that a hundred and twenty-two years had passed in barely the blink of an eye, yet now each minute seemed to take an eternity to tick away.

In the strangeness of his surroundings, the clock was the only thing in the room which had any significance for him. Why or how he had traveled through time, he didn't know, but he wished he could find the answers in the timepiece hanging on the wall.

"Have you ever lost track of time, Gabby?"

"Sure. Hasn't everyone?"

"Perhaps," he answered. Only he hadn't lost track of time. It had lost track of him. If time had simply passed, he'd be one hundred and fifty-six years old. He looked down at his hands. They were the hands of a thirty-four-year-old man, as was the face that had stared at him in the mirror this morning.

His bewilderment must have shown on his face for Gabby said, "Maybe you ought to lie down?"

Wood wondered if she would be this concerned for his health if she knew that he was not the prospective hired hand, Alfred Dumler, but a man who had been about to be hanged? It wasn't likely.

"I doubt rest is going to cure the jumbled mess I'm in," Wood said cryptically.

"What is it, Wood? Are you in some kind of trouble?"

The concern on her face tugged at his conscience. He didn't want to deceive her, yet what choice did he have? With no place to call home, he needed her help if he was going to find a way back to his previous life.

"I can't remember how I arrived here, Gabby. It's as if one minute it was Tuesday and then all of a sudden it was Thursday and whatever happened in between is gone from my memory," he said honestly.

"That's because you've been sick, Wood. From the heat. I'm guessing that you might have had to hitchhike part of the way in the hot sun and—"

"Hitchhike?" he interrupted.

She nodded. "I know you had planned to come on the bus, but maybe for some reason you couldn't take the bus and you ended up hitchhiking. Maybe you got as far as the interstate and had to walk the rest of the way with your suitcase. Spending hours in the sun dressed in heavy clothing could have brought on exhaustion."

Although he knew that wasn't the case, he nodded all the same. "It's important to me that I recollect how I came to be in your cornfield," he told her. "Who was the first person to find me?"

"That was Jeremy. I was waiting for you at the house in case you called. You were late, but then so was the bus."

"Perhaps then Jeremy can help me. It is possible that

my memory could return if I were to visit the place where he found me. Do you think he could be persuaded to accompany me to that particular location?''

"You mean the Nelson forty?"

Wood nodded.

"Jeremy's in school until three, but as soon as he comes home I'll have him take you there."

"I would appreciate that." He reached out to give her hand a gentle squeeze. "You are a kind woman, Gabby Davis."

She leaned closer to him and looked him straight in the eye. "I want you to be honest with me, Wood. You're not supposed to be in a psychiatric ward of some hospital right now, are you?"

"No, I'm not crazy, Gabby. You believe that, don't you?"

"I do," she said sincerely. "I wouldn't have brought you here for Hannah if I thought you weren't right, up here." She tapped a bony finger to her forehead. "And I thank you for not telling Hannah that I was the one who wrote to you."

"Are you certain this is the best plan for your situation?"

"Oh, yes," she said anxiously. "Hannah needs a man. It all comes down to the same thing. M-o-n-e-y," she spelled out.

Suddenly Wood had an uneasy feeling. Was this Alfred person supposed to help these two women with their financial woes? If so, his web of deceit could end up trapping him but good. What money he had was locked up in a bank in Missouri—or at least it was in 1876.

"I'm not a man of means, Gabby," Wood confessed soberly.

"I know that, Wood. I picked you because of who you are, not because of how much money you have."

Wood was afraid he had offended her. "Of course. I didn't mean to offend your integrity."

She dismissed him with a wave of her hand. "All that matters is that you and Hannah hit it off. Isn't that what's important in situations like this?"

"Yes, it is," he agreed, unsure what *hit it off* meant.

"First she needs to get used to having you around, then she'll see for herself what a special man you are…" she trailed off with a dreamy look on her face. "I think you're going to be just perfect for her."

Guilt punched Wood in the stomach. He had no intention of staying and becoming Hannah's "perfect" hired hand. "I mean no disrespect, Gabby, but Hannah appears to be eager for me to leave."

"Oh, no, she's not. She's agreed to let you stay for a couple of days."

"She told you that?"

"Oh, yes. And I'm hoping two days will lead to three and then four and so on and so on…" She gave him a shy expectant grin.

Wood didn't know how long he would need the Davises' hospitality. Hopefully, the real Alfred Dumler wouldn't make his presence known until Wood had traveled back to 1876.

"And if she wants me to leave after the two days are up?" he queried.

"That's where it's up to you to convince her to let you stay. Whether or not Hannah wants to admit it, she needs someone like you."

Wood was quite certain that Hannah wouldn't agree, but he didn't contradict the old lady. Right now Gabby Davis was his only ally.

"No matter how long I stay, I want you to know that I'll work for my keep."

"Until our plan works?"

If that plan included a job, Wood couldn't say no. "Yes, ma'am. What about Hannah? What do I do to convince her I can do the job?"

"First thing, you need to show her that you're smart. One thing she can't stand is foolishness." She wagged her finger at him. "And you have to show her you mean business. I'm warning you, it's going to be a challenge."

"You sound as if you want to help me," he said with a smile.

"I do," Gabby said. "But it's going to be tough." Gabby went on. "Hannah's a bit hard-headed at times. You spend an hour with me and I'll tell you what you need to know to fit in around here. But first we need to get you some clothes and a haircut." She appraised him for several seconds and added, "Well, maybe the hair's all right."

"And my mustache?"

"It looks like it's been there a long time."

Wood smiled and thought to himself. Oh, if you only knew how long.

"Where is he?" Hannah asked as she stepped into the kitchen and saw Gabby at the stove.

"Are you talking about Wood?" Gabby looked up from gravy she was stirring.

"Yes, I mean Wood." She slipped her baseball cap onto the rack near the door. "I don't suppose we're lucky enough to have him on the bus that left Stanleyville at ten."

Gabby shot her a reproving look. "He's resting. I think by tomorrow he'll be able to help you with the chores."

"I don't want him helping me with the chores," she retorted. "What I want is to send him packing. Oops, forgot." She gave her aunt a contrite look. "Can't pack when you have nothing to pack, can you?"

Gabby made a gesture as if she might whack Hannah with her wooden spoon.

"Just go tell him lunch is ready, will you?"

Reluctantly, Hannah went to fetch Wood from the bunkhouse. "Okay, Wood Dumler, time to get up," she called out, marching into the bunkhouse in a military fashion.

When there was no answer, she mumbled to herself, "My goodness, you do sleep soundly. Wood!" she shouted.

Still, there was no movement from the bunk area. As Hannah crossed the wooden floor, she saw him spread out on a cot, his stomach to the mattress, his torso bare. "I suppose I should be grateful he's at least wearing pants," she murmured as she approached the bed.

It only took a moment for Hannah to realize why he slept on his stomach. Dark, ugly bruises covered his back. She clutched her midsection, sickened by the thought of what kind of pain had been inflicted to cause the discoloration on Wood's back. He said he had fallen from a horse, but unless he had been dragged on the ground, she doubted any fall would produce so many contusions.

This time when she called out his name, he awoke. He seemed surprised to see her standing there. As he rolled to his side, he grimaced, obviously in discomfort. As soon as he saw the sympathy on Hannah's face, he tried to act as if nothing was wrong.

"Why does your back look like a stampede of cattle crossed it?" she asked.

"Perhaps one did." He reached for the shirt at the foot of the bed.

"Don't be flip with me, Wood."

"Flip?"

"I want a straight answer."

He stood, so that he towered over her, then leaned close and said next to her ear, "I encountered the wrong folks on my way to Minnesota."

If he had wanted to shock her, he succeeded. "You've been beaten." Hannah shuddered as she realized that he must have been bound and gagged. It would explain why there were rope burns on his neck and wrists.

He turned around, as if suddenly modest, to slip on his shirt.

"You need to put some dressings on your back," she advised him.

He reached over to the nightstand and grabbed the tube of analgesic creme she had given him that morning. "I've been using this."

"You need something stronger. Come with me."

"You don't have to..." He started to protest but she hushed him.

"Come with me," she ordered.

He did, following her across the yard and to the house. Gabby's eyes twinkled as she watched Hannah drag their guest by the hand, through the kitchen, the front of his shirt partially buttoned. Up the stairs they went, this time Hannah pushing Wood in front of her as they climbed.

Once they were in the bathroom, she had him remove his shirt while she rummaged through one of the cupboards. It didn't take long to find what she was looking for—a half-empty bottle of a yellow liquid.

"This is a strong liniment the doctor prescribed for me when I fell off the roof last fall. I had some bruises that looked almost as bad as those." She grimaced as she examined his back.

"What were you doing on the roof?"

"Trying to fix the TV antenna. It got all twisted around during a storm, and Gabby was upset because she couldn't watch her soaps," she said as she unscrewed the cap.

Wood had no idea what a TV antenna was or why Gabby would want to watch soap, but he could picture Hannah on the roof, and the thought sent a chill through him. "Forgive me for sayin' so, ma'am, but a woman should not climb a roof. That's man's work."

She poured a small puddle of the liquid into her palm and paused. "Just for the record, Wood, there is no man's work or woman's work here on the farm. It's just plain old work. Not that it matters, because in case you haven't noticed, I don't have a man. I am, however, a *capable* woman," she reminded him of his own words. "Now turn a bit and I'll put this on for you."

She had a gentle, soothing touch that had Wood closing his eyes as she spread the liniment across his battered and bruised flesh. It was a bittersweet experience, her fingers applying the balm tenderly to the painful contusions.

"Sorry," she murmured when he flinched from the discomfort. "Do you want me to stop?"

"No." He wanted her to rub not only his back, but his chest as well. And his arms, his legs... He shook his head at the improper direction his thoughts were headed.

It did no good. Hannah's touch created a physical reaction in him that couldn't be denied. He only hoped he could prevent her from seeing it.

He couldn't. As she finished his back, she craned her head around his front side to see if there were any bruises on his chest. As she did, she noticed the bulge in trousers that were already too tight for him.

"Well, I'll leave you to finish." She set the bottle on the cabinet, her cheeks red, her eyes avoiding his. "You can use this wherever you have soreness. I'd better go help Gabby with lunch."

Without another word or a glance in his direction, she left.

HANNAH ALWAYS CLEANED the kitchen after their noon meal, giving Gabby a chance to take her daily nap. Today she would have liked to exit the house as fast as possible. Lunch with Wood had been an unsettling experience. While Gabby had chatted with him as if he were a long-lost friend, Hannah had sat awkwardly, feeling as if she were the unwanted visitor, not he.

It was an unusual experience for her—being intimidated by a man. Normally with a couple of pointed looks and a few sharp words she could send the message that she was not a woman who wanted or needed a man's attention. But she didn't feel like her normal self when she was in Wood's company. Her emotions acted like the jumping beans Jeremy had brought home from the county fair—she never knew which way they'd move.

That's why when Gabby went upstairs to take her nap, she said to Wood, "You probably want to go back to the bunkhouse and rest."

Wood stared at her, twirling his fork between his fingertips. "I feel rested, thank you. Gabby said I should ask you what you want me to help you do."

There was something disturbing about the way he coolly looked her up and down as he spoke to her. She decided to take the offensive rather than let him put her on the defensive.

"Look, if you're feeling well enough to work, then I guess you're well enough to travel." She didn't want to be rude, but she wanted him out of her house.

"What about the job?" he asked.

"There is no job. Gabby should have never said that there was." Hannah started clearing the dishes from the table to avoid looking at his eyes. "I'm sorry if it's caused you any inconvenience, but that's the way it is."

He stopped playing with his fork. "This morning you told me I could stay a few days and prove that I can do the job."

"I changed my mind."

She could feel his eyes on her, but she refused to look at him.

"I should have known this was coming. It's because of what happened in the bath, isn't it?"

"Hardly," she denied vehemently. "I've seen naked men before, Mr. Dumler."

"That may be, but then why is it every time your eyes meet mine your cheeks turn pink?"

She turned to face him, determined not to blush. "You think I'm embarrassed?"

"It's understandable. Walking in on a man at a most private moment would cause any respectable lady's cheeks to blush." His dark eyes sparkled with amusement.

Hannah couldn't believe her ears! He was talking to her as if she had deliberately tried to sneak a peek at his private parts.

"Only because you didn't answer the door. I thought you might have fallen and bumped your head...or passed out or something," she explained, her voice rising as she clanged cups and glasses together.

"I dozed off for a few minutes."

Again, the memory of him in that tub of water flashed in her mind, and she felt her body warm. She wished she had never pulled that damn shower curtain open. But she had, and she had looked at him and as much as she wanted to deny it, she had seen *all* of Wood Dumler.

"It doesn't matter." She dismissed the subject, hoping that at the same time she could get rid of the image of him in that tub. She didn't. "What we should be discussing is when you plan to leave."

The sparkle of humor left his eyes. "Gabby warned me you might give me the heave-ho."

"Did she also tell you that I didn't answer your ad?"

He nodded. "She said you're too stubborn to admit you need help. She also said something about you wanting to prove that a woman can run this farm without a man."

"I can," she said with a lift of her chin.

"I guess I don't see why you wouldn't want another strong pair of hands."

"It's not the hands I object to, it's the body that goes with them," she retorted, then carried a stack of plates over to the sink.

He got up out of his chair and followed her. "Am I supposed to take that in its literal sense?"

He wanted to make her blush and he succeeded. "You can take it any way you like."

"Does that mean if I promise to keep my clothes on I can stay?" he asked.

Once again Hannah couldn't believe her ears. He was flirting with her. Unwanted, came a physical response that started somewhere in the vicinity of her stomach. It was a series of tremors she couldn't locate but she knew they were there just the same. She needed to squelch it quickly.

"This has nothing to do with what happened when you were in the tub," she stated in as dull a tone as she could muster. "I don't need your help."

"Because I'm a man?"

His proximity caused her pulse to flutter and she side-stepped him to collect the pots and pans from the stove. "Why is it when a woman doesn't want or need the help of a man, you men think it's a sexual issue?" she asked, slamming the dishes onto the cupboard with a clatter.

"Isn't it?" His dark brown eyes didn't waver from her face.

"No." She plunged her hands into the soapy dishwater to keep them from trembling. "For someone who desperately wants a job, you're not winning any points with the boss," she warned.

He stepped even closer and her heartbeat went up another notch. "Pardon me, ma'am, if I offended you. I was merely making an observation. I apologize for any inconsiderate comments I may have made. Attribute it to my ignorance. I've never been on a farm run by women."

His apology disarmed her. One minute he was flirting with her, the next he was sincerely contrite. "Maybe you'd have trouble working for a woman?"

"I don't believe I would."

"Have you ever worked for a woman before?"

"No, but that does not mean I would have difficulty working for you. I know this is your farm and you're going to do things your way. I respect that. I'm a hard worker, Hannah. I could help you if you'd let me."

When those brown eyes softened, so did her resistance. "I'm sorry, but the truth is I can't afford to pay another hired hand."

"All you have to give me is a roof over my head and three meals a day," he told her. "I don't expect any wages."

"That wouldn't be fair to you."

"It's all I need for now."

Hannah could hardly believe that she was considering saying yes. She knew little about him other than the fact that he had been beaten and now appeared to have no place to go other than her farm. Her common sense screamed not to listen to her heart that saw the plea for compassion in those compelling brown eyes.

"Let me think it over," she heard herself say.

WOOD SPENT most of the afternoon watching the clock. Ever since Gabby had told him Jeremy would be home at three-thirty, he had been edgy as he waited for the boy to return from school. Gabby thought he needed more rest, but what he needed was to find a way back to his sister. Right now, Jeremy appeared to be the only one with information that could possibly help him.

"Wow. You look different," the lad said when he saw Wood waiting for him on the porch steps.

"I had a bath." Wood stood, feeling uneasy in his twentieth-century trousers. "The clothes don't fit." He tugged on the cuff of the denim shirt.

Outlaw, who had been at Jeremy's side ever since he had hopped off the school bus, now transferred his affection to Wood, sniffing at his leg. Wood automatically reached down to scratch the dog's ears.

"Outlaw likes you. He's the one who found you after you got struck by lightning."

"Is that what you think happened to me?" Wood wondered if that hadn't been the reason why he had traveled from 1876 to 1998.

"You were next to this big old oak on the Nelson forty. Lightning ripped one of its branches right off." His eyes widened at the memory.

"Would you take me to the tree?"

"You want to see it?"

When Wood nodded, he gestured for him to follow. "Come on. I'll show you."

As they walked, Jeremy recounted in detail what had happened the afternoon of the storm. When they reached a large oak with a broken limb, he said, "There it is. Mom says it's probably the oldest tree on the farm. Look at how fat the trunk is."

Wood stared at the oak, trying to imagine what it had looked like one hundred and twenty-two years ago. Was this the tree from which he had hung?

Jeremy motioned for Wood to follow him. "If you come around this side you can see that it was hit by lightning one other time. It has a scar, see?"

Wood digested everything Jeremy had told him. Could this tree be the spot where his time travel had occurred? If it was, then it was possible that Jeremy's theory that he had been struck by lightning was correct. After all, Wood could remember sitting on the horse with a noose around his neck just as a bolt of lightning flashed in the sky.

"Where was I the first time you saw me?" he asked, surveying his surroundings.

Jeremy dropped down into the tall grass and spread his arms and legs. "You were lying just like this, with that tree limb right above your head."

Wood got down beside him, hoping to jar some memory that would answer his questions. Stretched out in the tall grass, he closed his eyes and willed his mind to recall what had happened.

"You know you're lucky you're not dead," Jeremy told him, sounding very adult-like.

"Yes, I am," Wood agreed soberly.

"Most people get killed when lightning hits 'em."

Similar thoughts had crossed Wood's mind. Why had he not died? It was true he had heard of instances where folks had survived being hit by the deadly bolt, but they were rare cases. So if it was lightning that had transported him forward in time, he had to question whether it would also take him back.

The more he thought about returning to 1876, the more grim the picture became. Not only would he have to worry about returning to the scene of the lynching where he could possibly die in the noose, he also had to fear that before he ever made it back in time, he could possibly be one of the not-so-lucky struck dead by lightning.

Wood racked his brain trying to think of any other means by which he could have time traveled. None came to mind. He had sat on the horse, seen the lightning bolt and then been whisked through time.

A horrible feeling of hopelessness swept over him. What were the chances that he would be struck by lightning twice? And even if he was, would it take him back in time or kill him?

When he had left Missouri all he had wanted was to find his sister. Now it appeared that was never going to happen. How was he ever going to rest not knowing what had happened to her?

The answer was he couldn't. He would have to find a way to get back. Even if it cost him his life.

Chapter Six

"Where's my baby book?" Jeremy asked as he sat down for dinner that evening.

Hannah frowned. "Why do you want that?"

"Because I have to do a family tree for history and write a report about what it was like to live in Minnesota at the turn of the century. My teacher says a baby book is a good place to start. You have one for me, don't you?"

"Yes, but I'm not sure where it is," Hannah fibbed, pulling a gallon of milk from the refrigerator. Like most mothers, she had kept a baby book, knowing that one day Jeremy might need to know the name of his paternal ancestors. Now that that day was here, though, she found it disconcerting.

"I can help you," Gabby volunteered. "I have several old Davis family diaries dating back to the original homesteaders. What information we can't find in my collection, we'll go look for at the library."

"You have a library in town?" Wood asked.

"Oh, yes. I worked there for almost forty years," she replied proudly. "If you want to know about local history, it's all there."

"I think history is boring. Don't you, Wood?" Jeremy asked.

Wood didn't answer. "Let me get that for you, ma'am."

Wood took the plate of steaming corn on the cob from Gabby's hands and carried it to the table. Then he held her chair as she sat down.

"Why thank you, Wood. How gentlemanly of you." Gabby beamed.

Hannah rolled her eyes. Before Wood had a chance to help her, she pulled out a chair and sat down.

"How come you call Gabby and my mom ma'am?" Jeremy wanted to know, the subject of history quickly forgotten.

"Where I come from, men address women that way out of respect," Wood answered.

"Is that why you hold the chair for them, too?"

"Yes."

"Not all women appreciate being called ma'am," Hannah said pointedly.

"She thinks it makes her sound old, but I think it's rather sweet, Wood," Gabby remarked, her face glowing. "A man with good manners is hard to find nowadays."

Hannah had to admit that Wood Dumler had social graces she wouldn't have expected for someone who arrived looking like a vagrant. It made her wonder if Gabby was right—he was simply a man down on his luck.

"Are you feeling better now that you've rested?" Gabby asked when Wood was seated across from her.

"I am."

Gabby turned to Hannah and said, "Aren't we lucky? Now that Barry's not going to be here for a few days, Wood can take his place."

"Why isn't Barry going to be here?"

"He called just before you came in and said he was taking Caroline to the hospital." For Wood's benefit she added, "Caroline is Barry's wife, and she's expecting their first child."

"But the baby isn't due for another month!"

"That's true, but her labor pains are five minutes apart. It looks like she's going to have a preemie."

Hannah felt as if someone had taken the wind out of her sails. She was counting on Barry for harvest. "That means I'll have to do the beans without him."

"What about Wood?" Gabby asked. "He's a little inexperienced with the machinery, but I bet you're a quick learner, aren't you, Wood?"

"I'm here to assist you in any way I can," he offered. "That is, if you want me to stay."

"Of course she wants you to stay," Gabby answered for her. "One woman can't harvest 400 acres of beans."

Hannah knew what Gabby said was true. Without Barry she had no choice. She looked up at Wood, who stared at her, waiting for an answer.

"He can stay," Hannah stated evenly. "Only until Barry returns."

"He'll need coveralls," Gabby pointed out. "I think Big Fred left a pair in that closet in the bunkhouse."

"Forgive me for saying so, ma'am, but Big Fred wasn't as big as you recall," Wood interrupted. He stood and pulled the pant legs out of his boots.

The bottoms of the legs stopped short of his ankles. Wood looked like a little kid whose mother refused to buy him new britches until the old ones had holes in the knees.

"Well," Gabby said, "I guess we need to take him to town, Hannah. He can't work in clothes that don't fit."

Hannah agreed. "We'll go tomorrow afternoon."

"It's not necessary. If you give me back my things, I reckon I can get by," Wood told them.

"I did wash your clothes, Wood, but you're going to need more than one set if you're going to work in the fields," Gabby assured him.

When they had finished eating, Gabby gave Wood his freshly laundered garments as well as Big Fred's coveralls which he eagerly took to the bunkhouse. While he changed,

Hannah pruned the rose bushes that grew alongside the house. At the sound of a screen door slamming, she glanced in the direction of the bunkhouse.

Wood was coming toward her, walking as if he had a wedgie. As she shaded her eyes from the setting sun, she realized he was walking funny because he could barely button the cotton shirt and the pants—well, she understood the reason for his scowl.

"What did she do to my clothes?"

"I'm sorry."

He chuckled but it was not a humorous sound. "This is worse than those other clothes you gave me to wear...." He looked down at the shirt cuffs that stopped about an inch from his wrists.

He appeared so comical Hannah had to stifle a giggle. "You can pick out another pair of pants and a shirt at my expense."

"You don't have to pay for anything. I'll work for whatever it is you give me," he said irritably.

"But it was our mistake."

"I told you. I don't accept charity. I work for whatever I get," he stated firmly.

She dusted off her hands and wiped them on her jeans. "Fair enough. We'll go first thing in the morning. Let me put my things away, and I'll show you where everything is on the farm."

When she would have bent over to pick up her knee pad and her garden shears, Wood beat her to it. As he stooped, however, the sound of fabric tearing stopped him in mid-motion. The crotch of his pants had come open at the seam.

Hannah's eyes met his.

"It isn't anything you haven't already seen, is it?" he said with a lift of one brow, then went back inside the bunkhouse.

Again, he had successfully turned the tables on her. She was the one who blushed, not him.

When he reappeared, he wore Big Fred's coveralls. Although they were old, she didn't need to worry that he'd pop any buttons or split any seams.

Wood, however, didn't look any less uncomfortable than before. "Now you look more like a farmer," Hannah remarked, wanting to chase away the uneasiness on his face.

"I look like a man wearing another man's clothes," he retorted. "But I do believe I am ready to work."

"Just about," she told him. "Give me your arms."

As he held them out straight, Hannah rolled back the cuffs until his forearms were bare. "There. That's better. Now what you need is a hat. Wait here." She went back into the house and found a brand new baseball cap one of the chemical companies had given her at a co-op meeting last spring. It was a bright yellow with the company logo emblazoned across the front in black.

"You'll need this when the sun shines," she told him.

Wood took it from her, eyed it curiously, then put it on, with the brim facing backward.

"Considering you're recovering from heat stroke, it might be wise to wear it the old-fashioned way."

He shrugged. "Jeremy wears his like this. I thought I might look more like one of the local people if I did."

Hannah could have told him that it wouldn't matter how he wore the hat. No one was going to mistake him for a local. When he had turned the cap around she said, "Okay, let's get started."

She led him around the long row of tall pines that separated their living quarters from the farm and took him through most of the farm.

As they stepped into the barn, several cats wandered over to greet them. "Here's where most of the animals are." For the first time all day Hannah thought Wood finally seemed at ease. "We have twelve stalls, but right now I only have six horses." They walked through the building and out the opposite end into the pasture where the horses grazed.

Most of them were at the far end fenced area, grazing. One silvery gray Arabian, however, stood not more than fifteen feet from them. "Who's this?" Wood asked, eyeing the horse with interest.

"His name is Bullet and I should warn you, he's rather highly strung."

Wood ignored her warning and approached the animal very slowly, his hand stretched out in front of him, palm down. At first the horse shied away, but Wood didn't give up. He continued to talk to him under his breath, crooning patiently until to Hannah's surprise, her skittish gelding allowed Wood to run his hand along his neck.

"He doesn't normally let strangers get close." Hannah couldn't keep the wonder from her voice.

"He knows I'm not a threat." His eyes pierced hers with the same message.

Wood spoke softly into the horse's ear and Hannah could see that whatever he lacked in machinery knowledge he obviously made up for in animal handling skills. First it was Outlaw, now Bullet. Could it be that Wood was as trustworthy as Gabby wanted Hannah to believe he was?

When Bullet moved away, Wood asked, "You don't have any work horses?"

She shook her head. "No one around here uses horses in the field. I've been thinking about getting a couple of draft horses, but they wouldn't be for work, just to pull my wagons at the shows."

Wood pushed the brim back on his hat and squinted. "What the heck is that?"

Hannah followed the direction of his gaze. "It's a pig."

"In with the horses?"

"What do you suggest I do with an eight hundred and fifty pound pig?" she asked dryly. "I won Wilbur at the county fair. He was just a little thing back then. I wouldn't have kept him, but ever since Jeremy saw the movie *Babe* he won't let me get rid of him.''

"He is big.''

Hannah nodded. ''Jeremy made him a box but he broke out of it so we had to put him in here with the horses. He likes to rut around for bugs in the manure pile.''

"He's going to start thinking he is a horse if you leave him out here,'' Wood warned her.

"Come here, Wilbur,'' Hannah called out to the pig, who snorted, then waddled over toward her. She slapped his backside and tickled the flesh behind his ears. ''You're a good pig, aren't you, Wilbur?''

"He gets much bigger he won't taste very good.''

"We couldn't eat him!'' Hannah exclaimed. ''He's Jeremy's pet!''

He chuckled, shaking his head in disbelief. ''A pig for a pet?''

"What's wrong with that?'' she demanded.

He simply shrugged, hiding a smile.

"What's so amusing?'' When he didn't answer right away, she added, ''Well?''

"You're sentimental.''

"And you find that funny?'' she asked, trying not to bristle.

"I find it charming.''

With one look from his dark brown eyes the atmosphere became charged with a sexual awareness. Her heart beat nervously as his eyes glittered with an emotion any woman would recognize. Desire. Not that it should have surprised her. Ever since he had first laid eyes on her there had been a flickering gleam of interest in them. And she would have had to have been blind not to notice the way his body had responded earlier today when she had rubbed liniment into his bruised muscles.

She was no stranger to sexual attraction, although it did seem to be a strange phenomenon. Why was it that she would be attracted to Wood Dumler, a man who didn't drive, who came from who knows where and whose past included a beating by God only knows what kind of people?

Yet she was attracted to him. That's why she was staring at his mouth and wondering what it would feel like to have those sun-parched lips on hers. Would that mustache tickle?

As if he could read her thoughts, he bent and brushed her lips with his. Surprisingly, they weren't rough, but soft and warm, with only the slightest hint of prickliness where the sun had left its mark. She trembled at the sweet stirring of desire that erupted inside her.

When her lips parted ever so slightly, he pinned her against the fence, a hand on either side of her. Hannah discovered that his mustache didn't tickle, but tantalized, tempting her to press her body closer to his and open her mouth to his tongue.

It had been a long time since any man had kissed her, and Hannah felt like a dieter being thrown a pound of chocolate fudge. Although kissing Wood should have been off limits, he tasted so good she couldn't resist the temptation to enjoy every moment of the pleasure. Her lips couldn't get enough of his and would never have left his had not Jeremy's voice rang out.

"Mom?"

Hannah could see the disappointment in Wood's eyes at the realization that their kiss had ended not by choice, but by an intruder. When he looked as if he wasn't about to let her go, Hannah pushed at his chest.

"We're out here," she called out just seconds before Jeremy appeared.

"You've got a phone call. It's Red Murphy." He handed her the portable phone.

Hannah glanced at Wood and realized that she had been kissing the man that she wanted Red to investigate. Only this morning she had called Red and left a message with the intention that he check Wood's background.

"You'll have to excuse me," she said to Wood, walking back toward the barn. "Red, hi. Look, this isn't a good time for me. How about if I call you later?"

After as brief a conversation as she could possibly make it, Hannah ended the phone call. Jeremy had returned to the house, leaving Wood alone in the pasture, petting Wilbur. A warm fuzzy traveled down Hannah's spine. Dressed in Big Fred's cast-off coveralls, he should have looked ridiculous. But he didn't. He looked good. Damn good.

And that was a problem. Only twenty-four hours ago she had wanted to kick him off the farm; now she was trying to figure out how not to be attracted to him.

Hannah was well versed in the art of putting men in their places. She'd had enough practice. It was time to nip this little attraction right in the bud. So they were curious about each other—that was normal and to be expected. But that was all that was going to happen.

She cleared her throat and said, "If you're going to work for me, I think it would be best if we both forgot what just happened."

"Yes, ma'am." Wood nodded at her and started for the bunkhouse. Then he turned around and speared her with a heated look. "Just to be sure, ma'am, which part do you want me to forget? The part where I kissed you or the part where you kissed me back?" As a wry smile creased his cheeks, he walked away.

WOOD HAD A RESTLESS NIGHT, most of it spent tossing and turning on the metal bed. Only twenty-four hours ago he hadn't been able to stay awake. Now he couldn't sleep.

But then what man would be able to rest after discovering he had been saved from death by a strange quirk of time. For that's what it had to have been. He still wasn't convinced it was the lightning, despite what Jeremy had told him.

If only he could remember what had happened after the noose had tightened around his neck. Over and over he replayed the details leading up to his hanging and his subsequent leap to the twentieth century. None of it made any sense. Why had he traveled through time and why had he ended up at the Davis farm?

The thought of not being able to return and never seeing his sister again he didn't want to contemplate. Not knowing whether she had wasted her life with an outlaw or returned to Missouri to live the life of a lady was a punishment he couldn't bear.

He punched his pillow for the hundredth time. If only he knew what had propelled him through time. Was it the something that old crone had given him? He remembered her pouring dirt into his hands and calling it the sand of salvation.

If it was the sand, he was in big trouble. Any traces of dirt that might have been on his hands had been washed away in Hannah's tub. At the memory of the bath, he felt a stirring in his loins. He smiled as he recalled the look on Hannah's face when she had pulled back that curtain. And the color that had been in her cheeks when she had seen the effects on his body caused by her therapeutic massage. And then there was that kiss.

With a great effort he pushed thoughts of Hannah from his mind. What he didn't need to do right now was complicate his predicament by taking a fancy to his hostess. Not that it was a fancy, exactly. More like a need to scratch an itch. She bothered him in a way no woman had bothered him in a long time. All that talk about there being no man's work or woman's work, just work. And those tight trousers.

He should never have kissed her last night, yet he hadn't been able to resist her invitation. For it had been an invitation. She had looked at him with the same wanting in her eyes that he had been feeling in his gut. The first time he had set eyes on her he had thought that she could be someone special. Then he had discovered that she belonged to 1998 and he belonged to 1876.

He rolled over, grimacing as he scraped his bruised back against the mattress. He wished he had Hannah to rub more of that liniment on his back. He smiled as he remembered how soothing her fingers had been as they had caressed his flesh.

He wondered if all women of the twentieth century were like Hannah. Bold enough to walk in on a man while he bathed yet shy enough to blush at the sight of his arousal.

Heavy breathing alerted him to the fact that Outlaw had crept closer to his pillow.

Wood scratched the dog behind his ears. "I'm in a pickle, aren't I?"

The dog moaned in agreement.

"If I go back to 1876 I'll never see Hannah again—not to mention I could hang. Yet if I stay, I'll never see my sister again."

Outlaw rolled onto his back, spreading his legs in a shameless request for Wood to scratch his belly. Wood complied.

Footsteps echoed on the wooden steps of the bunkhouse, and Wood noticed that the first rays of morning sun were peeking over the horizon. Outlaw jumped off the bed and ran to the screen door, barking excitedly.

"Wood?" Jeremy called out tentatively.

Wood swung his legs over the side of the bed. "Come on in. I'm up."

As soon as the door opened, Outlaw pounced on the boy, his tail wagging, his tongue bathing him with a wet welcome. "Mom said to tell you that if you want to take a shower before breakfast, you'd better hurry."

"I bathed yesterday."

"I know. Me, too. If mom had her way, I'd have to take a bath every day." He shivered at the thought.

Wood knew there was no point in upsetting his hostess. The path of least resistance—that's how he saw his role at the Davis farm. Until he found a way to alter time, it would be wise to do whatever necessary to please Hannah. "If she doesn't mind me using up the water, I guess I could take another one."

"Don't you have school today?" Wood asked, slipping his arms through one of the shirts Gabby had given him yesterday.

"The bus doesn't come until seven-thirty." Jeremy moved closer to the bed and glanced at the nightstand. He picked up Wood's pocket watch and studied it. "I've never seen a clock this small."

"It's called a pocket watch." Wood took it from him and slipped it into his shirt pocket. "It belonged to my father."

Also on the table were several coins he had had in his pocket at the time of the hanging. Jeremy eyed them curiously.

"I've never seen money like that. Is it foreign?"

Wood scooped up the coins from the table and shoved them into his pocket. "Nope, just old. Like the watch."

"Are you a coin collector?"

Wood didn't answer him. "You ask a lot of questions." He ruffled Jeremy's hair affectionately. "Let's go get some breakfast."

With Jeremy and Outlaw in tow, Wood headed for the house. As he crossed the dirt drive, his heart skipped a beat. He could see Hannah through the kitchen window, her blond curls falling about her face in disarray.

"Something smells good," he said to Jeremy, dragging his eyes away from the window.

"It's sausage. You're gonna like living here. Mom's a

good cook. She wins all sorts of blue ribbons at the county fair every year.''

Wood didn't know about how good a cook Hannah was, but she was definitely a sight for sore eyes. Again this morning she wore the tightest pair of trousers he had ever seen on a woman. Jeans was what Gabby had called them. Man teasers was what Wood would nickname them. Tucked into the waistband was a bright green shirt that emphasized every curve on her torso. Wood felt parts of his anatomy respond in a purely physical way. He quickly looked away.

Just as Wood was about to climb the porch steps, he felt a tug on his arm. In a whisper-soft voice Jeremy asked, ''Did you kiss my mom last night?''

Wood saw no reason to lie. ''I did.''

''I thought so,'' he said with a satisfied grin. ''I guess Gabby was right.''

''Right about what?''

''About the—'' he looked anxiously toward the house, as if worried that his mother might be able to hear. ''You know.''

Puzzled, Wood said, ''I'm afraid I don't know, Jeremy.''

He pulled Wood by the arm around to the side of the house. ''The mail-order thing.''

''The mail-order thing,'' Wood repeated.

Jeremy nodded vigorously. ''I told Gabby I didn't think it would work, but she said it's worked for lots of people, including my great-great grandfather. That's where Gabby got the idea to send for you. Of course, he sent for a girl, not a guy.''

As far as Wood knew, Gabby had advertised for farm help. So why did Jeremy refer to it as a mail-order *thing?* Before he could pursue the subject, Hannah's voice rang out on the still morning air.

''Jeremy, get in here for breakfast or you're going to miss your bus.''

As Jeremy scrambled into the house, Wood could only shake his head. This twentieth-century jargon confused him almost as much as the modern appliances. Apparently hired help was a mail-order thing in 1998.

So why did he have an uneasy feeling that Gabby and Jeremy knew something they weren't telling him?

Chapter Seven

"Okay, Wood. If you're going to stay, you might as well come out on the gleaner with me," Hannah told Wood after breakfast.

She could see by the look on his face that he had no idea what she was talking about.

"The gleaner is the combine. We're going to test the soybeans."

He nodded, but she doubted it was in understanding. "I thought Gabby said you had worked crop farms?"

"Not soybeans."

She sighed. "Half of my crop is soybeans."

"Then you better show me what needs to be done. I've always been a quick learner." He gave her a look that could only be classified as flirtatious. She didn't like it one bit.

When she snatched a pair of brown coveralls from a hook on the wall and started to unsnap them, Wood said, "You're not going to put those on, are you?"

What did he think, that she was going to strip in front of him? "I'm just slipping them over my jeans." She tugged on the garment. "Don't you have anything on underneath yours?" She eyed his coveralls suspiciously.

She realized from the sheepish grin that he didn't.

Again he had the upper hand. She was the one who broke eye contact, not wanting to notice how the coveralls clung to his frame, emphasizing his muscles and calling to memory what his naked body looked like.

When she went to climb the metal steps of the combine, Wood was right there at her side ready to give her a hand. "I don't need any help," she told him, then proceeded to miss a step and bump her knee. There was no way she would release the "ouch" on the tip of her tongue. With lips clamped shut, she climbed up the combine and perched herself behind the steering wheel.

"If you're going to ride along, you're going to have to sit on the armrest." She patted the cushion beside her. Wood climbed inside, folding himself to fit into the tight quarters. His nearness did funny things to Hannah's sense of equilibrium, and she wondered if she hadn't made a mistake telling him to come along this morning.

In the narrow confines of the cab, elbows bumped, thighs rubbed and no amount of effort was going to put any more distance between their two bodies. As Hannah drove down the dirt road, she tried to focus on explaining the operating instructions to Wood in a businesslike manner, but every time she caught a glimpse of his mustache she thought about what it had been like to have his mouth on hers last night and to feel those hairs gently brushing her skin in a most delectable way.

She pushed aside the pesky thought and concentrated on work. "We call this the eighty." She gestured to the rows of leafless plants on the north side of the road. "There are eighty acres of beans planted here."

"Plants look healthy," Wood commented and Hannah felt the sense of pride she always experienced whenever she drove the combine into the fields. To her left was an ocean of corn, the tassels rippling in the sun.

"As soon as we're finished harvesting the beans, we'll do the corn." Hannah nodded toward the tall stalks nearly ready for harvest.

"I don't think I've ever seen anything so beautiful," Wood stated quietly. "It's like a rainbow of gold."

Hannah met his gaze and felt an odd little catch in her chest. He had voiced her sentiments exactly. "That's why I love combining. How could I ever tire of looking at that?"

"How long have you been farming here?"

"Jeremy and I moved back seven years ago, but I only took over running the place after my grandfather died two years ago."

"When Gabby told me you were responsible for planting all that corn out there, I didn't believe her at first."

"You don't believe women can operate a farm?" she tried not to sound defensive, but he was dangerously close to hitting one of her buttons.

"I don't know anyone who runs a farm this large," he answered. "And yes, most women I know are too busy worrying about what dress to wear for which party to even consider there could be work needing to be done in a field somewhere."

She groaned. "Don't tell me. You like women to wear dresses."

"Is there something wrong with that?"

"This is 1998, Wood. Most of us are smart enough to wear clothes that suit the jobs we do."

His eyes drifted to the coveralls covering her from neck to ankle. "Nothing wrong with being smart."

Just for one fleeting moment Hannah didn't want to be smart. She wanted to be chic—which was a joke. Most of her wardrobe came from mail-order catalogs purchased for practical purposes, not for style. Until now, it hadn't bothered her that most of her time was spent wearing men's coveralls.

She mentally chastised herself. And it didn't matter now, either. She was a farmer and would show him what a damn good farmer she was.

She turned the wheels of the gleaner so that the front end was aligned with the planted rows. "We'll do a round and get the beans in the hopper. Then we'll use that bucket behind you to scoop some out and test them."

Wood glanced at the empty ice-cream pail and picked up the flashlight sized electronic instrument inside. "What's this used for?"

"That's the tester. It'll measure the amount of moisture in the beans. Before we use it, we'll test them the old-fashioned way." She motioned for him to climb down.

He waited for her at the bottom, offering her his hand as she followed him down the metal steps. She ignored the gesture. As she headed toward the back of the combine, she stumbled over a rut in the road. Wood steadied her with a pair of hands at her waist.

"Thanks," she murmured, sliding out of his grasp. During the instant his hands had been on her waist, her body had tingled with pleasure. She tried not to think what those hands might feel like on other parts of her body.

"Here's how my grandfather would test the crop." She reached for a bean stalk and pulled off one of the pods. "You squeeze this, then crack it at the top and bottom." She snapped the pod in two. "It should snap in your hand. Then you chew." She popped the bean into her mouth.

After only a few seconds, she spat the bean out. "Not ready."

"You can determine that by chewing?"

She nodded. "It has to do with how hard it is. But just to make sure I'm right, we'll do a round with the combine, then use the tester."

Back they went into the cab of the combine. When they had done a row of beans, she stopped. "Think you can climb up into the hopper and scoop me out a bucket of beans? All you have to do is use those two steps right next to the door."

Carefully, Wood did as she instructed, getting an ice-cream bucket full of shelled beans which he gave to Hannah. She unscrewed the cap on the electronic tester, filled it with beans, then poured them into the tester. She pushed a button and waited for the digital readout.

A number flashed in red across the minuscule screen. "See? Eighteen. We need a moisture content of thirteen before we harvest."

"Why is that?"

"We can't dry beans like we do corn," she explained. "We'll have to wait until the stalks dry off."

When they were back at the barn Wood reached into his pocket and pulled out a bean pod. He squeezed it, cracked it at the top and bottom, then snapped it in his hand. Next he put the bean into his mouth and chewed for a couple of moments before spitting it out.

"I hope nobody's going to eat these for breakfast." He gave her a smile that could only be called cocky.

Hannah didn't want to smile, but automatically her lips curved into a grin. She turned away so he wouldn't see, but it was too late.

"There's no reason why you can't smile while you work, is there?"

She faced him once more. "No."

"Good because you're pretty when you smile."

Hannah was no stranger to men's compliments, but this one made her extremely self-conscious. Not one to appreciate chivalry, she didn't want any man treating her as if she were a piece of china. She was a down-to-earth, no-nonsense, work-the-land kind of woman, not a hothouse flower.

She had no time to waste on flirting or small talk...even if Wood Dumler did have a pair of brown eyes that could make a woman's insides feel like scrambled eggs. He was her employee and she his boss.

"Look, we both agreed to forget what happened yesterday. We had a curiosity about each other, it was satisfied.

Now if you plan to work for me, you'd better trash the pick-up lines,'' she advised him.

Again he gave her that dumb look she had seen so often in the past two days. If she didn't know better, she'd think he didn't know what she was talking about.

"I do want to work for you," he said sincerely.

"Okay, then no more looking at me as if I'm some bimbo on a barstool waiting for you to make my day."

"Is that how you think I look at you?"

"Sometimes. And I don't need you to do the gentleman number on me, either."

"What gentleman number?"

"Holding doors, putting your hand on my elbow, helping me up the steps...that kind of stuff."

"Where I come from, men treat ladies with respect. I wouldn't be much of a man if I didn't open your doors for you. It's the proper thing to do."

Hannah sighed and blew her bangs out of her eyes. Of all the men for Gabby to find, why did it have to be an old-fashioned one?

"There's a time and a place for that kind of behavior, it's just not here. I'm not a lady, I'm your employer, and I want you to treat me like your employer. It doesn't matter whether I'm a woman or a man."

"It matters to me."

The look in his eyes echoed that sentiment and Hannah felt her body grow warm. "It shouldn't."

"What are you saying? That because I work for you I'm not supposed to have any manners?"

"This isn't about manners. You act as if I need you to watch out for me, like you're doing the manly thing watching out for the little lady. I told you, I'm no lady."

Before she could say one more word to the contrary, he pulled her into his arms and covered her mouth with his. Hannah clung to his broad shoulders as her body weakened in a most delicious way. Shivers of pleasure and a sigh of delight encouraged him to deepen the kiss. She knew she should push him away, yet she couldn't. It felt too good. She pressed her body closer to his in an instinctive invitation to intimacy. To her dismay, he was the one who pulled back.

"There's where you're wrong, Hannah. And if I weren't the gentleman I am, we'd be doing a whole lot more than kissing." His voice dropped into a husky, intimate tone that told Hannah that no matter how much she protested, she would always be a woman to him.

HANNAH WAS RELIEVED when Gabby offered to ride to town with them. The thought of sitting with Wood in the cab of the pickup was more than she could bear. Now at least Gabby could sit between them.

"Now where do you suppose he is?" she asked when they reached the truck and Wood was nowhere in sight. "I told him to meet me by the garage."

"I'll check out front." Gabby disappeared around the side of the house only to reappear a few minutes later with Wood in tow. "He was wandering around the other side of the house," she said in an aside to Hannah who simply shook her head in frustration.

Wood watched Hannah and Gabby climb up into the cab of the pickup truck, his face that same mask of suspicion he had worn the first time Hannah had seen him. Gabby slid across the bench seat and patted the dark upholstery.

"Come on up, Wood. There's plenty of room."

When he didn't move, Gabby asked, "Are you all right?"

Although he nodded and climbed inside, Hannah had her doubts. His face was pale and it suddenly dawned on her that the reason he didn't drive could have something to do with a traumatic car accident in his past.

"You better buckle up," Gabby told him. "Hannah's got a lead foot."

Wood sat perfectly still.

Hannah whispered to Gabby, "Better show him."

Gabby reached across his shoulder and pulled on the safety harness. "It hooks into this piece here." She latched it to the buckle extending from the seat.

When she started the pickup and backed it out of the garage, all the color drained from Wood's face. Had it not been for Gabby clutching his arm, Hannah didn't doubt for one minute that he would have leaped from the moving vehicle.

Hannah pulled out of the drive and onto the dirt road leading to the county highway. Out of the corner of her eye she could see Wood sitting as straight as a board, his knuckles clenched as his fingers clung to the seat belt.

Gabby kept up the conversation, rattling on about the neighboring farms and doing what Hannah thought was a first-rate job of selling the Stanleyville area. Wood didn't say a word.

When they reached town, Hannah parked the truck in front of the video store. Again Gabby had to help Wood with the seat belt, this time to unfasten it.

"You can take him to Carl's," Hannah told Gabby when all three were standing on the sidewalk. "I need to see Ed at the co-op. I'll meet you back here in say—" she paused to glance at her watch "—twenty minutes?"

"We should meet at the drugstore," Gabby suggested. "Wood needs some personal care items."

Wood stood silent, staring wide-eyed at the shops lining the main street. It made Hannah wonder how small the town was where he had spent most of his life. Gabby pushed her arm through Wood's, waved at Hannah, then led him up the street.

Hannah took care of her business at the co-op, then headed toward the drugstore which was on the opposite side of the street. As she passed the Cut and Curl, she saw Marlis gesturing frantically for her to come inside.

"We've all been dying of curiosity," Marlis said when she entered the shop, "we" being the other beautician and her customer, who both stared wide-eyed at Hannah.

"About what?" Hannah asked cautiously.

"That guy that's with Gabby. That's not her boyfriend, is it?"

"No, he's not." Hannah would have liked to walk out without saying another word, but she knew that the less she said, the more that would be misconstrued. "He's here to apply for a job."

"A job where?" Marlis wanted to know.

"At the farm."

Disbelief could be seen on the faces of all three women. It was Marlis who voiced their surprise. "You're hiring someone to work for you?"

"I might be. I'm not sure." Hannah was deliberately vague.

"We heard Gabby's helping him pick out clothes at Carl's," the other beautician commented, adding another permanent roller to the collection that already projected like porcupine quills on her customer's head.

Amazed at how fast the town grapevine worked, Hannah explained, "He lost his luggage on his way here."

"Where's he from?"

"Nebraska."

"And he's single?"

"Yes."

"Oh, good. We can use all the eligible men we can find," Marlis said with a smug grin.

"I haven't hired him yet," Hannah reminded her.

Marlis gave her a coy look. "Come on, Hannah. You wouldn't be buying the guy clothes if you didn't intend to hire him."

She would have explained how Gabby shrunk his only pair of pants, but really didn't want to say any more about

Wood Dumler. She knew his appearance in town would ignite a bonfire of curiosity the way it was.

"Does Red know you're gonna hire a good-lookin' guy like that?" asked Alice Zirbes, the customer who was having her hair permed.

"Red and I are friends, nothing more," Hannah stated for what seemed to be the millionth time. Why did everyone in Stanleyville insist on pairing her with the sheriff?

"Still, he ain't gonna like it," Marlis said. "I know you don't want to hear this, Hannah, but Red's got a thing for you and he's got it bad."

"That doesn't mean whom I hire is any of his business," she snapped a bit impatiently.

"So you are going to hire this guy then?"

Hannah grew more frustrated by the minute. "He's helping out until Barry returns."

"We heard about Caroline going into the hospital. They tried to stop the labor but last we heard she was dilated to seven."

"That baby's gonna come whether they want it to or not," Alice predicted.

"Rumor is Barry's looking at the Barton place," Marlis remarked.

"They're thinking about buying Herb's dairy farm?" Hannah felt a bit hurt that Marlis knew about it before she did. Only yesterday Barry had mentioned he was thinking about looking for a place, and now it seemed as if everyone in town knew he wanted to make an offer on Herb's place.

Hannah wished she had never stopped in at the Cut and Curl. All it had done was churn up her insides—as if Wood Dumler's appearance hadn't already done enough it.

By the time she walked through the front door of Kohler Drug, she was in need of antacids. She spotted Gabby at the checkout counter.

"Where's Wood?" Hannah asked, adding a roll of antacids to her aunt's purchases.

"He's outside on the bus bench. Didn't you see him?"

Hannah walked over to the plate glass window and glanced outside. The bench was empty. "He's not there."

A frown creased Gabby's forehead. She picked up the bag and hurried outside, looking up and down the street before saying, "Maybe he stopped into the café for something cold to drink."

"Does he have any money?"

"I gave him some."

Hannah's stomach lunged. "How much?" she asked uneasily.

"Just a twenty dollar bill."

"Well, he couldn't get far on that." Until now, Hannah hadn't considered the prospect that Wood could take her aunt into the bank and have her withdraw a huge sum of money. She sighed at the direction her thoughts had taken. Was she forever going to be suspicious of the man?

"Let's go look at Sally's." Gabby started toward the café with the green-and-white-striped awnings. Wood, however, was not in Sally's, or the Main Street Eatery or Beek's Pizza Palace.

"Should we check the bars?" Hannah asked with a lift of one eyebrow.

"I suppose we'll have to," Gabby reluctantly agreed.

Within ten minutes, every establishment including the bars in the business section of town had been visited, yet there was no trace of Wood anywhere. Hannah was about to give up when she spotted a tall man wearing a Stetson coming out of the library.

"Look." She pointed toward the north end of town. "That's not him, is it?"

Gabby squinted. "Yup, it is. He's wearing the hat I bought him."

They started toward the library, Gabby going on about how relieved she was they had found him. All Hannah could think about was how that Stetson had changed his appearance.

"Why did you buy him a hat? I gave him a cap," she said irritably.

"He wanted to pay for it himself, but I felt I owed it to him after shrinking his clothes like that." She lowered her voice. "He doesn't look like the same man, does he? Isn't it amazing what new clothes can do for a person?"

Yes, it was, Hannah couldn't help but notice as they approached Wood. No one would laugh at him now. He looked good. Damned good, Hannah thought, as something tightened in her stomach in response to his appearance. There was nothing sexier on a man than form-hugging jeans and a Western-style shirt. He was, as Marlis would say, "buff."

Annoyed that her body reacted physically to his, she took a flippant attitude. "Looking for some books to read in your spare time, Wood?"

He showed no reaction to her comment, but simply tipped his hat at both of them.

"I'm glad you stopped here, Wood," Gabby stated cheerfully. "Now I can go inside and say hello to Vivian and Sue." She placed a hand on Hannah's arm. "You don't mind, do you?"

Hannah wanted to scream yes, she did mind—that she didn't want to be left alone with Wood on Main Street— but Gabby didn't wait for an answer. She disappeared into the library leaving Hannah and Wood staring at each other on the sidewalk out front.

To Hannah's relief, the brim of Wood's Stetson shaded his eyes. She didn't want those eyes probing hers.

"Here. Let me carry those for you," he said, relieving her of her packages.

Hannah didn't bother to protest. It was too hot to argue.

"Maybe you want to go inside? It's cooler in there," he suggested.

Hannah already felt as if they were being watched. If she went in the library, she knew the scrutiny would intensify. Vivian and Sue were as bad as Marlis when it came to curiosity. All they needed was to see Wood fussing over her and they'd jump to all the wrong conclusions.

"I'd rather wait out here." She stepped around the corner to where the building cast a long shadow on the sidewalk and where they'd be less likely to run into anyone she knew.

"If we cross the street we can sit." He nodded toward the park on the opposite corner. "Or perhaps you don't want to be seen with me?"

"Don't be silly." As if to disprove his point, she crossed the street and sat down on a park bench.

Wood joined her, his thigh rubbing against hers as he sat down beside her. Silence stretched between them, becoming more awkward by the moment. Finally, he said, "Your boyfriend's watching us."

Hannah glanced across the park and saw Red Murphy in his squad car, watching the two of them. "Red is not my boyfriend," she repeated for the second time that day.

"Gabby says he'd like to be."

"Gabby should talk less about my private life."

"Then he is a part of your private life?"

"No—not that it's any of your business." She dabbed at the perspiration on her brow with the back of her hand.

"Forgive my inquiry," Wood said contritely.

Another awkward silence stretched between them. Hannah was acutely aware of the man beside her, as well as the one sitting in the sheriff's car around the corner.

Finally Wood said, "He must not have anything better to do. He's still sitting there."

"I'm sure it has nothing to do with us." Hannah shifted uncomfortably under the scrutiny.

"Looks to me like he wants to keep an eye on you."

"I told you. He's not there because of me."

"Then I must be the one he's watching."

Guilt had Hannah fidgeting. It was true she had told Red that she wasn't exactly thrilled with Gabby's choice of employees, but she had respected her aunt's wishes and not asked him to investigate Wood.

"Jeremy told me had you not tied me to the bed you would have called the sheriff to come get me."

"A woman can't be too careful nowadays," she said coolly. "You're just a stranger who put an ad in the newspaper."

He sighed. "I haven't run off with your silver yet."

Hannah's eyes met his and she felt mesmerized. All of her life she had relied on her intuition. Today it was telling her that this was a man she could trust. The problem was, she had spent a lifetime learning to distrust men.

"I haven't hidden my silver, have I?" she countered coyly.

Sparks of awareness ignited the hot summer air. "You don't need to hide anything from me," he said in a voice that was husky and deep, the way it had been when he had kissed her.

Oh yes she did, Hanna realized. She needed to hide her heart. For this was one man who had the power to find it.

"HAVEN'T YOU EVER WORKED on a farm with chickens before?" Jeremy asked as he led Wood into the church, the building where the chickens lived.

Wood shook his head. "You'll have to show me what needs to be done."

Jeremy carried an empty three-pound coffee can. "This stuff is oyster shells," he explained, putting a scoop of the feed into a narrow trough. "It makes the eggs harder." He set the coffee can down and picked up two gallon milk containers. "Now we get them water." He handed one of the jugs to Wood and led him outside to the spigot.

As they poured the fresh water into the drinking troughs,

Jeremy said, "So when Gabby wrote to you, did she tell you about me?" Jeremy asked.

Wood had no idea what the answer to that question was. It had been several days, and miraculously, Alfred Dumler hadn't shown up. What was even more extraordinary was that Wood had been able to continue the charade. He wondered how much longer he would be successful at pretending to be another man.

"Why don't you just come right out and ask me what it is you want to ask me?"

Jeremy shrugged. "Okay. Do you like kids?"

"Sure."

"Then you don't mind that Mom has me?"

"Why would I?"

Again he shrugged. "Not all guys like kids. My dad didn't. That's why he left us."

It was said so unemotionally that Wood wasn't sure if Jeremy was putting on a false show of bravado or if he really didn't care about his father.

"When was the last time you saw your dad?"

"I've never seen him."

Wood felt a rush of sympathy for the boy. Having lost his own father when he was fourteen, he knew what it was like to grow up without a dad. To this day there were times when he still felt empty at the thought of him. Although Jeremy behaved as if it didn't matter to him that his father was gone, Wood was almost certain it did.

"Do you play baseball?" Jeremy asked.

"I can."

"What about basketball?"

"No," Wood answered, not revealing that he had no idea what it was. "Sometime you'll have to show me how to play the game."

"You really want to?"

"Sure."

"Great!" As they walked past the bunkhouse, Jeremy

Welcome to the casino!
Try your luck at the roulette wheel ...
Play a hand of Twenty-One!

HOW TO PLAY:

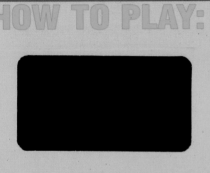

1. Play the Roulette and Twenty-One scratch-off games, as instructed on the opposite page, to see if you are eligible for FREE BOOKS and a FREE GIFT!

2. Send back the card and you'll receive TWO brand-new Harlequin American Romance® novels. These books have a cover price of $3.99 each, but they are yours to keep absolutely free.

3. There's no catch. You're under no obligation to buy anything. We charge nothing — ZERO — for your first shipment. And you don't have to make any minimum number of purchases — not even one!

4. The fact is, thousands of readers enjoy receiving books by mail from the Harlequin Reader Service® before they're available in stores. They like the convenience of home delivery, and they love our discount prices!

5. We hope that after receiving your free books you'll want to remain a subscriber. But the choice is yours — to continue or cancel, any time at all! So why not take us up on our invitation, with no risk of any kind. You'll be glad you did!

PLAY TWENTY-ONE FOR THIS EXQUISITE FREE GIFT!

THIS SURPRISE MYSTERY GIFT COULD BE YOURS FREE WHEN YOU PLAY

TWENTY-ONE!

It's fun, and we're giving away FREE GIFTS to all players!

PLAY Roulette!

Scratch the silver to see where the ball has landed—7 RED or 11 BLACK makes you eligible for TWO FREE romance novels!

PLAY TWENTY-ONE!

Scratch the silver to reveal a winning hand! Congratulations, you have Twenty-One. Return this card promptly and you'll receive a fabulous free mystery gift, along with your free books!

YES!

Please send me all the free Harlequin American Romance® books and the gift for which I qualify! I understand that I am under no obligation to purchase any books, as explained on the back of this card.

_____
Name (please print clearly)

_____
Address   Apt.#

_____
City   State   Zip

Offer limited to one per household and not valid to current Harlequin American Romance® subscribers. All orders subject to approval.   PRINTED IN U.S.A.

(U-H-AR-03/98)   154 HDL CE5Y

The Harlequin Reader Service® — Here's how it works:

Accepting free books places you under no obligation to buy anything. You may keep the books and gift and return the shipping statement marked "cancel." If you do not cancel, about a month later we'll send you 4 additional novels and bill you just $3.34 each plus 25¢ delivery per book and applicable sales tax, if any.*
That's the complete price — and compared to cover prices of $3.99 each — quite a bargain indeed! You may cancel at any time, but if you choose to continue, every month we'll send you 4 more books, which you may either purchase at the discount price...or return to us and cancel your subscription.

*Terms and prices subject to change without notice. Sales tax applicable in N.Y.

If offer card is missing write to: Harlequin Reader Service, 3010 Walden Ave., P.O. Box 1867, Buffalo, NY 14240-9952

BUSINESS REPLY MAIL
FIRST-CLASS MAIL   PERMIT NO 717   BUFFALO NY

POSTAGE WILL BE PAID BY ADDRESSEE

HARLEQUIN READER SERVICE
3010 WALDEN AVE
PO BOX 1867
BUFFALO NY 14240-9952

NO POSTAGE
NECESSARY
IF MAILED
IN THE
UNITED STATES

eyed it wistfully. "I wish I could sleep out here, too, but Mom won't let me."

She probably doesn't trust me, Wood thought. Aloud he said, "You're closer to the kitchen if you get hungry."

"I'm glad Gabby and you did that ad in the newspaper thing."

Wood smiled. It was nice to know this young man liked him even if his mother didn't. "Thanks, Jeremy."

"Have you ever been married, Wood?"

"Once."

"Was it like being in prison?"

"No. Why would you ask that?"

"Cuz that's what Mom calls it."

Wood wondered what kind of relationship Hannah had had with Jeremy's father that she would describe their marriage as a prison.

"Then how come you're not married now?" Jeremy continued to question him.

"My wife didn't like living in what she called the wilderness. She liked living in the big cities out East."

"At least that won't be a problem with Mom, will it." He gave Wood a knowing grin.

Wood frowned. What was the kid talking about?

"You know, I think Mom's beginning to like you. I heard her tell Gabby that you have possibility. Maybe she's going to like this whole mail-order groom idea."

Mail-order groom?

The words echoed like thunder. What was Jeremy talking about?

Fragments of conversations with Gabby Davis replayed in Wood's memory. "Hannah needs a man" not "Hannah needs a hired hand." "You're going to be perfect for each other" not "You're going to work well together."

Wood could feel moisture beading on his brow. Could it be that this Alfred Dumler hadn't come looking for work, but to marry Hannah Davis?

"Jeremy, you said you know the true reason why I'm here."

The boy nodded.

"Would you tell me?"

He gave Wood a puzzled look, then said, "You're going to marry my Mom. Well, you will if you can convince her this mail-order groom thing isn't a bad idea."

Chapter Eight

Marry his mother.

Gabby had placed an ad for a man—not to be hired help, but to marry Hannah. Alfred Dumler was a mail-order groom. And Wood was pretending to be Alfred Dumler—which meant Gabby expected him to marry her niece.

He shook his head and wondered if all folks in the twentieth century had such crazy notions. He had heard of mail-order brides, but women advertising for men? He shuddered. He supposed it went along with women not wanting men to protect them. What had happened in the last hundred and twenty-two years? Could it be there was a shortage of men?

Certainly Hannah didn't lack suitors. Wood would bet money that the sheriff would fill that position in a minute given the opportunity. So why had Gabby done such a thing? And without Hannah's knowledge?

"Wood?" Jeremy tugged on his sleeve, interrupting his musings. "You didn't answer my question."

"What was that?"

"Do you want to help me collect eggs tomorrow?"

"Sure."

"Good." Jeremy went on to explain that the chickens were his business, his college money. He even showed Wood the list of his customers and the prices he charged.

It was a needed distraction for Wood, who now found himself faced with not only being stuck in the wrong century but expected to enter an arranged marriage.

From Jeremy, Wood received a lesson in economics as he discovered inflation had made the little bit of money he owned nearly worthless. Why, Jeremy possessed greater wealth than he did.

"Can I ask you one more question?" Jeremy asked as he stood in the entrance to the chicken coop, finished with his chores.

"Okay, one more," Wood agreed, expecting it would be on the topic of the mail-order groom. It wasn't.

"Do you have any kids?"

"No."

"That's good. People who get divorced shouldn't have kids."

Wood detected a glimmer of sadness in the boy's eyes. Despite his stoic attitude, he was still a boy without a father. Wood's voice softened as he asked, "Do you miss your father, Jeremy?"

"No. I don't need him. I can take care of myself."

It was said with the same toughness Wood often heard in Hannah's voice. Like mother, like son, Wood thought, causing him to wonder if Jeremy's father could be the reason that Hannah didn't want men around. Or perhaps it was a twentieth-century thing. It was possible that women of 1998 disliked men. Possible, but scientifically unlikely. It was, however, a frightening thought.

"Jeremy, you need to finish your homework."

Wood turned and saw Hannah just outside the coop's entrance.

"All right, I'm going," Jeremy grumbled, calling out over his shoulder to Wood, "See you tomorrow."

As soon as he was gone, Hannah turned on Wood, "You don't need to feel sorry for us."

"What makes you think I do?"

"I saw the look on your face when Jeremy spoke of his father." She stiffened her shoulders. "We don't need anyone's pity. And especially not a man's."

"Every boy needs a father, Hannah," he said gently.

"Another one of the unwritten rules of the male sex."

"Perhaps it's the voice of experience. I've been a young boy without a father."

"And I've been a young girl without a mother."

So they had more in common than she wanted to admit. She knew the pain of being without a parent, although from the set of her shoulders he could see that she didn't want any sympathy from him.

"Why doesn't Jeremy have a father?"

She stiffened. "He does, it's just that the man chooses not to have a son."

"He doesn't want to be Jeremy's father?"

"Bingo." She walked away, pausing only to say, "We'll need to start early in the morning."

"Hannah, wait." He followed her, grabbing her by the arm. "I'm sorry. The only reason I ask about Jeremy is because I think he's a good kid."

"Yes, he is," she agreed. When she looked down at his hand on her arm, he released her.

"He misses having a father." Wood stated simply.

"I know." It was a muffled response that had him wanting to slide his arm around her and comfort her. He didn't.

"There's no chance that his father will ever return?"

She shook her head. "We met when I was eighteen. He was a hired hand who worked for my grandfather. Only here for the summer, but long enough for me to get pregnant."

"Doesn't he know that he has a son?"

"Oh, he knows," she said bitterly. "When my grandfather found out I was pregnant, he hired someone to help us find him. Not that it did any good.''

''You couldn't locate him?''

She made a sound of disgust. ''We found him—in a small town in Wisconsin where he had already found someone to take my place. He didn't care about me or the baby.''

For the first time he heard a vulnerability in Hannah's voice. ''I'm sorry,'' he said compassionately, placing a hand on her arm.

Only she didn't want his compassion. She slipped her arm out from his. ''I'm not. He was a jerk.'' The toughness was back in place. ''So now you know about Jeremy's father.''

''He's a fool.'' Wood shoved his hands in his pockets so he wouldn't be tempted to try to touch her.

''It doesn't matter. Jeremy's better off without him in his life.''

Wood didn't contradict her.

''As far as I'm concerned, no male role model is better than a bad one,'' she stated unemotionally.

''So now you hate all men,'' he deduced aloud.

Her eyes flashed. ''I don't hate men.''

''No? Sure sounds that way to me.''

''I just don't need them in my life. I know that's not what most men want to hear. They want to think women are helpless and can't make it without a man to take care of them. Well, this woman can take care of herself,'' she said boldly, as if in warning. ''You understand what I'm saying?''

''Yes, ma'am, I do.'' He moved toward her, his eyes pinning hers. ''So you can quit worrying that I'm going to try to get you out of those tight trousers.''

''I...I'm not worried,'' she stammered, backing away from him.

"Yes you are. Every time you look at me you act as if I'm going to rip off your clothes. You're more skittish than that silver Arabian in your pasture."

"Don't flatter yourself, Mr. Dumler," she said icily.

He moved closer to her until his face was only inches from hers. This time she didn't back away. She stood her ground, challenging him, eye-to-eye. Her breath was warm against his face, her chest pressed against his, tempting him to disregard his common sense. When her lips parted in an open invitation, Wood realized that she was enjoying their confrontation. She was challenging him to kiss her.

And if he were Alfred Dumler he would have. But he was Wood Harris and he belonged in 1876, not 1998. As much as he wanted to take Hannah in his arms and kiss her until those pretty little lips swelled to a deep pink, he was not going to do it. Because kissing Hannah Davis was not going to help him get back to his old life.

"You can put your mind at rest. If I'm going to rip off any clothing, it's going to be a skirt, not a pair of trousers."

His comment only fueled her anger. "That's exactly the kind of sexist remark I'd expect a man like you to make."

Wood wondered what a sexist remark was. Obviously, it was something distasteful to Hannah by the way she looked down her pretty little nose at him.

"If you expect to work for me, Mr. Dumler, I don't want to hear any of that macho posturing. Strut your stuff elsewhere or there will be no job, got it?"

"I believe I do," he replied soberly, although he had no idea what she was talking about.

She spun around and marched back to the house.

"Macho posturing?" Wood repeated as he watched her walk away. What in hell was she talking about? He shook his head in bewilderment.

No wonder Gabby had sent for a mail-order groom. Wood could almost feel sorry for the man who tackled the

job of marrying Hannah Davis. But then he remembered
how her lips had tasted…. At any rate, it wasn't something
he need be concerned about. He wasn't Alfred Dumler and
he was not going to be anyone's mail-order groom.

"I THINK YOU SHOULD let Wood have the loft," Gabby told
Hannah early one morning as she cooked bacon and eggs
for breakfast. "He's behaved like a perfect gentleman ever
since he's been here."

Hannah couldn't argue with her aunt when it came to
Wood's behavior. There was no lack of manners on his
part. *Gallant* was the word that often came to Hannah's
mind when describing him, which was the reason she figured Gabby was so fond of him.

"He seems perfectly content out in the bunkhouse,"
Hannah noted.

"There are no facilities out there," Gabby pointed out.

"Grandfather always made the hired help stay there."

"You said you weren't going to do things your grandfather's way," Gabby reminded her. "If we gave him the
loft we wouldn't even know he was in the house."

Hannah would know. Despite her resolution to treat
Wood as if he were any other hired hand, she hadn't been
able to keep her body from responding to his in a purely
physical way. He was too male and too handsome, which
is why she found herself thinking about him often, as if she
were a schoolgirl with a crush on the captain of the football
team.

It was bad enough that they had to bump elbows and rub
thighs in the combine, she didn't want to have to worry
about running into him in the privacy of her own home.
No, letting Wood stay in the house would only create more
tension between the two of them.

"You still don't trust him, do you," Gabby continued to
plead his case.

"I gave him the job, didn't I?" Hannah said wearily.

"Only because you were uncertain if Barry would be coming back."

"The point is, I did hire him even though he didn't know the first thing about corn or soybeans."

"You think he lied about his background?" Gabby's tiny mouth fell open.

"What I can't figure out is, if he has all that experience working on farms, why does he act as if he's never harvested before? Unless he's suffered some kind of a mental breakdown and can't remember."

"Oh, for goodness' sake! He's not mentally ill!" Gabby vehemently defended him. "Is that why you won't let him use the loft...because you think he's crazy?"

"No, I don't think he's crazy," Hannah answered honestly.

"Well, you shouldn't." Gabby was indignant on Wood's behalf. "You talk to the man every day. He's as normal as we are. And look at how good he is with Jeremy. You yourself said that once you show him something, he doesn't forget, that he has a sharp mind."

"He hasn't got a clue when it comes to chemicals."

"So they do things differently in the part of the country where he comes from. So what? Not everyone uses chemicals."

Hannah understood Gabby's defense of Wood. She wanted to think the best of him, too. She wanted to believe that she worried needlessly over his shortcomings.

"It isn't just the chemicals," Hannah continued. "There are times when he acts as if he doesn't understand what we're saying, like we're speaking a foreign language or something. And did you see the look on his face when Jeremy pulled out his calculator and asked him for help with a math problem? You would have thought he'd never seen one before."

"Because a man doesn't surround himself with electronic gadgets doesn't mean he's a mental patient on the loose," Gabby pointed out. "And he was able to help Jeremy with his math, without using a calculator. You saw how good he is with numbers."

"I want to trust him, Gabby, honestly I do, but..."

"I think you should quit looking for reasons to discredit the man. He's been a big help to us, especially with Barry not being here. And considering what we pay him, he's quite a bargain."

Hannah rubbed her forehead. "All right, all right," she snapped impatiently. "You've made your point. He can have the loft."

She didn't need to worry that she had made a mistake caving in to her aunt's pressure. When Wood came up to the house for breakfast, Gabby told him he was welcome to move his things into the house. To Hannah's surprise, he turned down the offer.

"I appreciate you thinking of my comfort, but I think it's best if I stay where I'm at," Wood told the two women.

"Why is that?" Gabby asked.

He looked her straight in the eye and said, "Because it wouldn't be proper."

"Proper?" Hannah looked at him over the rim of her coffee cup.

"Being you are two single women," Wood pointed out. "I wouldn't want to dishonor you."

Before Hannah could argue the point, Gabby gushed, "Why, how very sweet of you to worry about our reputations, Wood."

"I wouldn't want to make you the subjects of any gossip," he said nobly.

"I hadn't thought about that, had you, Hannah?" Gabby asked.

"You ought to know by now, Gabby, that I really don't

care what anyone says about me,'' Hannah answered, her eyes meeting Wood's in a challenge.

"But I do care,'' Wood insisted. "I'll not be the reason for your reputation being sullied.''

It had been a long time since any man had worried about her reputation. Hannah should have pointed out to him that the women's movement was supposed to have freed women from the need for such a defense. To her surprise, however, she found his chivalrous attitude endearing, not irritating.

Once again he found a way to touch her emotionally, and she didn't like it one bit. She shrugged, trying to sound indifferent as she said, "Very well. Stay in the bunkhouse.''

Wood could see that she was annoyed with his response to her invitation. When she left without him, slamming the screen door as she departed, he decided not to go after her, but to stay behind and talk with Gabby.

"I believe I've annoyed her,'' he remarked when they were alone.

Gabby grinned. "I know. Isn't it great?''

Puzzled, Wood asked, "You think it's great that she was annoyed?''

"Well, sure! It means she cares what you do, and that's a good sign, don't you think?'' There was a sparkle of satisfaction in her eyes.

"Gabby, are you deliberately talking in riddles?''

She came over and stood behind him, placing her hands on his shoulders in a reassuring gesture. "You don't know Hannah the way I do. Our plan is working. She likes you, Wood.''

"She doesn't behave as if she does.''

"That's because she doesn't want you to know that she's attracted to you.''

"You think she fancies me?''

"Oh, my goodness, yes. I've seen the way she looks at

you when she thinks no one else is looking. Take my word for it, Wood. Hannah's crazy for you," she whispered close to his ear, then she gave him a couple of affectionate pats and retrieved the coffeepot.

Wood thought there was only one woman crazy in the Davis household and that was Gabby. What made her think she could get a man-hater like Hannah to agree to marry any man?

When she would have refilled his cup with coffee, he stopped her. "No, I've had plenty."

"Okay." She returned to her place at the table, looking as if she hadn't a care in the world. "By the way, Vivian called from the library and said the books you wanted are in. I vouched for you so you could get the books." She took a sip of coffee, then said, "You should have told me you were interested in local history, I'd have shown you those diaries that Jeremy's looking at for his project."

Wood hadn't wanted to involve Gabby in his search for the past, not when there was the risk that he would come across information that would incriminate him in the murders of George and Mary Nelson.

"I appreciate the offer, Gabby, but you've already been so kind I can't ask for such a favor."

"Of course you can. Another place you can look is the historical society over in Creston. I could drive you there."

Wood knew that Hannah didn't want Gabby driving anywhere.

"And speaking of driving, has Hannah mentioned giving you lessons?" she inquired.

He shook his head. "I don't believe she has the time."

"It doesn't matter. I can teach you. There's really not much to it."

Having ridden with Hannah in the pickup, Wood knew Gabby understated the difficulty.

"First you need to pass a written test. We can probably

pick up a driver's manual at the courthouse on our way to the historical society. And you'll need identification.''

"What kind?"

"I imagine a birth certificate."

Wood wondered if public records dated back to 1852, the year he was born. "I'm afraid I lost that a long time ago."

"I'm sure there's a way to get a copy of it. Nowadays everything's done by computer. One phone call and—" she snapped her fingers "—it's here. Do you know the name of the hospital where you were born?"

"I was born at home," Wood told the truth.

"Oh! That could be a problem. I'll call Clara over at the courthouse and find out what you need to do." She scooted over to the telephone and was about to call when Wood stopped her.

"Gabby, I don't want to trouble you over this."

"It's no trouble, Wood." Again there was that innocence in her face.

"Learning how to drive isn't why I'm here."

"I know that, but you might as well do it. If you're anxious over taking a test, don't worry about it. Half the kids in the county drive without a license. The trick is not to get caught." She winked at him. "I'll take you out on the back roads and let you practice."

"All right. You can give me a few lessons, but no license. Not yet." Once he knew how to drive the car, he could go to the historical society on his own. He needed answers and he needed them soon. Life with the Davis women was getting much too complicated.

"WHEN YOU'VE FINISHED with that, I'd like you to sweep out the grain bins. The corn should be ready for harvest next week."

Wood turned at the sound of Hannah's voice and saw

her approaching, her skintight trousers having their usual effect on him. If he wasn't already in a sweat, he would be soon. It was getting harder and harder to ignore the fact that one look at her could make his blood pump as if he were running uphill.

"Just show me what needs to be done," he called out, keeping his eyes on the pitchfork as he continued to sling hay over the fence.

"Did you feed Wilbur?"

He glanced across the corral and saw the pig was slowly ambling toward him. "I'll get it as soon as I'm done here," he answered, pausing to lean on the handle of the pitchfork. He couldn't resist staring at the picture she made with her tight trousers and her bosom-hugging shirt. If he didn't keep his mind focused on what needed to be done, he could easily be distracted by her beauty.

"Fine. Come over to the equipment shed when you're finished." Her voice was cool, making him think that Gabby had to be wrong. Hannah was not thinking of him as anything but a hired hand. "By the way, I turned on the fence so be careful," she added, then started toward the machinery shed.

Turned on the fence? He was about to ask her what she meant when Wilbur snorted. Wood stuck the pitchfork in the bale of hay, then stepped closer to the wire fence.

"Come here, boy," he called out to the pig. He slipped a hand through the wire and the next thing he knew he was flat on his back on the ground. Hannah's face was over his, filled with anxiety as she cradled his prone figure in her arms.

"Wood! Talk to me! Are you all right?" she called out frantically.

"What happened?"

"You touched the electric fence. Didn't you hear me say I had turned it on?"

He grimaced. "You've got electricity running through that thing?"

"Fifteen hundred volts."

"Is that a lot?"

"Enough to give a person a good jolt, but I've never seen it throw anyone off his feet."

Still stunned, he asked, "I'm not dead, am I?"

"No, you're going to be okay. It's just that your body's had a shock, that's all," she answered sympathetically.

Wood's body tingled, reminding him of how he had felt when he awoke after the time travel. "What year is it?"

"1998."

He sighed. He hadn't gone back in time. But he hurt. All over. "Are you sure I'm not dead?" he said on a moan.

She pinched his cheek. "Can you feel that?"

"Feel what?" he pretended not to notice her touch.

A moment of panic flashed in her eyes until she realized he was fooling her. "Don't scare me like that."

He liked the look of tenderness on her face and he especially liked being in her arms. "It hurt like hell."

"I know. I've done it myself, although I still don't understand why it knocked you to the ground. I wonder if I should have someone come check it. Maybe there's more current going through it than there should be."

"There's obviously too much for a man." He grimaced as he tried to move.

"You are okay, aren't you?"

He was tempted to say no, for he enjoyed seeing the tender, caring side of Hannah Davis. "I'm okay," he told her, carefully sitting forward.

"You make a good nurse. You have a gentle touch."

She released him abruptly, as if suddenly embarrassed that she had been holding him, shoving her hands into her pockets.

He held his hands out, palm upward. "Don't put your hands away. Put them here, on mine."

When she hesitated, he said, "Go ahead. I want to show you something."

She placed her hands directly over his, leaving about an inch between their palms.

"Go on. Set them on mine," he urged.

She did as he instructed, then met his eyes. "They're tingling."

"As are other parts of my body." It was true. Wood felt as if every part of him tingled and not from the electricity that had coursed through his body. There was no longer any point in pretending. He wanted Hannah.

"Touch me here." He brought one of her hands to his chest and placed it against the pocket of his chambray shirt. "Can you feel it?"

"Your heartbeat is racing." She held his gaze. "It must be from the electrical shock."

He knew if he were wise, he'd agree. But he wasn't wise. He was entertaining foolish notions. "You're the reason it's thumping as if it wants to punch a hole in my chest. It was doing that before I ever grabbed the fence. All it took was for you to walk toward me in those trousers."

She sat back on her heels. "That is not the proper way to talk to your boss, Wood."

It was a weak-hearted protest. He knew it and she knew it.

"There are times when a gentleman must not worry about propriety," he murmured.

"And this is one of those times?"

"I do believe it is."

"Why is that?"

"Because you're a lady in distress."

She chuckled. "You're the one who's in distress, and I'm not a lady. I'm your boss. Remember?"

"All I see is a lady. A beautiful lady." Before she could utter another word, he had pulled her to him, his mouth urgently seeking hers in a hungry kiss that told her in no uncertain terms did he care that she was his boss. Nor did it matter that she hated men or that she was a woman from another century. All he could think about was the desire stirring in his loins.

Wood savored the taste of her, his tongue searching the interior of her mouth as she opened her lips, inviting an intimacy he hadn't expected. Although she felt tiny and fragile in his arms, there was nothing delicate about the way she made him feel. Or the way her hands drifted across his shoulders to his chest, toying with the buttons on his shirt until they worked their way inside to his warm flesh.

When he pushed her back against the ground, her voice was husky as she said, "This could be dangerous. Now I'm tingling, too."

He could see by the gleam in her eyes that she was teasing him, and he liked it. Gone was the tough, independent female boss. In her place was a sexy, self-confident temptress.

Once more he covered her mouth with his, amazed by the intensity of feelings she aroused in him. As the kiss lengthened, she pressed closer to him, her body soft and warm next to his. Wood loved the way she felt in his arms. She filled his senses, intoxicating him until all he could think about was touching her in every soft, sweet place he could find.

Whimpers of pleasure emerged from her throat as his hands molded her to him, sliding over her hips in a tantalizing exploration that had her arching toward him. With a boldness that came as no surprise to Wood, Hannah began her own intimate exploration. Fingers that had traced circles on his chest now made a descent down his abdomen. When they slipped inside the waist of his jeans, he could feel his self-control slipping away.

The jolt from the fence seemed like nothing compared to the current of desire that arced through him as she teased and tempted him. Wood couldn't get enough of her, the taste of those sweet lips, the smell of her orange scented hair mixed with the fresh aroma of hay.

She didn't stop him when his hand moved between them to her breast. Through the knit fabric of her shirt he could feel the nipple press against his palm. With each stroke, she purred in delight, pressing herself unashamedly against his throbbing hardness.

He lost all sense of time and place. All that mattered was the woman in his arms. When her hands moved inside his jeans, he didn't know how he would bear the excruciating pleasure.

But then she stopped.

It only took a moment for Wood to understand why. A brisk wind carried the first drops of rain. He rolled over and stared up at the ominous clouds hanging over them.

Hannah wasted no time in scrambling to her feet. "We'd better take cover."

Wood paid no attention. As lightning streaked the sky he realized that this was what he had been waiting for ever since Jeremy had shown him the Nelson forty. A thunderstorm.

"Wood, get in here!" Hannah shouted from the barn.

He didn't move, but stood in the pouring rain, watching the lightning dance across the sky, wondering if this storm could possibly be the vehicle that would take him back in time.

"Wood, come inside!" Again she screamed at him.

A bolt of lightning produced a crash of thunder that nearly shook the ground he stood on. As the storm crashed around him, he tried not to think about the wisdom of what he was about to do. If he was to return to 1876, he was going to have to risk his life.

Raindrops stung his skin, his heartbeat nearly choked him. He had to go back. To his sister. To the life he knew. He hesitated only a moment, then headed for an ash tree.

"Wood, what are you doing? Come inside, don't stand under the tree," Hannah screamed at him but he paid no attention. "Wood, get in here," she ordered him.

Again lightning flashed and thunder crashed. He thought about his sister, then he looked toward the barn and saw Hannah. She was running toward him, a look of panic on her face. When she reached him, she grabbed him by the hand and pulled him into the barn.

Her clothing soaked, her hair plastered to her head and water dripping over her face, she panted as she said, "Are you nuts! Don't you know how dangerous it is to be out in a storm and to stand beneath a tree?" She made a sound of disbelief and turned away.

"I'm sorry, Hannah. I—" Wood tried to apologize but she cut him off, spinning around to face him.

"Just when I start to think you're a normal guy you go and do something so stupid!" she shouted.

He tried to pull her into his arms, but she jerked away from his touch. "Oh, no you don't. You stay away from me, Wood Dumler."

"Hannah, I'm sorry. I didn't mean to frighten you."

"That's the third time you've kissed me and it's going to be the last," she declared emotionally. "I am your boss and you will not forget it." She took several steps backward, then added, "Now when this rain is ended, you will sweep out the corn bins and you'd better pray that the crop hasn't been ruined because if it is, I won't need you, and you'll be history." With those parting words, she spun around and went to the opposite end of the barn to wait out the storm.

Wood could only shake his head. If only she knew that he truly was history. Or was he? As he stared out at the stormy skies, he realized that he was more of a misfit than anything else. He didn't fit in the twentieth century yet he couldn't get back to the nineteenth.

And for the first time since he had discovered that he had time traveled through one hundred and twenty-two years he faced another dilemma. Did he want to go back to his old life? One look at Hannah reminded him that life in the twentieth century had something he never had found in 1876. A woman he could love.

Chapter Nine

True to her word, Gabby gave Wood driving lessons. After the first session Wood figured it probably would have been easier to go to the driving school rather than learn from a woman who called the turn signal that blinkie thing and got confused as to which position was reverse and which was drive on the shift lever.

If it wasn't for the fact that Wood wanted to visit the historical society, he wouldn't have risked learning to operate Gabby's car. However, he knew that the only way he could go without arousing suspicion would be to go alone. And without any other means of transportation, he had no choice but to accept Gabby's offer.

Wood had checked out several books from the library, including one on meteorology which explained the causes and effects of lightning. Instead of giving him hope of finding a way to use lightning to travel through time, he had only become more doubtful that he would survive should that be the vehicle to take him back.

In Wood's stack of books were several biographies of Jesse James as well as eyewitness accounts of the James Gang's raid on the bank of Northfield. Nowhere did he find any mention of his sister.

So far his search for information on his sister had been fruitless. From a visit to the county courthouse he had learned that there were no death records for a Hannah Elizabeth Harris or a James Woodson Harris.

Wood knew the historical society might be his last hope. Although Gabby had offered to take him there once harvest was over, Wood knew he couldn't wait. He left a note for Hannah and borrowed the keys to Gabby's car.

Wood wasn't sure which was the greater risk—driving an automobile on roads he had never traveled, or skipping out on working for Hannah. However, once he was at the historical society, he forgot about both. It was there he found the personal diaries of the Nelson family. Wood avidly searched for any mention of his sister Hannah. It was there in a journal entry dated September 22, 1876.

It was written by George Nelson's son, a doctor who had returned home from New York after his father's death to settle his estate. He wrote that he had met the woman of his dreams, a Miss Hannah Harris from St. Louis, Missouri. There was only that one entry. Nothing more.

Wood read on, hoping to find another mention of what happened to Edward Nelson. Had he courted Hannah and made her his wife? Was she living as a doctor's wife in New York? They were questions which haunted Wood, as did his own fate.

The only mention of George Nelson's murder occurred in an entry where Edward stated that his parents' murderer had escaped justice. Did that mean that Wood was still the person they thought had killed them?

Wood was about to leave the history center when he noticed a museum display titled "Making Journalism History." Curious, Wood stepped inside. In the center of the room were various printing presses. Also on display were typewriters and telegraphs and other office furniture from the early days of publishing.

Lining the walls were front pages of newspapers throughout Minnesota's history. Wood paused under the numbers 1876 and his heart nearly stopped. There on the front of the *St. Paul Tribune* was his photograph beneath a headline that read, "Missouri banker suspected of killing two."

Wood would have read the entire article, but a couple of women were about to step beside him. Worried that they'd recognize him, he left the display and returned to the resource room. Within minutes, the information clerk had shown him how to find the microfiche of the newspaper and make a photocopy of the article. Wood folded the paper, tucked it in his pocket and took it back to the farm.

HANNAH WAS GOING to fire Wood. The man was out of his mind. He had to be. Ever since he had arrived at her farm he had pulled one crazy stunt after another. Now today he had left her high and dry. And for what? To run personal errands? From what he had told her, he didn't have a personal life. So where had he spent the day?

While Gabby prepared dinner, Hannah paced in the kitchen while she waited for his return. Fuming. Fussing. Ready for a fight.

"I'm sure he wouldn't have left if it wasn't important," Gabby said in Wood's defense.

"Nothing is more important to me than getting that crop in," Hannah tossed at her. "Or have you forgotten that we could lose the farm if we don't get it to market?"

"We're not going to lose the farm," Gabby said with an annoying calmness. "If I know Wood, he'll work twice as hard tomorrow to make up for today."

What Hannah didn't need was for her aunt to defend the man she was about to can.

Only she didn't fire Wood. She couldn't. When he walked through the kitchen door, looking like a stray puppy in need of a place to lay his head, Hannah's anger dissolved. She couldn't hit a man when he was down—and he definitely was down. He looked as if he had lost a huge battle.

But it wasn't just sympathy that kept Hannah from letting him go. Another emotion had coursed through her when he had walked through the door. Relief. Ever since she had found his note that morning she had harbored the fear that he might simply drive away in Gabby's car and never return. It was a possibility she hadn't wanted to face. And not because she'd be shorthanded for harvest. Or because he had Gabby's car.

She wanted him to be a part of her life. And that was a problem for a woman determined to rely on no man.

"I would be grateful if you could forgive me for my absence." His voice was flat, his face expressionless.

"I needed you today, Wood. Where were you?" There was no anger in Hannah's voice, just concern.

"I would appreciate you not inquiring about my personal life," he answered politely.

"I believe I have a right to know when it affects your work here at the farm," she kept her voice even, despite feeling hurt by his reply.

They stood facing each other until Gabby stepped between them. "It's time for dinner. I'm sure Wood will feel more like talking after he's had something to eat."

Hannah didn't think so, judging by the look on his face. Although he said nothing as to his whereabouts, he did behave like the gentleman he always was at dinner. Despite her request that he not treat her like a lady, he pulled out her chair for her, then fussed over Gabby in his usual manner.

"We'll need to work after dinner," Hannah announced.

"Wood, you look tired," Gabby remarked, giving Hannah a look that asked how she could even suggest such a thing.

"I am capable of working this evening, ma'am," he answered.

"What about my game? Last night you said Wood could play basketball with me after dinner," Jeremy reminded his mother. "You promised."

Hannah had always made it a point not to break her word to Jeremy. Therefore, she had no choice but to agree to one hour. "But only one hour," she specified.

While Hannah and Gabby cleared away the dishes, Wood and Jeremy played basketball. As much as she tried to avoid glancing outside, Hannah was at the window more than she was the sink. Jeremy patiently demonstrated different shots to Wood, who listened with the same attentiveness he always gave Hannah whenever she explained the work around the farm.

"They're having fun, aren't they?" Gabby commented as the sound of laughter spilled into the kitchen.

"Jeremy loves basketball," Hannah said wistfully.

"He likes Wood. Go ahead. Admit it."

Hannah sighed. "Yes, he likes Wood. There. I've said it. Are you satisfied?" She stepped around her great-aunt to retrieve the broom from the closet.

Gabby grinned smugly and folded her apron neatly before slipping it into a drawer. "It's good for Jeremy to have a man around the house."

Hannah paused in the middle of her sweeping, leaning on the broom handle to ask, "I'm not going to fire him. Are you satisfied?"

"You'd be foolish to let him go when you don't know how long Barry will be gone. Besides, he fits in here. I know you don't want to admit it, but he does."

Hannah was beginning to think Wood might fit in at the farm. It seemed crazy to her that she should want to trust someone who had arrived under such bizarre circumstances and had exhibited rather odd behavior, but the truth was, despite everything, her intuition told her Wood was a good man. However, she wasn't quite ready to admit that to Gabby.

"We both know you're going to have to replace Barry. Why can't that someone be Wood?"

"Oh, Gabby, it's not as simple as you think," Hannah said on a sigh.

"Oh, I think it is," she said with a giddy look on her face. "He's a man of character. It's there in his nose."

Hannah hoped her aunt was right.

WOOD WAS NOT HAPPY with the way history remembered him. He wasn't a cold-blooded murderer or even a thief, which is what the newspaper article had insinuated. His mysterious disappearance left a cloud of suspicion that had folks not remembering that he had been a man of integrity whom they'd often turned to for help, but wondering if he had stolen and killed to save his sister.

Not the way any man would choose to be remembered. If there was one word that he would want etched on his tombstone it would be *honest*.

Not that it mattered now. There probably was no tombstone. Why would there be? With the exception of a couple of cousins in Chicago, Hannah was his only kin. More than likely his disappearance had simply emancipated her from what she regarded as an interfering brother. She certainly wouldn't search for him the way he had searched for her.

Falling off that horse and through time may have saved him from death, but it had put him in a predicament no man would envy. Using another man's identity and deceiving the people who had shown him kindness. What irony it was—in 1876 he had lived as an honest man only to be regarded as a man without honor. Now in 1998, he lived a lie yet Gabby regarded him as an honest man.

A man she wanted to marry her niece. As Wood waited outside for Hannah, he debated whether he should tell her where he had been and why. With all the newspaper clippings he might be able to convince her he wasn't crazy but simply a man out of time. But she'd also learn that he had been wanted for murder. And he didn't doubt that she'd realize the reason for the rope burns on his neck and wrists had to do with a lynching, not a beating.

No, she'd never trust him if she knew the truth. And right now more than anything else he wanted to earn Hannah Davis's trust. He knew it wasn't going to be easy. When she came outside, she barely spoke a word to him.

"You're angry with me." Wood had to walk briskly to keep up with her as she strode across the gravel drive.

"As I said, I needed you today."

"You have my apology. I'll work as late tonight as you believe is necessary."

"The beans can't be harvested at night. Corn yes, soybeans no." She cut across the grassy knoll separating the chicken coop from the grain bins and headed toward the machinery shed. "And another thing, you shouldn't be driving Gabby's car. You don't have a license."

"Gabby said lots of people drive these back roads without a license."

"That doesn't make it right." She stopped outside the large metal shed and said, "Wait here."

A few minutes later out came a truck with Hannah behind the wheel. She pulled up alongside Wood, and called out to him. "Hop in."

Wood did as she instructed, and had barely shut the door when she took off down the dirt road. Even though he had ridden in her pickup and Gabby's car, Wood wasn't quite prepared for the experience, although Hannah handled the truck as easily as she did any of the other machines. He noticed that except for the steering wheel, few things inside the truck resembled Gabby's car.

"I figured as long as you've been sneaking around driving Gabby's car, you might as well learn to drive this so you can haul the corn for me,'' she told him, then came to an abrupt halt.

Dust erupted like a giant cloud. Wood thought he saw Hannah stifle a grin, making him wonder if she didn't know the effect the ride had on him.

"This is a stick shift." Her hand rested on a ball atop a stick protruding from the floor. "You don't move this until you press in the clutch. It's the pedal to the left of the brake. The trick to getting started is to release the clutch as you step on the gas. Like this." She put the truck in first gear and slowly moved forward.

Wood listened intently to her instructions, trying not to be distracted by the way the setting sun cast its golden glow on her blond curls. It didn't help that she smelled like orange blossoms, or that her pink shirt clung to her curves in a most tantalizing way. She was pretty, and even though she could be as stubborn as a mule, she had a way about her that could make a man's blood rush through his veins until he ached.

Maybe it was the fact that she was capable. He had never met a woman who could run an entire farm by herself. But it wasn't just the physical labor she tackled. Hannah was strong, inside and out. And it was that thought that oddly he found comforting. Those tiny hands on that big steering wheel maneuvering this giant piece of metal as if it were a kettle on the stove.

She was gutsy. And bold. Yet feminine.

Again he thought about Gabby's plan to marry Hannah off to a man she had ordered from an advertisement. Would she ever agree to such an arranged marriage?

For one brief moment Wood saw himself in front of the justice of the peace with Hannah. What if he were her husband, working beside her on the farm, acting as a father to Jeremy? He would be a better husband than Alfred Dumler.

Mostly because he knew the important things any husband of Hannah's should know. Like not to talk to her too early in the morning because she woke up crabby. And not to let her know that you were watching out for her even though you were. And what soft spots on her body could cause her to moan when caressed by a man's fingers.

"Wood? Are you hearing anything I'm saying?" she demanded, interrupting his daydream.

"Sure," he lied.

"Good. Then we can trade places." She climbed out of the truck and came around to his side.

As he walked around the front of the truck, he told himself he was crazy to even be thinking about marriage to Hannah. He could make no plans for his future when he didn't know what century he'd be in tomorrow. Even had he wanted to stay in 1998, there was no guarantee he wouldn't be catapulted back to 1876. And there was still his unresolved guilt. No woman would want a husband who had been branded a murderer.

As Hannah patiently talked him through the operation of the truck, Wood kept telling himself he didn't want to be a permanent fixture in 1998. However, one brush of Hannah's breast against his shoulder as she leaned over to work the clutch had him feeling less sure of himself.

As the truck bucked like a bronc, Hannah laughed. "I think you need more practice." It was the first time since he had been at the farm that she actually appeared to be having fun. Although he knew her smile could light up her face, he hadn't realized that laughter would make her positively glow in a most captivating manner.

As they laughed together over his attempts to drive the truck, he realized that he was captivated by Hannah—a woman who needed no man in her life. A woman who wanted only to be his boss. A woman of a time period to which he didn't belong. It was a sobering thought.

As he drove the truck back to the farm, he said little. He concentrated on working the clutch and the gas pedal to keep the truck running smoothly. When Hannah suggested she be the one who parked the vehicle in the shed, he willingly relinquished control.

"Is there anything else you'd like me to do?" Wood asked her as they stood outside the equipment shed.

"I'd like you to tell me where you were today. Wood, if you're going to work for me, I need to know that I can depend on you."

Wood wanted to reassure her and tell her she could count on him to get the job done. But the truth was she couldn't depend on him being there. Time had seen to that. The helpless feeling that had plagued him ever since he had time traveled raged within him.

All of his life he had been a responsible person. Hell, he hadn't even missed a single day of work until he had left in search of his sister. When he committed to a job, he saw it through to the end.

Only now that aspect of his life had been yanked right away from him. As long as he was caught in this time warp, he was not in charge of his life. It was an awful feeling—this uncertainty—especially for a man who had always been certain of where he was going with his life.

"I told you I had to take care of some personal business," Wood evaded answering her question.

She sighed. "Wood, why did you really come to this farm?"

Her question caught him off guard. "You know I don't remember what happened…" he trailed off, again avoiding saying too much.

"Okay, I've accepted that happened, but why did you stay?"

"Because I need work."

"But why here? What makes a man leave Nebraska and answer an ad for help in a state hundreds of miles away?"

He shrugged. "Things happen."

"What do you mean things happen?" He could see she was growing impatient.

He sighed. "If you must know, I've been looking for my sister. She ran off with a man and I've been trying to find her. That's why I chose Minnesota."

He ran a hand over the back of his neck to ease the tightness in his muscles.

"How old is she?"

"Eighteen. Too young to know what love is," he said cynically.

Hannah didn't contradict him. "And this man she's with?"

"He's in his thirties and an undesirable character."

"Is that why she ran away? Because you disapprove of him?"

"Don't make me sound like the bad guy here. If you met this man, you'd know why I'm concerned. He's trouble." He wanted to tell her more, that his sister was involved with a member of the gang of outlaws who followed Jesse James, but how could he explain any of it without revealing that he was an 1876 man living in 1998? As much as he wanted to confide in Hannah, it was a risk he simply couldn't take.

"That may be, but if she's eighteen, she's legally an adult. She'll have to live with the choices she makes. I don't think there's probably much that you can do," she said pragmatically.

"You may be right," he agreed, but for a totally different reason.

"Do you have any idea where she might be?"

He shook his head. "I've traveled through Missouri and Iowa looking for her, but I haven't had any luck this far.

I've pretty much given up hope of finding her at all," he confessed, silently adding, *Until I go back to her life time.*

"Maybe you should talk to Red Murphy. Even though she's legally of age, he can probably run a trace on her," Hannah suggested.

What Wood didn't need was for the sheriff to become involved in any part of his life. He was sorry he had brought up the subject of his sister. "It's something I prefer to do on my own. I'm not going to give up."

She nodded in understanding. "Thanks for telling me. I know it's not always easy to talk about something so personal." She started toward the house but he stopped her.

"Hannah, did you ask because you're my boss or because you're a woman?"

"Both."

ONCE THE HARVEST BEGAN, there was little time for anything else. Everyone rose early and went to bed late, even Gabby who took charge of the meals while Hannah worked in the field with Wood. When it rained one afternoon, Hannah took the opportunity to run errands in town.

She deliberately avoided walking past the Cut and Curl, not wanting to answer the questions she knew Marlis would ask about Wood. What Hannah didn't expect was that she'd run into the beautician at the bank.

"Hey there, Hannah. Aren't you looking good," Marlis gushed as they met in the lobby.

"I look tired," Hannah corrected her. "We've been harvesting past midnight every day this week."

"By *we* I suppose you mean Wood Dumler and you, right?" There was a sparkle in her eye Hannah didn't want to see.

"He has been helping out now that Caroline's had her baby and Barry's had to spend so much time at the hospital. Have you seen little Alicia? They said she might be able to come home next week," Hannah remarked, wanting to direct the subject away from her hired hand.

"Oh-oh. You haven't heard."

"Heard what?"

"Barry and Caroline are going to have to take her to Rochester. She needs some sort of surgery. Something to do with her heart. They say it's not as serious as it sounds, but it sure does sound awful, doesn't it?"

"I didn't realize there were additional problems. I'll have to give them a call and see if there's anything I can do."

"Lucky for you Mr. Dumler was around to take Barry's place." Marlis refused to let the conversation stray from Wood.

"Yes, it was a good thing." She reached in her purse for her keys. "You'll have to excuse me, Marlis. I have a whole list of errands to run." She tried to sidestep around the other woman, but Marlis wasn't about to let her cut their conversation short.

She placed a hand on Hannah's arm. "Wait. You just can't run off without telling me all about him."

"About who?" Hannah feigned ignorance.

"Wood Dumler."

"There's nothing to tell, Marlis," she said on a note of boredom.

"Is that why Red's been grumpier than a bear with a sore paw?"

"Wood is my employee, Marlis. Nothing more, nothing less," she stated firmly.

The beautician eyed her curiously. "Are you sure about that? Because like I told you earlier, I think he's awful cute, but I wouldn't want to cut in on someone you've got first rights to."

"I have no rights when it comes to Wood," Hannah emphasized.

"Then why don't you send him on down to Lenny's Place on Saturday nights?"

"He's free to do whatever he wants in his spare time," Hannah said primly.

"I heard he's been hanging out at the historical society over in Creston."

That was news to Hannah.

"Apparently he's interested in local history," Marlis remarked.

"Doreen said she had to special order all sorts of old newspapers and things for him. He wanted to find out about the Jesse James Gang."

Hannah shrugged. "So he's interested in history."

"Maybe he's planning to stay awhile, what do you think?" she said with a sly grin.

"I hope he stays through harvest, anyway."

"Janell over at the county courthouse said he was at the records office, too."

Hannah knew the other woman was pumping her for information, but she refused to rise to the bait. "He must have had business there."

"At birth and death records?"

Hannah herself was curious, but wouldn't admit that to Marlis. "I believe it's best not to pay attention to gossip. Now if you'll excuse me, I really do need to get going."

"Good luck with your harvest," Marlis called after her retreating figure, but Hannah wasn't thinking about combining. Her thoughts were on Wood. He hadn't struck her as the kind of man who'd spend his free time at the historical society reading history books.

The visit to the courthouse could explain where he had gone the day he had borrowed Gabby's car. But what had he hoped to find in records? Did he think his sister had died?

It was an awful thought. Hannah had to push it from her

mind because she realized that she was in danger of getting emotionally involved with Wood Harris. Not a smart thing to do. He was just another employee.

Or was he?

"GABBY, WHAT ARE YOU doing here?" Wood asked when the old lady knocked on the screen door of the bunkhouse. Normally Jeremy was the one who woke him, but this morning Gabby's was the first voice he heard.

"I need to talk to you, and I don't want Hannah to hear," she said through the screen.

Wood opened the door and ushered her inside, pulling up a wooden chair for her to sit on.

"Is something wrong?" he asked, sitting across from her on the edge of his cot.

"Now that you and Hannah are getting along so well, I think there's something I should tell you. It's about the will."

"Will?"

She nodded soberly. "Her grandfather's. You know that Hannah took over the farm when he died?

"Yes. She told me there's been a Davis on this land ever since it was homesteaded."

"That's true, and it's been one of the most prosperous farms in the county...until recently."

"Are you saying Hannah's not doing well?"

"Oh no, she's doing a fantastic job, considering what she had to start with. The problem is not her fault. You see, my brother—her grandfather—left her in a pickle."

Wood frowned. "He was in debt when he died?"

"No, not at all. He was one of the wealthiest farmers in the county."

"Then why is Hannah having financial troubles?"

"Because he didn't leave her any money. That's all in a

trust that she can only get if the terms of his will are met,'' Gabby explained.

"So he gave her the farm yet he really didn't give her the farm?"

Gabby nodded solemnly. "She's had to take out all sorts of additional loans to keep the place going."

Wood rubbed a hand along his stubbly jaw. "Can't she meet the terms of his will?"

Gabby threw up her hands in frustration. "She won't. She's too stubborn."

Wood knew Hannah was hardheaded, but he also knew she was intelligent. Surely she wouldn't let an inheritance go simply because of pride? "That doesn't sound like the Hannah I know."

Gabby harrumphed. "You haven't heard the terms of the will."

"Then perhaps you'd better tell me," he urged her.

She lowered her eyes as she said, "In order to collect the bulk of the estate, she has to marry."

"Ah." Suddenly the picture was clear in Wood's eyes. The reason Gabby had placed an ad for a mail-order groom was so that Hannah could collect her inheritance.

"You've been around Hannah long enough to know that she doesn't think she needs a husband, and now that her grandfather has made it a necessity to have one in order to collect the rest of the money needed to run the farm, she's determined to make a go of the farm without help from anyone."

"Admirable, but not necessarily wise," Wood commented with a wry grin.

"My thoughts exactly," she said flashing him a smile. "I like you, Wood. We think alike. Of course, I knew that the minute I read your first letter. Now you can see why I had to advertise for a man."

"You decided to find Hannah a groom so that she wouldn't lose the farm."

She nodded. "Yup. A man looking to be a partner on the farm. And you answered, bless your heart!" She flashed him an endearing grin of gratitude.

"If I marry Hannah, she collects her inheritance."

Gabby nodded vigorously. "She's entitled to it, and if my brother hadn't been such a stubborn old man, he wouldn't have put that stupid provision in the will. But he was as old-fashioned as the rest of his generation and he honestly didn't think that a woman could run a farm this size by herself."

"But didn't Hannah prove that to him before he died?"

"Oh, no. When she and Jeremy moved back here, my brother ran the farm and no one—especially not a woman—was going to take over his duties. Despite all the help she gave him, he never would admit that she was just as capable as any man."

"She is that," Wood agreed.

Gabby sighed enviously. "I could never do what's she's doing. That's why my brother left her the farm and not me. He knew that she'd manage it the way it should be done."

"Yet he wanted it done his way," Wood noted.

Gabby nodded. "So that's the situation, Wood. Either Hannah marries, or she never collects the money needed to save the farm." Gabby folded her hands in front of her on the table and looked at him as if he were their last hope.

It was an unsettling thought. Pretending to be Alfred Dumler, mail-order groom, when he thought it was simply a whim of an old lady was one thing. But now that Wood knew the marriage involved saving the livelihood of three people, his pretense took on a new dimension.

"Knowing this about the will doesn't change anything, does it?" She looked at him anxiously.

"You want to know if I'm still willing to marry Hannah?"

She nodded eagerly, anticipating his answer.

Wood felt a stab of guilt. Gabby truly was a sweet little old lady who didn't deserve to be the victim of his deception. He was pretending to be a man who had come to the farm of his own free will to answer an ad for a mail-order groom.

"I can't promise you anything, Gabby," he said honestly. "But you have my word I'll do whatever I can to help Hannah hang on to the farm."

After he had uttered the words, he knew how hollow they actually were. What could he do? Marry Hannah? Even if she agreed, which was unlikely, how could he possibly wed a woman from another century?

Chapter Ten

Every day Jeremy took the same route home from the school bus. And everyday he saw fewer rows of corn.

That's why on this particular day his steps were a bit slower as he walked past the tall rows of corn. The end was near. The golden stalks, many of which towered over him, would soon be gone, which is why he sat down and unzipped his school bag.

He pulled out a granola bar. He would much rather have had a candy bar, but his mom said they were empty calories. He unwrapped the snack bar and tossed the paper in the direction of his open school bag. It missed and he had to crawl on his knees and retrieve the errant wrapper.

As he did, he saw another piece of paper. Something white. Curious, he snatched it from between the corn stalks. It was an envelope—a letter—but most of the writing had been smudged by rain.

One thing that wasn't smudged was the return address label. It must have been plastic coated. Jeremy read the name. Alfred Dumler. Had Wood mailed this letter a long time ago and it had never arrived?

He thought for a moment, then remembered the day Wood had arrived. Gabby had dropped the mail. Could this be a piece that had been in that bunch?

Jeremy's brows drew together. He studied the smudged postmark. It said September something...

Maybe he should open it. It wasn't like anyone would know. And besides, it was probably all run together just like the address.

He ripped open the envelope and extracted the single piece of paper. It said:

Dear Hannah,
I've had a change in plans. I won't be able to come
on the 10th of September, but I still plan to visit.
Would October work for you? Please write and let me
know.

It was signed Alfred Dumler.

"YOU DON'T LOOK so hot," Gabby remarked when Hannah came in for dinner one evening.

"I don't feel so hot, either," Hannah admitted, dragging her feet across the floor to the sink where she filled a glass with water.

"I hope it's not that flu bug going around. Mabel said both of her grandkids had it—ran a fever for three days, couldn't even get out of bed."

"Mom, you can't be sick. Tomorrow's my birthday," Jeremy reminded her.

"I'll be fine by tomorrow," Hannah assured him. "I just need to take some aspirin and lie down for a bit."

Only she wasn't fine the following day. No amount of determination was going to get her aching muscles and joints to move from the bed. When Gabby took her temperature, the thermometer read a hundred and two.

"Yup, it's the flu," she diagnosed soberly.

"It can't be. I have too much to do."

Gabby added another blanket to her bed. "It'll still be there when you get up."

"But it's Jeremy's birthday. We're supposed to camp out." She shuddered as chills racked her body. "Maybe if I sleep this morning I'll feel better by dinner."

Only Hannah didn't even wake up for dinner. Except for a couple of brief visits to the bathroom, she didn't get out of bed until after nine o'clock that night. Still weak, she slipped her feet into a pair of moccasins and padded down the stairs.

The house was quiet. Jeremy's birthday cake sat on the kitchen table, iced and decorated, but uncut. Hannah found Gabby sitting in her den, reading an Agatha Christie novel.

"Why didn't someone wake me?"

"We figured you needed your rest. How are you feeling?"

Hannah sank down onto the love seat. "Still woozy." She dropped her head into her hands. "My head aches. My throat's sore, too."

"Are you hungry?"

She nodded. "Where's Jeremy?"

"Wood took him camping," Gabby replied.

That brought Hannah's head up with a jerk. "You let them go?"

"Is there a reason why I shouldn't have?"

Hannah looked at her aunt's innocent face and didn't even bother trying to explain. "I don't want Wood taking Jeremy camping."

"Why not? Just the other day you told me you thought he was good with Jeremy."

Hannah groaned. "That doesn't mean I..." She trailed off in a groan.

Gabby put her book aside and got up to fuss over Hannah, who had kicked off her moccasins and brought her legs up onto the love seat in a half-lying, half-sitting position. "You shouldn't be out of bed. You're not well at all."

"I'm tired of being in bed," Hannah moaned.

"Maybe, but you need your rest." Gabby patted her hand. "Let me get you a couple of those pain relief tablets—you know, the ones that help you sleep."

"I don't want to sleep," Hannah protested, but Gabby paid no attention.

She disappeared only to return with two tablets and a glass of water. "Here. Take these."

Hannah did as she was told, hating the way her body had betrayed her. She had no time to be sick. Especially not now.

"*I* wanted to take Jeremy camping on his birthday. We were supposed to ride over to the creek and pitch his tent, roast hot dogs and marshmallows, tell ghost stories...." Then she did something rare. She cried.

Gabby reached for a box of tissues and comforted her. "There now, there's no need to feel bad. It's not like Jeremy's birthday was ruined. We're going to have the cake tomorrow when you're feeling better."

"But it's a tradition and it's been broken." With a supreme effort, Hannah pushed herself to her feet. "I've got to go find them."

"Don't talk nonsense," Gabby scolded. "What you need is to get back to bed."

Hannah paid no attention to her aunt's advice, wandering into the kitchen with her aunt trailing behind her. At the door she pulled her jacket on over her nightgown and slid her feet into her boots.

"Hannah, you're not being rational. You can't go out when you're sick," Gabby argued.

"I have to make sure Jeremy's all right." She shoved her hair up beneath her cap, then grabbed her keys from their usual peg on the wall.

"But you shouldn't be driving. Those pills will make you sleepy," Gabby fretted.

Hannah didn't say another word, but headed for the garage where she climbed into the pickup. She had to rest her head against the steering wheel before she could muster up the energy to start the truck.

As she drove down the dark country road, she thought she truly hated Wood. He had pushed his way into their lives, intruding where he wasn't wanted, making himself useful, making himself needed.

Well, she didn't need him. She needed no man, and she was going to make damn sure that her son didn't need him, either. She knew exactly where to look—it was the spot she and Jeremy had camped out on his past five birthdays. Near the creek, behind a thicket of elderberry bushes. They had made their own firepit, lining stones in a circle so they could roast hot dogs and marshmallows.

Sure enough. Smoke billowed from the glowing embers of a fire. Hannah killed the engine and walked the rest of the way on foot. A light shone in the small domed tent with two heads in silhouette.

When she peeked inside, she found Jeremy and Wood stretched out on their stomachs, a checkerboard between them.

"Mom! What are you doing here?"

Hannah stumbled inside. "Happy birthday."

"Mom, you look awful!"

From the way Wood stared at her, Hannah knew she must look pretty bad. He looked his usual handsome self. In fact, in the light of the lantern, he was so darn good looking she could have—

Suddenly she realized that she hadn't even brushed her teeth all day or combed her hair. And she was in her nightgown. She wanted to turn around and leave, but she felt awful. And dizzy. And tired.

"Mom, why are you here?" Jeremy repeated.

"I want to camp out with you."

"But you're sick."

"Not really. I'm tough." It was the last thing she said before crumbling at their feet.

"It's a good thing the tent is big enough for three, huh?" Jeremy said to Wood as he zippered a groggy Hannah into his sleeping bag.

"I think maybe we should take her back to the house," Wood said to Jeremy.

"No, I'm camping out with Jeremy. It's his birthday," she protested wearily.

Wood placed his palm over her forehead. "She's feverish," he said to Jeremy. To Hannah he said, "Jeremy and I are going to take you home. If I know Gabby, she's walking the floor worrying about you."

"I just saw Gabby. She gave me some tablets," Hannah murmured sleepily, nestling against Wood's shoulder.

"I think she's tired," Jeremy said in a low voice. "Maybe we should just let her sleep here with us. I can open up my sleeping bag and we can share."

His offer tugged at something inside Wood's chest. "I'm not sure this is the best place for your mom. The ground's going to be damp by morning," Wood told him, even though the thought of Hannah spending the night in his arms was an attractive one.

"Then we'd better take her home," Jeremy agreed.

Wood could see that Hannah was going to fight him on the matter.

"No, I don't want to go home. I can stay here." She struggled briefly in an attempt to convince them she felt all right.

They weren't convinced.

"Hannah, be sensible," Wood spoke to her as if she

were a child. "You and Jeremy can camp out another night."

"Does that mean I have to go home, too?" Jeremy asked Wood in a whisper.

More than anything Wood wanted to stay at the house and make sure Hannah was going to be okay. But he didn't want to disappoint Jeremy, either.

"Let's get your mother home first and then we'll talk about it, okay?"

Hannah stirred briefly when Wood carried her to the pickup. Swaddled in his sleeping bag, she rode between Jeremy and Wood, her head falling against Wood's shoulder.

"You drive a stick pretty well," Hannah murmured as Wood maneuvered the truck down the dirt roads.

"I had a good teacher," he answered, liking the feel of her body leaning against his.

As soon as they arrived back at the home place, Wood carried her into the house, up the stairs and deposited her in her own bed, while Gabby fluttered behind him, mumbling her concern.

"Do you think she needs a doctor?" Wood asked as Gabby removed her jacket and tucked her back into bed.

Hannah's eyes fluttered open. "I don't need a doctor. I told you, I'm fine." She tried to sit up, but collapsed against the pillow.

In an aside to Wood, Gabby said, "She's always bullheaded when she's sick. Thank goodness she doesn't get sick often."

"I want to get up," Hannah protested, although not a single limb moved. "I'm hungry."

"I warmed up some chicken soup for her. I'll get it," Gabby said, and started toward the door.

Wood stopped her. "You stay here. I'll go."

"It's on the stove. And you'd better bring her some more

juice. Oh, there are some soda crackers in the cupboard next to the refrigerator, and she'll need a napkin,'' Gabby gave him instructions.

"Would you all stop acting like I'm some kind of invalid?" Hannah complained. When she would have swung her legs over the bed Wood sat down beside her.

"You are going stay in bed and do exactly as you are told. Got it?"

"Are you forgetting who's boss here?" Hannah challenged, although it was a pretty weak one.

"You're not my boss tonight. You're a woman who's too stubborn to admit she needs help."

"And what are you going to do about it?"

"I'm going to get you the soup and you're going to eat it. Understand?"

"Yes."

Her submission caught him off guard. As she fell back against the pillow, her blond curls no longer springy, her face pale, Wood thought he had never seen her look more beautiful.

"I'll be right back," he announced to the three of them, then went downstairs to get Hannah's soup.

As he gathered the things for her tray, Wood realized how comfortable he felt in the Davis kitchen. In a short time he had become a part of their family, and surprisingly, it was not the uncomfortable place he thought it would be. Unfortunately it was not a place he could consider as permanent. Even if he wanted to stay, time threatened to take him away.

When Wood returned to Hannah's room, only Jeremy was there. "Where's Gabby?" he asked as he set the tray down on the nightstand beside the bed.

"She said she was tired and she was going to bed," Jeremy replied.

"I don't need Gabby to feed me," Hannah announced irritably.

"Not when you have me," Wood told her.

"You're not going to feed me, Wood Dumler."

"And who's going to stop me? You?" He chuckled. "You can't even fluff up your own pillow. How are you going to battle someone my size?"

"Jeremy?" Hannah turned to her son for help.

"I'll be right back, Mom. I have to go to the bathroom," he said, then disappeared out the door.

"You better sit up," Wood said patiently, putting his arm around her shoulder and pulling her forward so he could prop her pillows behind her.

When her covers slipped downward, Hannah tugged them back up. "You shouldn't be in here at all. I'm in my nightgown and it's sheer."

Wood grinned. "I know. You came out to the tent and climbed into my sleeping bag, remember?"

She blushed. "Why are you doing this?"

"Because I like taking care of you, Hannah," he told her, then reached for the bowl of soup.

She had no response to that statement.

"Now open up and let's get this food inside you."

To his surprise, Hannah did exactly as she was told. Although she didn't finish all of the soup, she did eat her soda crackers and drink her juice.

"Feel better?" Wood asked as she slid back down in the bed.

"Yes, thank you."

"Think you'll be all right?"

"Yes."

"Good. That means Jeremy and I can leave." He didn't miss the apprehension that flashed in her eyes. "You can trust me to take good care of him, Hannah."

She didn't say a word, and he wondered if she did trust

him or if she simply didn't have the strength to argue with him. As Wood turned out the light, he dropped a kiss on her forehead.

As he left the room, her small, sickly voice called out, "Hey! I'm still your boss."

Wood grinned to himself.

WHEN WOOD AND JEREMY got back to the campsite, they played more checkers, roasted something Jeremy called hot dogs over the open fire and told spooky stories. All the while Wood's thoughts were never far from Hannah.

"We've done a pretty good job keeping the secret, haven't we?" Jeremy asked Wood as they lay in the tent, the only light coming from a gas lantern. It had been a while since they had spoken on the subject of the mail-order groom, and although Wood had hoped that Jeremy had disregarded the idea, it was obvious he hadn't.

"I'd say you're a man who can be trusted to keep information to himself," Wood answered.

"I'm not a blabbermouth like some of the kids at school."

There was a small moment of silence, then he added, "I haven't even told anyone you're not Alfred Dumler."

Wood's heart skipped a beat. Momentarily stunned, he could only look at Jeremy.

"It's okay. I like you, anyway."

"What makes you think I'm not Alfred?"

He reached into his backpack and pulled out a ragged-looking envelope. "Because I found this." He handed it to Wood, who read its contents.

"How long have you had this?" he asked when he had finished.

"Since Wednesday."

"Three days, yet you didn't say anything to me?"

"I couldn't. Mom was always around."

Wood nodded in understanding. "My real name is Wood Harris," he said quietly.

"So how come you're pretending to be this Alfred guy?" There was no censure in his question, just curiosity.

Wood didn't know what to say to the boy. He exhaled a heavy sigh, then said, "It's a long story and a complicated one. Believe me, Jeremy, I have a good reason for using another man's name."

"You don't owe some people a bunch of money, do you?"

Wood shook his head. "No, why would you ask that?"

"Because I once saw this show on TV where this guy had to change his name because he had stolen all this money and the cops wanted to—"

Wood interrupted him. "Jeremy, I can promise you the reason I'm not using my real name has nothing to do with anything you've seen on TV. You know the kind of man I am."

"Yeah. You're too nice to be a crook. Mom says you won't even accept all the money that's owed you. She thinks it's because you feel sorry for her, but I think it's because you don't need it."

Wood tapped his chest with his fingertips. "It's what's inside here that makes a person who he is, not a name. Whether I'm Wood Dumler or Wood Harris, I'm still the same man who has worked on your farm for the past month."

Jeremy nodded in agreement. "You don't need to worry. I'll keep your secret."

"I hope one day it won't have to be a secret."

"Does that mean you won't be the mail-order groom if that happens?" Anxiety edged his words.

"I'm not sure, Jeremy." he answered honestly.

"But if you're pretending to be a mail-order groom now, it must mean that you think it's a good idea, doesn't it?"

"I want to help your mother in any way I can."

"Does that mean you plan on staying? That you want to be my dad?"

Wood didn't miss the fact that Jeremy didn't ask if he wanted to marry his mother, but rather did Wood want to be his father. It was a delicate situation Wood found himself in. He didn't want to hurt the boy's feelings, yet he didn't want to mislead Jeremy, either.

"It's not a question of whether I want to be your father," Wood told him as he watched shadows dance on the canvas. "It's whether your mother and I are suited to each other."

"But you like her, don't you?"

"Sure I do."

"And she likes you."

"She told you that?"

"No, but Gabby says Mom watches you when you're not looking and that's a sign that she's taken with you," he said earnestly. "I think that's why Gabby went to bed and left you to feed mom the soup. To make it...you know—" he grinned shyly "—romantic."

Wood didn't doubt Gabby had played matchmaker. He only hoped that she was right about Hannah's feelings for him. However, he suspected that the reason Hannah had her eye on him probably had to do more with her being worried he might steal something rather than her being taken with him.

"Liking someone and wanting to marry him are not the same thing. Your mother doesn't appear to be a woman who's going to take kindly to someone sending for a groom for her without her knowledge," Wood pointed out.

"Gabby's not sure we should ever tell her."

Wood frowned. "She'd rather I be a hired hand than your mother's husband?"

"Uh-uh. She thinks nature should take its course. If you

and Mom fall in love and get married, then my mom doesn't need to know that Gabby advertised for a husband for her," Jeremy said on a yawn.

Wood reached up to turn off the gas lantern. "I'm certain everything will work out in a reasonable amount of time. You and I need to get some sleep if we're going to be any help to your mother tomorrow."

Jeremy groaned in protest as darkness filled the tent, but Wood noticed it was only a matter of minutes before the boy had fallen asleep. Not so for Wood. Long after the light had been extinguished he thought about Hannah and the way she had looked when she had arrived at their camping spot.

It was nice to know that the smart, strong, capable Hannah could be foolish at times. He shook his head. And she thought she didn't need a man to take care of her.

THE FOLLOWING MORNING was Sunday and Wood filled in for Hannah for a second time. He took Gabby and Jeremy to church, leaving Hannah to sleep in.

When she did finally awake, the sun was streaming through her window. At the sight of the nearly empty soup bowl, she realized that last night hadn't been a dream. She had gone out to the campsite and Wood had carried her home. He had fussed over her in a way no man had ever fussed over her, and to her surprise, it didn't leave her angry, but feeling rather special. Maybe old-fashioned men weren't such a pain in the butt after all.

Gingerly, she climbed out of bed to discover that her legs weren't wobbly and her head wasn't throbbing. She crept downstairs to the kitchen where she made herself toast and a cup of tea. Then she tried to remember where she had left her moccasins.

In Gabby's den. Sure enough, there they were, stuck partway beneath the flowered love seat. Hannah bent down

on her hands and knees to retrieve them, when she noticed
the corner of a magazine sticking out beneath the ruffled
skirt. It was a farm journal which Hannah would have
tossed into Gabby's magazine rack if a piece of paper
hadn't fallen out.

Curious, Hannah read what it said. It was an invoice for
an ad billed to Gabby. Suspicion replaced curiosity. Hannah
opened the magazine to the classified section and scanned
the small print until she found one that had been circled in
pen.

"That pig!" She dropped the magazine.

HANNAH HEARD GABBY'S CAR return from church. As she
glanced out her bedroom window, she saw Jeremy and
Wood head for the chicken coop. Gabby was nowhere in
sight. Hannah could only guess that she had stayed after
for donuts and coffee and that Mabel would be bringing
her home.

It was probably better that Gabby hadn't come home.
Hannah preferred to vent her anger on Wood, the *mail-
order groom*. She shivered at the thought. Everything he
had done since his arrival had been with one goal in
mind—getting her to the altar. The solicitous behavior, the
interest in her son, the intimate moments they had shared…

She took a deep breath and marched outside, the farm
journal in hand. He and Jeremy worked side by side, carefully submerging the freshly gathered eggs in a metal tub
of water and placing them in one of the half dozen cartons
lined up in a row on the grass.

"Hi, Mom. Wood's helping me with the eggs," Jeremy
said when she came out of the house.

"You'll have to finish later. I need to speak to Wood,"
Hannah said briskly.

"Are you mad about something?" Jeremy asked.

"Jeremy, just go inside."

"But my eggs…"

"I'll take care of your eggs."

Slowly Jeremy headed for the house, pausing on the porch steps to say, "Wood didn't do anything wrong. He couldn't have…"

One stern look from his mother had him slipping inside without another word.

"You must be feeling better. You're acting like the boss again," Wood commented, rising to his feet.

"Boss? Don't you mean *wife?*" She held up the farm journal. "I saw Gabby's ad."

"That's why you look like you want to tear my heart out and eat it for breakfast."

She chuckled mirthlessly. "Believe me, your heart does not interest me."

"I'm sorry to hear that."

"How could the two of you…" She trailed off at a loss for words.

"Gabby was worried that you were going to lose the farm," he said in the older woman's defense.

"I know what motivated Gabby. What I want to know is what kind of a man answers an ad for a groom?" Hannah was so angry she could barely stand still, moving restlessly back and forth.

But more than anger, she felt hurt. Just when she was beginning to think she could trust Wood, she discovered that he had been lying to her from the start. No wonder he had flirted with her. And all that gallant behavior…and the kisses. It was all an act. To convince her to marry him.

"I'm sorry, Hannah."

His apology did little to calm her. "You still haven't answered my question. What kind of man are you to agree to marry a woman you've never met?"

"I never thought I was going to marry you when I came here," he replied.

"You didn't come here looking for a wife? Well, golly gee, Wood, why not tell another lie?" she drawled sarcastically. "It's not like you haven't been lying since the day I met you, is it?"

"I couldn't tell you the truth," he admitted. "I knew you would send me away. And then there was Gabby."

She waved a finger at him. "You leave Gabby out of this. We're talking about you coming here under false pretenses—pretending you needed a job."

"I did need a job."

"You were after more than that," she sneered. "No wonder you said you'd work for nothing. You had your eyes set on bigger stuff—like owning half of this farm."

"You're wrong about me, Hannah," he said quietly.

"Am I?"

"Yes, and I'd appreciate it if you'd stop looking at me as if I'm one of those bugs Wilbur ruts around for in the manure pile," he retorted.

"At least those bugs serve a purpose," she spat back. She was behaving like a shrew, yet she couldn't help herself. How could he have duped her this way? Insinuating his way onto the farm, endearing himself to Jeremy and Gabby, reminding her that she was a woman....

That was the part that bothered her more than anything. Wood Dumler hadn't just filled a void at the farm, he had filled an emptiness in her life. And she hated him for it.

"I want you to pack up your things and be gone by tomorrow morning." She finally was able to quit wiggling and stand perfectly still, her arms folded across her chest.

Wood heaved a long sigh. "I'm a good worker, Hannah. If you don't want the marriage thing, I can understand that, but at least let me help you with the harvest."

"I don't need your help," she said through tight lips.

"Yes, you do," he contradicted her. "Don't send me

away over some ad that doesn't mean anything to either one of us.''

She stared at him in disbelief. "How can you say that? You came here thinking you were going to marry me!"

"I didn't!" he protested.

"You didn't answer Gabby's personals ad for a husband?"

This time he was the one who shifted restlessly from foot to foot. "This situation isn't what it appears to be."

She raised a hand in the air. "I don't want to hear any more lies, Wood. There's nothing you can say that will change my mind. I'll write you a check for the wages you have coming. It should be enough to get you a bus ticket back to Omaha or wherever it is you want to go." She started gathering up Jeremy's egg cartons.

Wood tried to help her, but she pushed him away. "I don't want to go anywhere. It's true I came here under false pretenses, but my goal hasn't been to get you to marry me."

"Oh, no? What about the kisses?"

"I kissed you because I wanted to. That was the only reason," he said sincerely.

"Yeah, right," she drawled sarcastically.

When she nearly dropped a dozen eggs, he again tried to take the cartons from her hands, but she wouldn't let him. "Will you please let me help?"

"No." Stubbornly, she carried all the cartons in her arms, holding the top one in place with her chin.

He rushed to get the door for her. As soon as she had set the eggs down, she returned to the porch. "Just in case you didn't understand anything I've said, you're fired."

When she would have turned around, he grabbed her by the arm and pulled her to him. Before she could utter a word of protest his mouth was on hers, hot and demanding. Energy warmed her insides, vibrating from the top of her head to the tip of her toes. A thrill unlike any she had ever known swept through her as his large hands pressed her against his hardness. Her hips tilted involuntarily. She groaned, not in anger, but with pleasure.

She wanted more than his kisses. Much more.

Not so Wood. He ended the kiss just as abruptly as it had begun.

"A woman as pretty as you doesn't need to advertise for a husband," he told her, then turned and walked away.

She went inside, her body trembling. She took a long cool drink of water, her face still flushed. Jeremy sat at the table, his face lined with worry.

"Did you know about this?" she asked, assuming he knew what "this" meant.

The guilty look on her son's face told her he did. "I like Wood, Mom. He's a pretty neat guy."

"Jeremy, don't even utter that man's name in my presence or I..." She stopped speaking as the sound of a car door slamming could be heard through the screen door. A few moments later Gabby bounced in. One look at the faces of Jeremy and Hannah was enough for her to know that something was definitely amiss.

"How are you feeling?" she asked Hannah.

"I'm hot and it's not because I have a fever." She poured herself a cup of coffee, then sat down.

"She knows why Wood is here, Gabby," Jeremy said quietly.

"Oh-oh." Gabby dropped down onto a chair at the table, looking very much like a schoolgirl who had been caught chewing gum in school.

"An ad for a husband?" Hannah could only stare at her great-aunt in disbelief. "How could you do such a thing?"

"You know why." She kept her voice low.

"Grandfather's money?"

Gabby nodded solemnly. "I didn't want you to lose the

farm.'' Moisture gathered in the corners of the old lady's eyes, causing Hannah's anger to dissipate.

As goofy as the idea was, she knew that Gabby's intentions had been good. She had simply wanted to help save the farm.

''We're not going to lose the farm,'' Hannah reassured her aunt, patting the wrinkled hands.

''Are you going to make Wood go home?'' Jeremy wanted to know.

''He's leaving in the morning,'' Hannah replied.

Gabby and Jeremy groaned in unison.

''Aw, Mom, come on!''

''He lied to me,'' Hannah said in her own defense.

''So did me and Gabby,'' Jeremy pointed out. ''We knew about the ad, but we didn't say anything because we knew this is just what you would do. You'd send Wood away, and we didn't want that because we think he's neat.''

''He is a rather remarkable young man,'' Gabby added her two cents' worth. ''He's good with animals, and you're never going to find anyone who's willing to work for so little money.''

''He didn't know what a soybean was until I showed him,'' Hannah reminded them.

''But he works so hard.''

''He's not staying,'' Hannah said firmly, ignoring the woeful pleas in the eyes of the two people at the table.

''You don't have to marry the man, but don't you think we should at least keep him on through the harvest?'' Gabby asked.

''We'll get by. We did last year.'' Hannah got up to get the bottle of aspirin from the cupboard.

''Last year you had Barry full time,'' Gabby reminded her.

''He'll help with the corn harvest.''

Hannah was about to pop a tablet in her mouth when

Gabby said, "Now I know you're not thinking clearly. You know that Barry and Caroline's baby is scheduled to have surgery next week. He's not going to be able to come back to work here."

"Then I'll harvest the corn by myself. Jeremy will help me," Hannah stated stubbornly.

Gabby rose to all of her four feet eleven inches and looked down at her niece seated at the table. "Hannah Marie Davis, you're being bullheaded. You have a perfectly reliable man willing to work for you, yet you're going to let him go because of your pride. Now, I have a say in this farm and my say says we keep Wood on at least until harvest is over."

"I vote with Gabby," Jeremy piped up.

"You don't have a vote," Hannah informed him.

"He should have," Gabby declared.

"How come I don't have a vote?" Jeremy demanded.

"All right, you have a vote," Hannah snapped in frustration.

"Good, then it's two yeses and one no which means Wood stays, right Gabby?" Jeremy looked to his great-aunt for confirmation.

"Is he right?" Gabby looked at Hannah.

"All right. He can stay. But only until harvest is over." Hannah knew her aunt was right. She couldn't afford to let Wood go at this time of the year. No matter what her personal feelings were, she needed another pair of hands. Wood's hands. But only for harvest. Not for anything else. And especially not for holding her.

"YOU GET TO STAY." Gabby's face beamed as she made the announcement.

"I bet I have you to thank for that, don't I?" Wood said affectionately.

"And Jeremy."

"Then I owe you both a debt of gratitude." He hugged Gabby, then said, "Do you know where Jeremy is?"

"Outside somewhere," Gabby told him. "I was just about to do laundry. If you bring your things over, I'll wash them up for you."

"Gabby, you are a gem." Wood tipped his hat, then went to retrieve his dirty clothes.

Gabby relished his compliment. There was nothing she wouldn't do for Wood. In her opinion, she had picked out the best mail-order groom possible for Hannah. It was true that her original plan had been for Hannah and Wood to fall in love, but all things considered, at least Hannah hadn't sent him away. Gabby knew that no matter what Hannah said, she liked having Wood around. It was only a matter of time until she realized what a good husband he'd make.

A short while later Gabby smiled to herself as she carried a basket of laundry to the basement. In it were Wood's work clothes. He had asked her on several different occasions if she would show him how to use the washer and dryer.

She had refused, telling him it was no bother for her to include his laundry in with Jeremy's. As she sorted through jeans and shirts, she hummed a song from her childhood. In and out of the pockets of shirts and pants her fingers traveled to the rhythm of the music.

When she found a folded up piece of paper in one of Wood's shirt pockets, she couldn't resist taking a look at it. Carefully peeking at one corner, she discovered a photocopy of a newspaper dated 1876.

"This must be what he was looking for at the library," Gabby mused aloud. Curious, she unfolded the rest of the paper, then gasped.

"Oh, my!" Her hand flew to her mouth. Staring at her

was a picture of Wood Dumler. Her narrowed eyes read the caption and the two-column story.

"Oh my!" she repeated again. "This can't be...it just can't be," she said, shaking her head. "Or can it?"

She folded the clothes that had been in the dryer and placed them in the straw basket. Then she went upstairs.

"Gabby, are you all right? You look awfully pale," Wood remarked when he saw her coming. He hurried to relieve her of the burden. "What are you doing carrying that? Didn't I tell you to wait for me to lift those baskets for you?" he gently scolded her.

"I'm fine," she told him, although her legs wobbled a bit.

He could see that she was unsteady and helped her to a chair. "You better sit. Can I get you anything? Some water?"

She shook her head, then reached out and patted him. First his arms, then his shoulders, his cheeks, his ears. "I can't believe it."

"Gabby, what's wrong?"

She reached into her apron pocket and pulled out the photocopy of the article. "I found this when I was washing your clothes."

Wood didn't need to look at it to know what it was. Gabby's face said it all. He sat down beside her, taking his hands in hers. "I don't know why or how it happened. One moment I was in 1876, the next 1998."

"Then it's true?"

"Yes."

"Oh, my!"

And for the second time in two days a Davis woman fell into Wood's arms.

Chapter Eleven

Wood carried Gabby outside onto the porch where she could get some fresh air, setting her down on the swing.

"Gabby, talk to me." He patted her hand. "Come on, Gabby, wake up."

Befuddled, she opened her eyes and glanced at her surroundings. "Oh, Wood," she said on a long sigh. "Thank goodness. I'm here. On the porch. That means it must have been a dream." She giggled nervously. "Oh, you wouldn't have believed the dream I had." She straightened, patting her curls. "I was doing the laundry and..."

Wood knelt beside her, once more taking hold of her hands. "Gabby, it wasn't a dream."

"What?"

"That afternoon you and Jeremy found me in your cornfield...I didn't come from Nebraska. I came from the year 1876."

She gasped. "Oh, my! Hannah was right. You've escaped from a mental hospital, haven't you?" She yanked her hands away from his, fear filling her eyes. "Where is Alfred Dumler? What have you done to him?" she demanded in alarm.

"I've never met Alfred Dumler, and I don't know why he never showed up that day," Wood answered truthfully.

"Then why are you pretending to be him?"

She looked so fragile and confused, Wood was afraid she'd faint on him again. "Because I knew if folks found out who I really am, they would think I'm crazy, just as you do right now."

"But you must be crazy," she whispered, her cheeks paper white. "No one can travel through time. That only happens on TV or in the movies," she insisted, her lips quivering.

"You saw my picture in the newspaper."

"So you look like some man from 1876."

"No, I am that man, Gabby. I know it sounds preposterous, but if you'll listen, I will tell you how I think it all happened."

At first he thought she might say no. She looked as if she wanted to get to the nearest telephone and call Red Murphy.

After a few minutes of contemplation, however, she said, "That's why you were afraid to ride in the pickup—because you had never even seen an automobile before, had you?"

He shook his head. "Or a combine or a radio or TV or a computer."

"That newspaper accused you of doing some awful things."

"I could never hurt anyone. You believe that, don't you?"

She rose to her feet, swaying slightly. Wood automatically reached out to steady her. She didn't push him away.

"Come inside. If we're going to talk, I think I'd better make me some tea."

ONE THING WOOD DISCOVERED that afternoon was that although Gabby appeared to be a bit dotty at times, her mind was as sharp as a tack. She pulled out history books and quizzed him about life in 1876 until she was satisfied that what he said was indeed the truth. Wood figured it helped that her great-grandmother's personal diary mentioned the murder of George and Mary Nelson and how she believed an innocent man had nearly hung for the crime.

That evening at dinner Gabby was unusually quiet, causing Hannah to worry that her great-aunt might be getting the same flu bug that had sent her to her bed. Gabby assured her she felt fine, that she simply had a lot of things on her mind.

Wood could only hope that she wouldn't tell Hannah everything they had discussed that afternoon. Although he had requested she not reveal how he had arrived at the Davis farm, she had made no promises. All she had said was that she needed time to think about what she should do next.

That's why he was surprised when she sought him out at the bunkhouse that evening. "We need to find Alfred Dumler," she told Wood, the tone of her voice telling him she definitely thought it was an urgent matter needing their attention.

"Gabby, if we do that, Hannah's going to know I'm not Alfred," Wood pointed out.

"I don't want to bring him here. I want to find him so that I can tell him not to come," she explained.

"You don't need to worry about it, Gabby," Wood told her.

"Why not?"

"Because Jeremy found a letter from him." Wood pulled the soiled envelope from his pocket and handed it to Gabby. "He found this in the cornfield just the other day. Apparently it had been there for some time. Jeremy thought it might have been dropped from the mail on that day when you first found me."

"It's from Alfred Dumler," Gabby said, noting the return address. "Then Jeremy knows you're not Alfred?"

Wood nodded soberly. "But he doesn't know about the time travel."

Gabby unfolded the letter and read it. "Alfred says he's been detained and perhaps I could let him know if October would be a better time."

"What are you going to do?" Wood asked.

"I'm going to write and tell him not to come. We don't need him. We have you."

"Then you want me to stay?"

"I do. I like having you around," Gabby admitted shyly. Then she looked Wood in the eye and asked, "The question is do you want to stay?"

"I do."

"Does that mean you haven't given up on our plan?"

"I thought you would have given up on it by now."

She patted his hand. "Things happen for a reason, Wood. I believe you were sent here to help us save the farm."

He sighed. "Didn't you see Hannah's reaction when she found out about the ad?"

"She was steamin' mad." Gabby chuckled. "I expected that. She hates the idea of marrying just to get the money, but I'm telling you, Wood, time is running out. You yourself heard her complain that corn prices are at an all-time low. If they don't pick up, it could mean disaster for the farm."

Gabby looked at Wood as if he were some sort of knight in shining armor.

"How can I make plans for a future here in 1998 when I have no way of knowing if I'll be taken back to 1876?"

"I might know of a way to find out the answer to that," she told Wood.

That piqued his curiosity. "What is it, Gabby?"

She pulled a small square of newsprint from her pocket and handed it to him. "There's a psychic coming to Spring Valley."

Wood read the advertisement, which claimed a Madame Duvalee knew the answers to questions you had about your past and future. "Do you know this person?"

"Heavens, no. She's from California. She's on a tour and Creston is one of the places she'll be. She's giving a demonstration, but she's also going to be talking to people one-on-one."

"And you think I should go see her?"

"Yes. She could have the answers you're looking for regarding the time travel."

Wood wasn't as confident as Gabby, but he didn't believe he should rule out the possibility, either.

"If you want, you can take my car," Gabby offered. "Until then, you need to not waste a single minute of the time you do have with Hannah. You are a little bit in love with her, aren't you?"

"What man wouldn't be?"

"Then in the meantime, I suggest you stay out of thunderstorms." She gave him an impish grin.

Wood knew it was nothing to take lightly. The thought that at any moment he could be tossed into another time period kept him in constant uncertainty. Although Gabby wanted him to follow through as Hannah's mail-order groom, he knew it wasn't an easy decision to make. The last thing he wanted to do was cause hardship for Hannah.

Maybe it was a risk he needed to take. If he married Hannah, he could repay all of them for helping him during a time when he had nowhere else to turn. If he couldn't save his sister, he could at least help the Davis family save their farm.

As to whether time chose to be cruel a second time, he had no way of knowing. For now, he would do what he could to protect the folks he cared about. And he did care about Jeremy, Gabby and Hannah.

Especially Hannah.

He would be her mail-order groom. She would get the money, he would get to spend what time he had in 1998 with Hannah. Sounded like a fair exchange. Now all he had to do was convince her that she needed him to be her husband.

DURING HARVEST, it wasn't uncommon for Hannah to eat her lunch in the field. Each morning she would fill the wooden picnic basket with food and the thermos full of cold lemonade, grab a lap robe from the closet and head for the gleaner.

When Barry worked the fields with her, lunchtime was nothing more than two workers breaking for a bite to eat. With Wood, however, eating off a blanket in the middle of a cornfield took on a new meaning.

Hannah had always loved the peace and solitude of being in a field of tall stalks of corn waiting to be harvested. It was one of her very favorite times of the year, when clouds drifted lazily in the autumn sky, and the corn glistened as if it were dusted with gold. The fact that Wood shared her sentiments only added to her enjoyment of the moment.

Hannah wished she could stop thinking about how good it had felt to be in his arms. But every time those big hands picked up a sandwich or cradled a cup, she was reminded of how they had felt on her skin. As much as she wanted to deny it, working alongside Wood in such close proximity was a bittersweet experience.

Adding to her discontent was the fact that Gabby had brought Wood here to be her husband. Hannah still bristled every time she remembered the reason Wood had kissed her was because he wanted to convince her to let him be her mail-order groom.

She longed for the end of harvest. Once she no longer needed his help, she could let him go and put an end to her aunt's misguided attempts to save the farm. She supposed she should be relieved that his true purpose for coming was finally out in the open. At least he had accepted that she had no interest in marrying anyone—inheritance or no inheritance.

He had stopped flirting with her for one thing. Although he still opened doors and did all sorts of gentlemanly things, he gave her no indication that he still hoped to become her partner.

That's why she was so stunned when one afternoon during lunch he brought up the subject.

"I happen to agree with Gabby on this whole issue of your inheritance," Wood said casually, trying not to put Hannah on the defensive.

She gulped the remainder of her sandwich. "I would suspect you do."

"Marriage is not a prison," he said earnestly.

She chuckled sarcastically. "Do you know something I don't?"

"I have been married."

"And correct me if I'm wrong. It didn't work out."

She was a tough one. Wood had to grant her that. "Only because we didn't have a common goal."

"Oh, and you think we do?" She raised an eyebrow.

"Yes, even though you don't want to admit it," he answered, fighting the urge to pull her into his arms and show her just how much in common they had.

"I thought we had settled all of this when I told you you could stay on through harvest," she said wearily.

"We did, but I believe the subject merits reconsideration."

"Why?"

"For two reasons. One is your financial situation."

That touched a raw spot in Hannah. "Wait a minute. If you think I'm going to marry you so that I can get my grandfather's money, you're one hundred percent wrong.

First of all, I don't need that money, and no matter what Gabby's told you, I'm not going to lose the farm if I don't get it. Secondly, there are any number of single men in Filmore County I would consider before I married a man I hardly know.''

"But you haven't married any of the men in Filmore County—not even Red Murphy,'' he reminded her calmly although he felt anything but calm.

"And I'm not going to marry you!'' She tossed her empty plate into the lunch basket with more force than was necessary.

"Is it not true that if corn prices remain where they are now, you are going to suffer the biggest loss ever?''

"Yes, but I'll get through it. Farmers have bad years and survive.''

"And sometimes they lose their farms. Hannah, you can eliminate that risk by getting married,'' he argued.

"I could but I won't,'' she said stubbornly.

"You're going to just let all that money go to a charity?''

"Gabby told you about the deadline?''

"Yes. You have exactly nine days left.''

"It doesn't matter. I'm not going to comply with my grandfather's wishes just to get money.''

He leaned back, a piece of straw dangling from his mouth as he said, "The way I see it, this isn't about money. It's about the struggle your family's endured to keep their land, to not surrender to grasshoppers or droughts or floods. It's about your heritage, Hannah, something that's so important to you that you're willing to bust your back working rather than accept your grandfather's money.''

"Don't you mean submit to his terms?''

He pointed a finger at her. "That's exactly what I'm talking about. You talk as if you're in a duel with him, trying to prove that you can outlast him.''

"I am.'' Her eyes flashed passionately.

"He's dead, Hannah!"

"It doesn't matter. If I marry, he wins."

He threw up his hands in frustration. "You are one stubborn lady."

"I think it's a ridiculous idea—marrying someone in order to collect an inheritance." She scooped up the remains of their lunch and tossed them into the picnic basket. When he tried to fold the blanket for her, she snatched it out of his hands. "I can do this myself."

"Yes, ma'am."

"And quit calling me ma'am."

He stilled her busy hands and looked in the eyes. "What part of respect is it that you dislike?"

She looked suitably chastised. "Most men I know don't treat women the way you do."

"They should."

She pulled her hands away from his. "I think we're straying from the topic of conversation."

He sighed. "On the subject of marriage, here's the way I see it. You can marry me, collect your inheritance, and nothing has to change. You have my word that I won't make any claims on you financially."

She thrust a hand to her hip. "Are you saying you'd sign a prenuptial agreement?"

"A what?"

"A contract saying that what you bring into the marriage is what you take out," she explained.

"I'm not looking for money from you, Hannah."

"What are you looking for?"

"A place to stay. That's the second reason why I think we should reconsider the marriage idea. You can use an extra man to help you, and I need a roof over my head."

"For how long?"

He shrugged. "Until you want me to leave or until I figure out a way to find my sister. It would essentially be the same setup we have now, except you would be able to eliminate a great deal of your debt.''

She bristled at his statement. "And what would you know about my debt?" She shook her head. "I should have known. Gabby."

"I do have eyes and ears," he reminded her with a wry grin.

"You talk as if marriage isn't a serious legal contract. Most couples know each other for years before they marry. I know so little about you, yet you expect me to trust you enough to enter a marriage."

Wood knew that she had a valid point. Ever since he had arrived at the farm he had been keeping things from Hannah. For a good reason, but he had still been deceptive.

"Forgive me if I haven't been completely truthful with you, Hannah," he said sincerely.

"I'd like you to be direct with me right now, Wood. If you expect me to even consider a legal arrangement like the one you're suggesting, I need some honest answers from you."

He sat back against his heels and spread his arms. "All right. I'll do my best."

"What is your background? And don't tell me farming. I know what your references say, but you are no farmer."

Wood knew that the time had come for him to reveal his past. If he was going to put her in a situation where she could one day have her husband drop out of sight, she needed to know why.

He shoved his hands out in front of her, palms upward. "Most of the work these hands have done has been with numbers."

"You're an accountant?"

"No, a banker. At least I was at one time."

"A banker." Hannah gazed at him in amazement. "No

wonder you didn't have a clue about the soybeans. You faked your references?''

He took a deep breath and said, "No. I'm sure Alfred Dumler is a fine farmer. It's just that I'm not Alfred Dumler.''

Hannah could only stare at him in disbelief. "If you're not Alfred, just who are you?''

"My name is James Woodson Harris. Wood.'' He took a deep breath, trying to figure out how to tell her how he came to be lying in her cornfield. "I didn't lie when I said I didn't remember how I got here. It's just as I told Gabby. One day I was looking for my sister, the next I was flat on my back in your cornfield.''

Skepticism caused her eyebrows to lift. "You're saying you can't remember how you got here?''

He shrugged helplessly. "Like I told you before, I woke up one morning and part of my life had disappeared.''

He searched her eyes for one glimmer of understanding, but all he saw was apprehension. He wondered how he would ever be able to convince her that the newspaper article that had branded him a murderer was erroneous. She'd remember those bruises on his neck and wrists and any hope of earning her trust would be forever gone.

"If you have amnesia, you should have seen a doctor.'' Again there was uncertainty in her tone.

"And how would a doctor help me?''

"He could give you a physical exam for one thing—see if you've had any head injuries that might have caused you to lose part of your memory.''

He shook his head. "I don't think a doctor's going to be able to tell me anything that will help me.''

She sat quietly for several moments. "I wish you had told us who you were right from the beginning.''

"It was easier to let you assume I was Alfred Dumler. I needed a place to stay and, like you, I thought Gabby had answered an ad for a hired hand. Considering my circumstances, it was the only option I thought I had," he explained.

"The truth didn't merit any consideration?"

He sighed in exasperation. "I was homeless, without money and not feeling well. Even when you thought I was Alfred Dumler you wanted to have me hauled to the nearest insane asylum. How do you suppose you would have reacted had I told you the truth?"

Hannah knew he had a point. "But to take another man's identity..."

"I only took his name, Hannah. The man you know is me, Wood Harris, not Alfred Dumler. I'm the one who has worked with you till the wee hours of the morning. I'm the one who helps Jeremy with his homework and plays cards with Gabby. And I'm the one who wants to see that you get what's rightfully yours—your inheritance."

To his surprise she didn't give him an outright rejection. "I need to think about all of this," she told him, gazing past him to the corn stalks, waving in the breeze.

"I understand."

She folded up the blanket and gathered up the picnic basket.

"You take the combine. I'll drive the truck," she told Wood.

He saw it as a positive sign. For weeks she had been training him to run the combine. Now he was finally getting his chance. She finally trusted him with the most expensive piece of machinery she had. Now the only question was would she trust him with her heart.

JUST WHEN HANNAH THOUGHT they'd finish the harvest in record time, the rains came. Steady, cold rain that made it impossible to work in the fields. All Hannah could do was sit on the porch swing and stare dismally out at the gray skies and hope that tomorrow would be dry. If it wasn't bad enough that corn prices had dropped, now the weather threatened to keep her from getting her crop in at all.

Ever since she had been a small child Hannah had liked to sit on the porch and listen to the rain. She thought the sound of the drops hitting the roof were like mood music. Today those drops sounded relentless, a perfect background for her own emotions.

Two days had passed since Wood had proposed to her, yet she was no closer to making a decision. She wished she could forget about the stupid deadline of the will, but it hung over her head, pounding on her subconscious just like the rain pounded on the roof.

Although Hannah had thought of little else during those two days, she hadn't arrived at any conclusions. Her pride demanded that she ignore her grandfather's wishes and fight to keep the farm without his help. But then her intellect reminded her that it was difficult enough making ends meet without the added pressures of more debt.

And there was Wood himself. Every instinct she had tempted her to trust him, despite the fact that she knew so little about him. Marrying a stranger should have appalled her. Yet it didn't. It actually intrigued her.

He had made it sound like a business arrangement, which should have suited Hannah just fine. Intellectually Hannah knew it was exactly what she should have wanted to hear, but emotionally it felt like a rejection. She caught herself wondering what it would be like to have a man who would fuss over her and make her feel as if she were the most important woman in the world. Someone who would bring her coffee in bed and kiss her awake, someone she could talk to late at night and fall asleep in his arms.

The men in her life had never proved to be very reliable. Her own father had left when she was only seven, discontented with life on the farm. After her relationship with

Jeremy's father, she had dated few men. None had proved they were any different. Just like the hired hands that came and went, so did the loves in her life.

Experience had taught her not to trust her heart to the care of a man. Now here she was contemplating marriage. Of course it wouldn't be a real marriage. It was a business arrangement. It would have a prenuptial agreement, a legal contract and, after a certain amount of time, a dissolution.

"Why don't you come inside and have a cup of hot chocolate with me?" Gabby called out through the screen door, interrupting her musings.

The chain on the swing creaked as Hannah slowly rocked back and forth. "Are there any of those fudge brownies left?"

"I just made another batch. And this time I frosted them."

It was a temptation Hannah couldn't refuse. She scrambled inside, shrugged out of her rain gear and hung it in the entry.

"You just got over the flu and now you've gone and got your hair wet." Gabby scolded her, setting a steaming mug of hot chocolate in front of her niece.

Ever since Hannah's own mother had died when she was only twelve, Gabby, despite being single and never having been a parent, had assumed a maternal role in Hannah's life. The problem was that Gabby was more of a mother hen than her own mother had been. Even though Hannah was an adult woman with a child of her own, Gabby often treated her as if she were still a twelve-year-old. At times it irritated Hannah. But not today. Today with the cold rain and her emotional uncertainty, she found Gabby's concern comforting.

"It's a good thing you made me something hot to drink." Hannah wrapped cold hands around the warm cup and inhaled appreciatively.

"We're running out of time." Gabby set a plate with six brownies on the table.

"I think we'll get all the corn in," Hannah said, blowing on the steaming chocolate before taking a sip.

"I'm not talking about the harvest. I'm talking about getting your inheritance."

Hannah sighed. "Oh, that."

"Yes, that."

"I still have time."

"Then you haven't ruled out marriage?" Gabby asked eagerly, taking the chair opposite Hannah.

Hannah was a bit surprised that Wood hadn't told Gabby about his marriage proposal. The fact that he hadn't was another point in his favor. He had left it up to Hannah to spread the news—if there was any news to spread.

"Wood and I have discussed the possibility of getting married." She scooped up a tiny marshmallow with her fingers and plopped it in her mouth.

Gabby's face brightened. "Then you're not angry with me for bringing him here?"

Hannah was about to tell Gabby that she wasn't responsible for bringing Wood to the farm, but thought it would be better not to say anything. "No, I'm not angry."

Gabby exhaled a long sigh. "Good. We need to pull together if we're going to save the farm. When will the wedding be?"

"I haven't said there's going to be a wedding. I said I'm considering it."

"You'd better hurry."

"It's still seven days until the deadline."

"Yes, but have you forgotten there's a five-day waiting period for a marriage license in Minnesota?"

Hannah had forgotten. "That means I only have two days to make up my mind." She smoothed fingers across her brow.

"Not if you want to drive across the border into South Dakota. There's no waiting there."

Hannah shook her head. "I can't take a day off now— not during harvest." She groaned. "I just wish I had more time to think this through."

"Your grandmother used to say that it didn't do much good to dwell on a decision. She would tell me to make up my mind and not worry. Nothing was irrevocable."

That may have been fine for her grandmother, but Hannah always planned things out methodically. "I don't know. Maybe I shouldn't have been so quick to discourage Red," she said thoughtfully over her mug of chocolate. "At least I've known him most of my life and he's—"

"Boring," Gabby finished for her. "Wood is a hunk. I've heard the gals in town talk about him."

Hannah agreed. He was a hunk, which was what was so frightening.

"Hannah, your great-great-grandfather had a mail-order bride. He knew her less than a week when they became husband and wife, and their marriage lasted over forty years."

"He probably wasn't marrying her to collect an inheritance," Hannah retorted.

"No, he needed someone to cook and clean for him. Is there much difference?"

Hanna chewed on her lip. "If there were more time, I'd hire a private investigator to check into Wood's background."

Gabby pooh-poohed the idea. "To find out what? He's been living with us for over a month now. Can't you tell what kind of man he is? I can."

Hannah sighed. "I guess if I go through with it, I'll have to accept him on blind faith."

"As I see it, you're like one of those contestants on the game show who get to choose between three doors. Door number one has nothing behind it. You choose it, you're in the same pickle tomorrow as you are today—in debt and without your grandfather's inheritance.''

Hannah raised an eyebrow. "And door number two?"

"That has any one of the men you know from Stanley-ville standing behind it. If you choose it, you get the money to pay off your debts and a man who will be in your face forever. Even if you divorce, he'll live within a few miles of us. And everyone in town will know about it, too."

"You think I should take door number three, don't you?"

"That's where Wood is standing. If it works out between you and Wood—"

"That's not an option, Gabby. I said it was going to be a marriage in name only," Hannah interrupted her.

"Okay, I hear you," she snapped a bit impatiently. "When you want to be rid of your paper husband, the man behind door number three will leave town."

"Gee, what a deal," Hannah drawled.

"It's up to you. One, two or three?" Gabby slid the plate of brownies in Hannah's direction. "I know which door I'd take."

Maybe Gabby was right. If she married a stranger, there would be no problem when it came time to dissolving the marriage. Wood would leave, and she wouldn't ever have to face him again, which was not going to happen if she were to marry someone from Stanleyville.

Long after they had finished their brownie break, Hannah's thoughts were still on Wood Harris. As much as she wanted to trust him, he still hadn't told her much about his past. Maybe he truly did have a bit of amnesia. It was possible. If only she could be more like Gabby and Jeremy—accepting him without any reservations.

There was no denying that Gabby did trust the man. Hannah had no doubt she would have loaned him money had he asked. Hannah was grateful he hadn't asked. To his credit, he worked hard for everything he had and disliked when Gabby gave him gifts.

Then why was it that Hannah couldn't let go of her reservations about him? She wanted to blame it on the fact that he had lied about his identity, but the truth was, it was the fact that he had kissed her and let her believe that he was interested in her romantically when all he had wanted was to marry her—for convenience sake.

That hurt.

HANNAH HAD MADE her decision. Wood could tell by the way she avoided looking at him during breakfast. Not that she ate any food—another clue that she was ready to give him an answer. Most of the action on her plate had involved pushing her scrambled eggs from one side to the other. She was nervous—which Wood interpreted as a good sign. If she was going to reject his offer, she'd do so with her usual bold approach.

As soon as Jeremy had gone to school, Gabby discreetly excused herself from the kitchen. Hannah got up to get herself another cup of coffee. Wood waited patiently, wondering what was going through her head. He was seeing her in a white dress, flowers in her hair, a smile on her face.

"I've come to a decision regarding my grandfather's will," she began the conversation, clutching her cup with both hands.

The muscles in Wood's stomach tightened as he waited for her to continue.

She took a sip of coffee, then said, "Corn prices dropped again yesterday, and if this rain doesn't let up I'm not going to get my crop out of the field before the snow flies. I don't want to lose this farm." It was as if she spoke to the coffee, not him.

"Are you saying you want to go through with the marriage?"

After what seemed like an eternity, she said, "Yes."

Wood felt as if Wilbur had been sitting on his chest and finally moved off him. Ever since he had proposed to Hannah, there had been an awkwardness between them. Maybe now things could finally return to the way they used to be.

"I'm pleased to hear that," he told her.

She looked at him. "Are you?"

"Yes. I want to marry you." It was the truth. At first he had been wary of Gabby's plan, but now, knowing how it was going to benefit Hannah, he saw it as a logical step for both of them. Besides, he was already more than a little in love with her. And once they were married, he'd be able to tell her the whole truth about his past. There would be no secrets between them.

"Just so long as you know it's not going to be a real marriage," she warned.

Wood felt as if Wilbur had sat back down on his chest. "But how are you going to collect on your grandfather's inheritance if it's not legal?"

"I didn't say it wouldn't be legal. I said it wouldn't be real. We'll be husband and wife in name only." Again she avoided his eyes, but the color in her cheeks confirmed what Wood suspected.

"In name only?" he repeated.

"Yes. You're the one who told me nothing would have to change. We could continue as we are now. That means you'll work for me and sleep in the loft."

He could see her hands shake as she raised her cup to her lips and took another sip. Well, his insides were shaking, too. Out of anger and frustration. What kind of a marriage would it be if he slept in the loft? How would he ever be able to tell her the truth, to earn her trust, to win her love?

"Being the gentleman you are, I'm sure you can respect my wishes on this matter," she said evenly.

Wood did not feel very gentlemanly right now. He wanted to remind her that she was the one who had put her hands in his trousers when they had been rolling around in the hay. Sleep in the loft?

Wood wanted to tell her to forget the whole thing. But he couldn't. Because whether or not she wanted to be a wife to him, he still wanted to be her husband.

"You have my word I'll not force my attention on you," he said quietly.

"Thank you. Then we can go ahead with the plans. You're going to need a copy of your divorce decree," she told him.

"Why?"

"You need it to get a marriage license." She looked at him expectantly. "Is it going to be a problem getting a copy?"

He frowned. "I doubt I can obtain a copy of the divorce decree by tomorrow."

"I think if you call the courthouse where it's filed they might be able to get a copy faxed to the records office here," Hannah suggested.

Faxed? Even if what she said was possible, how would he explain the date on the divorce decree?

"Are you sure it's necessary? It was a long time ago."

"I'll call and check with the license office." She checked her watch. "It's too early to do it now. We'll call later."

Wood nodded, although he still wasn't used to the telephone technology. He'd had to go from telegraph to telephone to a wireless cell phone—over a hundred years of technology—in less than a week.

"And after we get the license?"

"We'll get married here, at the farm. We can't afford to

take any time away from harvesting. We can get a minister to come here."

"What about witnesses?"

"There's Gabby."

"And Jeremy?"

"I guess he'll be there, too." She didn't look at him as she spoke, but busied herself with clearing away the dishes from the table. "I've talked to my attorney. He's drawing up the necessary papers that need to be signed."

"You mean the prenuptial agreement."

"Yes. There's something else I think you should know."

"What's that?"

"The terms of my grandfather's will say I need to stay married for one year. If we go through with this, you'll have to agree to stay here during that time. After the year is up, you're free to go."

A kernel of doubt began to sprout in Wood's mind. "And if I leave before then?"

"I'll forfeit my inheritance."

It wasn't what Wood wanted to hear. If it were at all possible, he would uphold his end of the bargain. The problem was, what if time played another cruel trick on him and sent him back to 1876. What then would happen to Hannah?

"What if something neither one of us has any control over separates us?" he asked.

She finally looked at him. "You mean death?"

He nodded, knowing that if he went back to 1876, he certainly would be dead in 1998. The problem was, would Hannah and her lawyers know?

"The only way I lose the inheritance is if you and I divorce or legally separate. So you see, I really am dependent on your good faith. I'm the one who loses everything should you decide to drift."

"Is that what you think I am? A drifter?"

"I don't want to think that."

She slammed a stack of plates into the sink and turned to face him. "Look, this is not an easy decision for me to make."

He could see she was trembling. "You're not scared, are you?" He hadn't thought of her as being afraid of anything.

"Of course I'm scared," she said in an uncharacteristic display of emotion.

Despite his resolution not to touch her, he pulled her into his arms, cradling her head against his shoulder. "There's no need to be. I'd never hurt you, Hannah," he said softly against her hair. "You have to trust me. This will all work out."

They stood in each other's arms, as if seeking reassurance from each other. It felt so right to have her warm body close to his that Wood placed a kiss on the top of her head. Then on her forehead, her temple, her cheek.

When he would have captured her mouth, she pulled back. It was the slightest of hesitations, but all that Wood needed to remind himself that he had promised there would not be a physical side to their relationship.

He released her. "Forgive me. I have overstepped my bounds. You have my word. That will never happen again, and I will do everything in my power to see that you are not compromised."

"Forget it," she called over her shoulder as she walked away from him. Without another comment on the subject, she reached for her hat. "We need to get to work. Just because it's raining doesn't mean there isn't work to be done."

He stopped her with a hand on her arm. "I thought you said we need to go get the marriage license."

She rubbed her forehead thoughtfully. "We can go after lunch."

Wood could see by her attitude that it was just another

day to her. He reminded himself that he would be wise to keep that in mind. The marriage was nothing but an arrangement—nothing more, nothing less.

As he watched her slip on her rain jacket, he only hoped that this arrangement didn't backfire on both of them.

"Aren't you coming outside?" she asked when he made no move to put on his jacket.

"In a minute. I need to talk to Gabby first," he answered.

She nodded, then headed for the machinery shed where she told Wood she would be waiting for him. One of the trucks needed an oil change.

But Wood's thoughts were not on mechanics. As if he didn't have enough to worry about. He had thought he only had to stay in 1998 five more days, that once he had signed the marriage certificate, Hannah would get her inheritance and it wouldn't matter if time sent him back to 1876.

Now he had learned that he needed to be in 1998 for one year or his marriage to Hannah would net her nothing. Would he still be on the Davis farm a year from now? There was only one question that took priority.

How in the hell was he going to get divorce papers from the nineteenth century?

Chapter Twelve

"We have a problem, Gabby," Wood announced uneasily. "Hannah says I need a copy of my divorce decree in order to get a marriage license."

"Oh, that is a problem, isn't it?" She tapped her fingers on the kitchen table. "Maybe there's a way around that. Let me call Janell over at the courthouse."

Wood waited while she made the phone call, wondering what all the "aha's" and "oh I see's" meant. He soon found out.

"Janell said that you don't need a divorce decree when your ex-wife is dead. She would be dead now, right?" Wood nodded and she added. "Then all you need is a copy of the death certificate."

"Which is just as hard to get as the divorce decree."

Gabby raised a wrinkled hand. "Wait a minute. I haven't told you everything. You only need the death certificate if she died within the last twelve months."

Wood's face brightened. "Then I don't have a problem."

"I'm afraid you do. You still need either a driver's license or a birth certificate."

Wood groaned.

Gabby tapped one bony finger against her lips in contemplation. After several moments, her eyes lit up. "I think I have an answer," she stated simply.

"You want me to get a driver's license?"

"No, there's not enough time. What you need is a new birth certificate. One created especially for you."

Wood could hardly believe his ears. "You think we should forge one?"

"Not us. Wait here." She disappeared from the kitchen only to return a few minutes later carrying a skinny little blue book. "Look at this."

Wood read the title. *How to Find a New Identity.* He leafed through the large print and came to the conclusion it was a handbook for criminals. "Where did you get this?"

"At a flea market." She quickly added, "Not as in fleas that make dogs scratch. Flea market is a term used for a sale which is usually an open market that has second-hand things. Being a collector of books, I thought it was rather interesting that someone could actually publish a book on how to find a new identity."

"Maybe they should have titled it *How To Get Away With Being A Crook*," he quipped.

"There are legitimate reasons for wanting a new identity," Gabby said naively.

"Like mine?"

She nodded vigorously.

He rubbed a hand along his jaw. "It sounds rather risky."

"The book claims it's foolproof."

Wood wasn't as convinced as Gabby. "And if it doesn't work?"

"How can it not work? So what do you think? Do we do it?"

"We?"

"I'm going to help."

Wood felt a bit guilty at the thought of dragging such

an innocent old woman into such an unsavory business. "Are you sure you want to do this?"

Gabby took the book from his hands and flipped through the pages. After a couple of minutes of reading she said, "It's just as I thought. We're going to have to go to the city."

"Stanleyville?"

"No, Minneapolis. It's a couple of hours away by car."

"But I have to work with Hannah this morning," Wood reminded her. "And we're getting the license this afternoon."

She glanced at her watch. "You let me handle Hannah. Go get your jacket and meet me out back, okay?"

IT HAD BEEN A LONG TIME since Hannah had wanted a man. After Jeremy's father had deserted her, she had dated a series of men whom Gabby had labeled misfits. Hannah had agreed with her nomenclature, but for a different reason. Gabby, in her rose-colored glasses, hadn't found fault with any of the men, but simply said the relationships didn't work because Hannah's personality hadn't fit with theirs. Hannah wasn't quite so charitable. She thought the men were simply misfits.

With Wood she didn't have such feelings. Partially because he was so unlike any of the men she had dated. He had made no promises, other than to uphold his end of the bargain—a bargain that included marriage.

Only this was not going to be a real marriage. It was a sham. A fake. A scheme to get her grandfather's money. The closer the hour drew near for them to exchange vows, the more uneasy Hannah became.

Deception. She hated it. Her grandfather, as manipulative and eccentric as he had been, had written the terms of his will with no hidden agenda. He honestly believed that she needed a husband. That Jeremy needed a father.

Now she was doing just what he wanted her to do—get married—but for all the wrong reasons. Hannah knew that in one year's time—if not sooner—Wood Harris would be gone. No man had ever stayed in her life for more than a year. Why should he be any different?

Gabby had insisted Hannah and Wood not see each other on the day of the wedding. Both had worked in different fields. Jeremy and Wood had eaten their dinners in the bunkhouse while Gabby tried to coax food into Hannah at the house.

Tired from the harvest and stressed from the emotional roller coaster her emotions had traveled, Hannah soaked in a scented tub, while Wood used the shower in the loft. Gabby carefully choreographed their movements, convinced that if they saw each other their marriage would be doomed.

Hannah wanted to point out that it already was, but she didn't have the heart to burst Gabby's bubble. She knew her aunt actually thought pretty much the way Hannah's grandfather had—that once Hannah married she'd fall in love with her husband. That's why she did everything in her power to make the wedding a special event.

She arranged for Marlis to come to the house to fix Hannah's hair. The last person Hannah wanted to see on her wedding day was the hair stylist, but again, she gave in to the whim of her seventy-five-year-old aunt. Despite Marlis pumping her for information, Hannah found that having someone else wash and dry her hair was relaxing.

However, as the hour approached for the ceremony to begin, her nerves continued to slowly unravel. Her uncertainty grew until just before she was to get dressed, panic threatened to overwhelm her.

"I can't do this, Gabby. You're going to have to be my proxy at the wedding ceremony." She clutched her stomach which she felt sure was going to erupt before long.

Gabby clicked her tongue. "Hannah Marie Davis, you will do this with the dignity and grace you inherited from the long line of women in this family." She opened the closet door and pulled out an ivory satin wedding dress. "Put this on. It was your mother's."

Hannah fingered it lovingly. "Where did you find it?"

"It's been in the attic." She fussed with the satin-covered buttons. "I had to steam it to get all the wrinkles out, but I think it'll be all right."

Hannah shook her head. "I don't feel right about wearing it."

"Why on earth not? Your mother loved you. If she were here, she'd be giving it to you herself."

Hannah had to wipe a tear from her cheek. "She would be so disappointed in me if she knew what I was going to do."

"You shush. She would admire you for the courage you've shown these past three years."

"You don't think it's bad luck? I mean, look what happened to my parent's marriage," she said unhappily.

"Just because your father left your mother doesn't mean he didn't love her," Gabby insisted.

Hannah stared at her. "Why do you always defend him? He left us because he didn't want the responsibility of a wife and child. He wanted to do his own thing," she said with a sneer.

"He wasn't as bad as you want to paint him to be," Gabby answered. "I believe that had he not been killed in that car accident, he would have come back to both of you."

Hannah sighed. "I guess we'll never know, will we?"

"No. Now let's see how this is going to work." She unbuttoned the dress and held it so Hannah could step into it.

"How do you know it's going to fit?"

"We'll make it fit...just like we're going to make your marriage fit," Gabby said quietly, pulling the satin bodice up and adjusting the sleeves over Hannah's bare shoulders.

"For a year you mean."

Gabby didn't answer. She tucked and pinned while Hannah stood trembling. When she was finished, she turned Hannah around so that she faced the mirror and asked, "Well, what do you think?"

Hannah couldn't get a single word past her throat. Standing before her was a bride—a beautiful bride. Her trembling increased.

"Wood is going to be so surprised," Gabby said gleefully. "He's never even seen you in a dress."

The mention of Wood nearly caused Hannah to run for the bathroom. "I can't do this, Gabby," she cried, wringing her hands.

Gabby grabbed a hold of her trembling fingers. "Yes, you can and you will. Think of Jeremy."

"I have thought of him, and that's what's so disturbing. He's become fond of Wood. If Wood leaves after a year, what will that do to him?"

"He won't leave," Gabby stated confidently.

"The agreement is only for one year."

"He won't leave," Gabby repeated. There was a rap on the door.

"Gabby, is Mom ready?" Jeremy's voice called out.

"We'll be right down," Gabby called back. Then she looked at Hannah and said, "If you don't go through with this, tomorrow your grandfather's inheritance will be gone forever."

Hannah swallowed with difficulty, then nodded. "I'm ready," she said with more courage than she was feeling. When she would have walked out the door, Gabby stopped her.

"Wait. Your headpiece." Out of a floral box came a tiara

made of baby's breath and violets. Gabby carefully set it on Hannah's blond curls. "That's the something blue. This is the something borrowed." She removed her gold watch from her wrist and handed it to Hannah. "You can't wear that old work thing with a wedding dress."

Hannah unfastened the thick leather band of her digital watch and replaced it with Gabby's slim gold bracelet. Then she hugged her aunt, kissing her on the cheek. "Thank you."

Hannah expected the justice of the peace would be in the living room. To her surprise, however, the house was empty. When she looked at Gabby, the old lady smiled and pulled her by the hand as if she were a child being dragged to school by her mother. Once they were outside, Hannah saw a horse-drawn buggy.

"Whose idea was it to get this out of storage?" she asked as Jeremy offered his hand.

"Probably the mice," Jeremy gave his bow tie a tweak. "Come, Madam. Your pumpkin awaits," he said with a formal bow.

"I thought the ceremony was going to be here," Hannah remarked when she and Gabby were both seated on the worn leather seat.

"You said on the farm," her aunt reminded her, clutching Hannah's hands to still their trembling. "Relax. Everything will work out just fine."

Jeremy took them to the only field that hadn't been harvested. There, with the setting sun painting a flaming backdrop of color, bronze corn stalks stood tall in the autumn air. However, it wasn't nature that took Hannah's breath away, but a man dressed in a black tuxedo.

"When did he get the tux?" she whispered to Gabby.

"That morning we went to the city. Doesn't he look handsome!" Gabby gushed.

"Yes." Hannah's voice was weak. Her mouth was dry.

Her hands were moist. And if she wasn't careful, she was going to cry. Partly because it was exactly the kind of wedding she would have arranged, had she been marrying for love. But more than that because when she saw Wood waiting for her, she realized that she wanted him to be marrying her for all the right reasons, and not for the sake of an old man's will.

As Jeremy stopped the carriage, Wood came to help them climb down. First Gabby, then Hannah.

"You are a beautiful bride. I am truly a lucky man," he said as he put his hands around Hannah's waist and lifted her to the ground.

His touch sent a tremor of pleasure running through her. "Thank you," she croaked, still unable to find her voice.

As Hannah linked arms with Wood, the sound of music filled the air. Jeremy had brought his boom box and was playing one of Hannah's favorite country-western songs, John Michael Montgomery's "I Swear."

"Considering everything that's happened, I thought this would be a good spot for the ceremony," Wood whispered in her ear as he escorted her to where the minister waited. "I hope you don't mind."

She shook her head, too choked up to speak. Throughout the entire ceremony, she felt as if she could cry. She didn't know how she got through the vows. When Wood repeated, "As long as we both shall live," her eyes met his. They looked sincere and determined, as if he truly wanted to stay married to her for as long as he lived. When he placed a thin gold band on her finger, he squeezed her fingers reassuringly, as if reaffirming his feelings for her.

Hannah almost forgot that it was a fantasy until the minister pronounced them husband and wife and Wood made no attempt to kiss her. The marriage certificate was signed, good wishes were bestowed upon the newlyweds and

Gabby, Jeremy and the minister hopped into the minister's pickup and left.

"I think they have a surprise planned for us," Wood told her when Hannah would have protested them leaving.

He pulled her by the hand over to the carriage, where, spread out on the ground was a plaid blanket. In the center was a bottle of champagne, two flutes, a knife and the smallest wedding cake Hannah had ever seen.

Wood tugged on his ear. "I had a feeling the two of them had something up their sleeves."

"We don't have to stay out here," Hannah told him, feeling ridiculously embarrassed by the setup.

"You don't think they might feel bad if we..." His voice trailed off, as he waited for her to say something.

"I suppose they might." Hannah shifted, annoyed and uncomfortable. "Are you thirsty?"

"My mouth is a bit dry," he confessed.

"Mine, too. I guess we might as well drink the champagne."

He shrugged. "Sure, why not?" He reached for the bottle. "I'm not sure I know how to open this."

Hannah noticed a hand towel folded neatly beside the glasses. "You need to work the cork carefully." She handed him the towel. "Put this over the top in case it pops."

Despite his insistence that he would probably spill it, Wood managed to open the bottle with little fuss. He filled both of the flutes, then made a toast.

"To us." His eyes held hers as their glasses clinked together, and Hannah, although she hadn't even taken a sip, felt effervescent inside.

"Mmmmm. It's good," she said, quenching the dryness and appreciating the warm fuzzy feeling the liquid produced.

"More?" He held up the bottle and she shoved her glass in his direction.

"I didn't eat much dinner," she confessed, the champagne relaxing her.

"You want to eat the cake?"

Hannah giggled. "Why not?" She dropped down onto the woolen blanket, her skirt puffing out all around her. "I feel like Cinderella."

"Cinder who?"

Hannah took another sip of champagne. "Cinderella. I thought everyone knew about Cinderella."

"Not me," he admitted.

"She's this poor girl who can't go to the ball until her fairy godmother changes her rags into a beautiful gown."

Wood cut a sliver of cake. "Was Gabby your fairy godmother?"

"She wanted to be. That's why I'm wearing this dress and you're wearing that tux and we have the carriage and this—" She made a sweeping gesture with her arm that encompassed the champagne and cake picnic.

"We have no plates or forks," Wood told her, a piece of cake in his hand.

"Don't need any. The groom is supposed to feed the bride." She leaned toward him, her mouth wide open, inviting him to place the cake in her mouth. However, as he was about to shove it in, she swayed, and he missed his target. Icing glazed her cheek and outlined her lips.

Hannah giggled. "You don't have very good aim, Wood. Here. I'll show you."

She cut a piece of the cake and said, "Open wide."

He did as she instructed, but she deliberately missed his mouth, smearing the cake on his chin. "Oops!" She gave him an impish look.

"Very funny," he drawled.

Hannah laughed as his tongue snaked out to lick the frosting from his face.

"Now what do we do? We have no napkins." He swiped at his chin with the back of his hand.

"Nope." She reached for the hand towel and waved it temptingly in front of him. "Just this towel." When he would have reached for it, she snatched it away, hiding it behind her back. "I think I like the way you look with cake on your face," she said impudently.

"Give me that towel, Hannah," he ordered her, but she paid no attention.

"Uh-uh. Have some more champagne, Wood. It's really good." She took another drink while her other hand remained behind her back.

A devilish fire lit his eyes, but she paid no attention. "Don't make me take it from you, Hannah," he said in a dangerously seductive voice.

She should have heard warning bells. Maybe she did hear them and paid no attention. At any rate, she was unprepared for the speed at which Wood's arms wrapped around her waist in an attempt to get the towel.

"Come on, Hannah. Give it up," he coaxed as the two of them playfully tumbled onto the blanket—she holding fast to the towel, he trying to pry it loose from her fingers. They wrestled like a couple of teenagers fighting over a loose football.

Knowing her defenses were being stormed, she used the only tactic she had. "Ouch, you're hurting me," she cried out, feigning pain.

He immediately loosened his grip on her, allowing her time to slide out from beneath him. "I'm sorry. I didn't mean..." He began to apologize only to realize she was laughing, not crying.

"Why, if that wasn't the most low-down, dirty..." He started to crawl toward her, like a lion stalking its prey.

Aroused by the look in his eyes, Hannah said, "I told you, Wood. Chivalry will get you nowhere." She inched her way backward until she reached the edge of the blanket.

"Are you saying I should just take what I want?"

Although she knew she was playing with fire, Hannah couldn't resist asking, "What is it you want?" She dangled the towel in midair. "This?"

With one quick grab he snatched the cloth from her hand and tossed it aside, his eyes never once leaving her face. "You're tempting me, Hannah."

"Tempting you to what?" she taunted.

"To forget that I promised not to touch you."

She hooked her hands over the back of his shoulders, unconsciously offering herself to him. "Is that why you didn't kiss me when the minister pronounced us husband and wife?"

"Did you want me to kiss you?"

"Not if it would have been fluttery and soft like this." She barely brushed his mouth with hers, "Then, no. That's an obligatory kiss and I don't want any man to feel obliged to kiss me."

"No chivalrous kisses?"

"Definitely not."

"What if it had been a wild and hungry kiss given only because the man couldn't resist making you his?"

She trembled at the thought, her lips quivering, her breasts heaving. That slight movement was all it took for Wood's resistance to abandon him. He captured her mouth with his in a kiss that sealed their marital contract. For Hannah it was an exquisite torment, as the intimate exploration of his tongue made her long for another gratification.

She found herself at the beginning of a passionate journey, being pulled along by emotions that refused to listen to anything but the seductive pull of anticipation. Wood's hands ignited a flame she had forgotten burned deep inside her.

Even though her body rubbed against his, she couldn't get close enough to satisfy the craving for his touch. Moaning softly, she encouraged the exploration his hands made as they traced patterns of intimacy in places she thought would never know the pleasure of a man's touch again.

She wanted more, much more than the kisses that only fueled her growing desire for him. Frantically she forced open the buttons on his shirt, loving the heat that greeted her fingers as they roamed across his bare flesh. When her hands found the waistband of his trousers, he shuddered.

"Does this mean you don't want our marriage to be in name only?" he asked huskily.

Just when Hannah thought she was on the brink of surrender, his words snapped her back to reality. She snatched her fingers away, as if they had been burned.

He tried to recapture the moment, saying, "It's all right. I don't mind. Hell, I want you so bad I ache."

Hannah rose to her feet, turning her back to him. "This wasn't supposed to happen. If we hadn't been drinking the champagne…" She fumbled with the buttons that had come undone on her dress.

"I want to return to the home place," she told him, avoiding his eyes.

Wood felt as if he'd been punched in the stomach. For just one moment he had thought that they might have truly celebrated their union. Now he could see that she wanted nothing to do with him other than to have his name on the marriage certificate.

They said little on the way home. Once they were back at the house, Wood saw how wrong he had been to think she wanted anything more from him. Hannah was as brusque as she had been the first day he had arrived at the farm. Gabby was the one who showed him where he would sleep—for it had been decided that he would take the loft in the house. Hannah's husband couldn't sleep in the bunk-house, and for all appearances he needed to be Hannah's husband.

Wood undid the buttons on the stiff shirt, remembering how Hannah's fingers had slipped between the pearly fasteners, sending a river of fire through his blood. He kicked off the rented shoes and sank down onto the bed, wondering what was going through her mind at that very moment. Was she thinking about how close they had come to consummating their marriage?

If only he hadn't asked that stupid question. *Does this mean you don't want our marriage to be in name only?* Why couldn't he just have let things happen? Because he wasn't used to women taking the aggressive role in sex. Although it had caught him off guard, it had also excited him. But then nearly everything Hannah did aroused him.

As he hung up his jacket, he remembered the box inside his pocket. He had meant to give it to her during their champagne picnic, but he had forgotten about it in the heat of their passion. He stared at the silver wrapping paper. Iridescent foil, was what the clerk had called it. All Wood knew was that it was unlike any paper he had ever seen—just as Hannah was unlike any woman he had ever known.

If only he could find the key to her heart. Instead of sleeping alone in the loft, he could be spending the night with his bride. That's where he wanted to be. In her arms, with her warm body next to his. He closed his eyes. If he didn't stop thinking about her, he would never be able to sleep.

But then why should he? It was his wedding night. No, it was *their* wedding night. And they needed to settle something once and for all. He was tired of her body saying one thing and her mouth saying another.

Barefoot, he padded down the stairs to the second floor. It was dark except for a narrow strip of light beneath Hannah's door.

With a sharp rap, he called out in a whisper. "Hannah, open up."

When she answered, she wore a flimsy, pink nightgown that gave a certain part of Wood's anatomy a quick jolt. She made no attempt to cover up, but simply said, "Is anything wrong?"

He swept her up into his arms, kicking the door shut with his foot. As he carried her to the bed, he kissed her, his mouth hungrily demanding a response. Her lips opened, inviting him to take what he wanted.

Into a tangle of sheets their bodies fell, shifting and gliding until they were stretched out side by side. He was all over her, loving the taste of her. Starting at her neck, then her shoulders, pushing aside the flimsy pink nightgown to find a rosy nipple. Velvety sighs of pleasure encouraged his tongue to caress her hot flesh.

With one easy movement, she lifted the garment over her head and sent it sailing to the floor. She grinned at the sensual surprise in his eyes. If he had thought she was sexy in her tight trousers, naked she took his breath away. Although he could have marveled in her beauty, she was not about to lie idle. She planted a trail of kisses over his face and throat, then unzipped his trousers. As he kicked his way out of the legs, her hands made a journey of discovery across his stomach, up and down his thighs until they found their target.

Never had Wood met a woman who behaved so boldly in bed. He trembled as she wrapped warm fingers around his erection.

"I love what you do to me," she murmured huskily.

"Shouldn't I be the one saying that?" His breath came out shakily as she stroked his swollen flesh.

"You make me feel like a woman."

"That's never been a question in my mind," he said, as once more he took a nipple into his mouth, his tongue circling it delicately.

Slowly he caressed her burning flesh, tracing her rounded curves, gliding downward to the center of her desire. As his fingers found her moist, intimate spot, she quivered and arched her body invitingly. Whimpers of pleasure urged him to explore her wetness, the sensitive folds of flesh inviting his touch.

With a brazenness he found irresistible, she guided his swollen flesh into her, moaning as the intensity of his need thrust him deep into her center. They melted together, their bodies suspended somewhere in time as the ageless rhythm of a force neither could control took over.

Their bodies raced in search of pleasure, forward and back in an incredibly sweet blending. She pulled him deeper and deeper, melting his heart, melting his soul. There was nothing else in the world that mattered except the exquisite sensations of being one with her. It was a journey to another dimension, one he didn't want to see end. But neither one could stop the rush of ecstasy that ruled their actions, pouring out of them in an overwhelming urgent need. Just when he thought she had sent him over the edge, he felt something he had never felt before, an explosion so magical it shook his entire body.

Hannah kissed him tenderly on his cheek. "I think Gabby was right. We fit."

Wood smiled lazily. "You are one bold lady, Mrs. Harris." He kissed her nose. "I was wondering how I was going to be able to fall asleep tonight, but after that..." He sighed contentedly.

She ran her hands over his damp back. "Sleep? Why Mr. Harris, have you forgotten what night this is? There's no such thing as sleep on a wedding night."

WOOD AWOKE EARLY the next morning, although he wasn't sure he had even been asleep. It had been a wonderful night with Hannah. He raised himself up on one elbow and stared at the lovely picture she made next to him, her blond curls fanned out on the pillow.

He glanced at the clock beside the bed. When he had made an appointment with Madame Duvalee, he had never expected that this morning he would be lying beside Hannah in her bed. As much as he wanted to stay with her, he knew that if he were going to talk to the psychic, he needed to go now, for she would be leaving town by the end of the day.

He carefully rolled off the bed and tugged on his pants. Then he climbed the steps to the loft, grimacing as each riser creaked under his weight. He changed out of the formal wear and into a pair of jeans. As soon as he was dressed, he headed downstairs.

As he expected, Gabby waited for him in the kitchen. "You're still going to go?"

Wood nodded.

"I thought that since you and Hannah..." A grin tugged at the corners of her mouth.

"You know?"

"I'm a light sleeper and the stairs creak."

"You were right, Gabby. She doesn't hate me."

She flung her skinny arms around him in a hug of joy. "Didn't I tell you the two of you would be a perfect match?" She pulled back and studied his face. "So why are you going to see Madame Duvalee?"

"Don't you see? Now that Hannah and I are married, more than ever I need to know how I got here. If she is a true psychic, as the paper says, then I have to talk to her."

Gabby looked uneasy. "I suppose you're right," she told Wood, although he could see that she really didn't agree with him.

"Are you going to let me take your car?"

"Of course." She walked over to the cupboard and pulled out a set of keys. "Be careful that no one sees you."

"I'm not driving into Stanleyville," Wood reminded her, tossing the keys into his pocket.

"I know, but you'll be on county roads."

"I will drive slowly," he assured her, smiling to himself as he recalled one of the lessons Gabby had given him and the thrill he had experienced to have so much power at his fingertips.

"What do I tell Hannah when she finds you're not here this morning?" Gabby asked.

"That I had an errand to run," Wood answered, then blew her a kiss on his way out the door. "See you in a couple of hours."

WHEN HANNAH AWOKE and found herself alone in the double bed, she wondered if she had dreamed that Wood had spent the night with her. Then she saw her nightgown in a heap on the floor, and she knew that the aches in her muscles had nothing to do with work. She and Wood had spent a good portion of the night making love in ways Hannah had never dreamed possible. The memory sent a rush of warmth through her.

So where was he? she wondered. When she glanced at the clock, she saw a small foil box on the nightstand. Circling the package was a gold ribbon that had a tiny wedding bell in its bow.

Hannah carefully undid the wrapping and opened the box. Inside was a miniature locket. Engraved on the back were the words "To Hannah from Wood" along with the date of their wedding.

Hannah's heart swelled with emotion. He had bought her a wedding gift, yet she had given him nothing. Today she would remedy that. First, she needed to see him.

It was with a spring in her step that she showered, dressed and hurried downstairs. Expecting to find Wood in the kitchen, she was disappointed to see only Jeremy and Gabby.

"You look happy," Gabby commented, exchanging a conspiratorial glance with Jeremy.

"I am happy," she confessed with a grin, then poured herself a cup of coffee.

"Did you like our surprise?" her son asked as she sat down at the table. "Gabby made the cake but I helped her frost it."

Hannah nearly blushed as she remembered what had happened as she and Wood had eaten the confection. "It was lovely."

Jeremy caught her totally off guard with his next question. "Now that you're married, will I get to change my name to Harris?"

Hannah glanced at Gabby, as if she should have the answer. "I guess I hadn't thought about it until now," Hannah answered honestly.

"I think it'd be kinda cool to be Jeremy Harris. Then everyone at school would know I have a father."

Hannah was at a loss for words. Although she knew Jeremy was fond of Wood, she hadn't expected that he'd view their marriage as permanent. After all, he knew about the provisions of the will. It was an unsettling thought, especially when Hannah realized that she, too, was thinking her marriage could be permanent.

She wasn't even sure how Wood truly felt about her. How could she know if he planned to adopt Jeremy as his son? Just because he had made passionate love to her didn't mean he would stay forever.

"You'd better eat your breakfast and get to your chores," Gabby advised Jeremy.

"Where is Wood, anyway?" Hannah finally asked.

"He's not here."

"What do you mean he's not here?"

"He's not *gone,* if that's what's put that look of horror on your face," Gabby answered. "He's just not here at the moment."

Hannah relaxed. "You mean he's outside."

"Not exactly." She was saved from having to answer by the ringing of the telephone. Gabby scurried to answer it. Hannah listened to her end of the conversation.

"Oh, no." A pause. "Okay." Another pause. "Uh-uh. I understand." Then still another pause. "We'll go find out."

When Gabby hung up the receiver, her cheeks were pale.

"What's wrong?" Hannah immediately asked.

"That was my friend Mavis from Spring Valley. She said she just saw Red Murphy handcuff Wood and take him away in his car."

Chapter Thirteen

"This doesn't make any sense. Why on earth would Red arrest Wood?" Hannah asked Gabby as the pickup kicked up a trail of dust on the dirt road leaving the farm.

Gabby sat wringing her hands together, wondering if she should tell Hannah about the forged birth certificate or if she should let Red be the one to break the news. For Gabby was certain that the reason Red had taken Wood in was because he had somehow found out about their little adventure into the clandestine side of life.

"Do you know why Wood was in Spring Valley in the first place?"

Hannah's questions had Gabby squirming. "I believe he had an appointment."

"What kind of appointment?" When she didn't answer, Hannah asked, "Gabby, do you know who he was going to see?"

After another long silence, Gabby said, "Madame Duvalee. She's that psychic they've been talking about on TV." She had to clutch the door handle as Hannah took a curve a little too fast for Gabby's peace of mind.

"Why would he go to see a psychic?"

Gabby wanted nothing better than to explain the whole situation. The problem was she had promised Wood she wouldn't mention his time travel to another soul. He had vanted to tell Hannah in his own time—when he was convinced she would accept the truth. Only now Red Murphy hreatened to take that decision out of his hands.

"Gabby, *do* you know why he went to see this Madame Duvalee?" Hannah asked a second time.

Gabby needed to make a decision. Now. "There's something I need to tell you before we go any farther," she told Hannah. "Pull off the road."

"Can't you tell me while I drive?"

"I think you'd better pull off the road for a few minutes."

Hannah parked the pickup on the gravel shoulder of the highway. Then she turned to her aunt. "All right. What has our hair standing on end?"

"I think Red picked up Wood because he found out he had a forged birth certificate, which I helped Wood get in Minneapolis last week so he could buy a new identity because he really is Wood Harris, not Alfred Dumler."

"Wait a minute. This doesn't make sense. If he really is Wood Harris, why would he need to buy a fake birth certificate?"

"Because his was too old," she answered weakly.

"I told him we could call the courthouse and have one faxed."

Gabby tugged on her lower lip with her tiny teeth. "He couldn't do that."

"Why not?"

Her voice was barely above a whisper as she said, "Because then everyone would have figured out that he was born in 1842."

"You mean 1942," she automatically corrected her. "Are you saying that Wood is really fifty-six years old?" Her mouth dropped open in disbelief.

"No, he wasn't born in 1942, I said *1842*," she repeated, her voice rising. "He's a hundred and fifty-two years old.

He time traveled from 1876. That's why he had to preten
to be Alfred Dumler because you already thought he wa
crazy, and if he tried to tell you he was a time traveler, yo
would have had him locked up. But he's not crazy, and h
really is Wood Harris. It's just that he's in the wrong cen
tury.'' The words came out in such a rush that she was ou
of breath by the time she had finished.

Hannah stared at her great-aunt in disbelief. ''You're no
making any sense.''

''I know it's hard to believe. I fainted when Wood tol
me. Who would have thought time travel was possible?''

Hannah's jaw tightened, and she tapped several finger
on the steering wheel. ''Now let me see if I have thi
straight. Wood used to live in 1876 until that day you foun
him in the cornfield, which was the day he time travele
He doesn't know how or why he got here, but thought he'
better pretend to be Alfred Dumler, the mail-order groom
you had advertised for in the farm journal.''

Gabby nodded in agreement.

Hannah's eyes narrowed suspiciously. ''And the real A
fred Dumler—what happened to him?''

''Oh, he couldn't come. He wrote me a letter but it go
lost that day of the storm and Jeremy only found it la
week.''

''It was conveniently lost, eh?''

''What's that supposed to mean?'' Gabby asked.

Hannah sat there slowly shaking her head. ''Gabby, yo
don't really believe all this stuff, do you?''

''Of course I do. It's true!''

''It's a scam.'' Hannah slapped the steering wheel wit
her palms. ''I can't believe it. I've been taken in by a co
man!''

Gabby gasped. ''Wood's no con man! Hannah, it's tru
He's from 1876. That's why he acted so strangely when h
first arrived. Everything was foreign to him—all the appl

ances, the vehicles, the machinery. Why else do you suppose he would have asked for a horse to ride to town?'' She wanted to explain all the puzzling circumstances of the past month, but Hannah wanted no explanations.

She was too angry to listen to anything Gabby said in Wood's defense. She started the pickup and did a U-turn in the middle of the highway.

''Where are you going?'' Gabby's cheeks grew even whiter.

''Back home. Wood Harris can figure out how to get himself out of jail,'' she said stubbornly.

''He's your husband!''

''Not for long.''

Gabby gulped air as if she were a fish out of water. ''You're driving too fast! Hannah, turn this truck around this minute,'' she ordered in her sternest librarian's voice, her knuckles white as she clung to her purse. Hannah slowed the vehicle, but she didn't turn around.

''Hannah, you have to listen to me. Wood's no con man. It's the truth. He time traveled,'' Gabby pleaded with her.

''The only thing he's done is bamboozle both of us. And Jeremy.'' Anger put two red spots on Hannah's cheeks.

''He most certainly has not!'' Gabby protested indignantly. ''He's a good man who's caught in a time warp.''

Some of Hannah's anger dissolved at the sight of her seventy-five-year-old aunt nearly in tears. It wasn't Gabby's fault that they had been taken in by a con man. She was just an old lady with a big heart, who didn't always make the sharpest decisions.

Hannah took a deep breath, trying not to let her emotions overrule her common sense. ''He's caught in a jail which is where he should be.''

''You're wrong, Hannah. Wood's a good man.'' Gabby refused to give up her defense of the man. ''Now turn this truck around and take me to that jail.''

"No. I won't do it."

"I never thought I'd see the day when you would be a coward."

Hannah chuckled mirthlessly. "You think I'm afraid to go see Wood?"

"Aren't you?" When she didn't answer, Gabby pressed on. "Hannah, he's your husband. You at least owe him the right to give you his side of the story. How's it going to look if you don't even go get him out of jail?"

"Like I woke up and smelled the coffee," she retorted

"No, it's going to make you look like a fool."

"I am a fool. I trusted him." As hard as she tried, Hannah couldn't keep the hurt from her voice.

"All right. If you don't want to pick him up, at least allow me to go set the record straight. I'm the one who helped him get the forged documents."

"No."

"All you have to do is drop me off at the front door. You don't have to come inside. I'll take care of everything."

"No."

Gabby would have stamped her foot had it reached the floorboards of the truck. As it was, she was too short and had to settle for a stern scolding. "Are you going to tell me what I can and cannot do?"

Reluctantly Hannah stopped the pickup. She mumbled something under her breath, then made another U-turn.

"Thank you," Gabby said primly.

"You're welcome."

They were the only words spoken until Hannah parked the truck in front of the courthouse.

"Are you coming in with me?" Gabby asked.

It was a challenge. Hannah could see it in the old lady's eyes. The C word still hung in the air between them. Gabby knew that if there was one thing Hannah hated, it was to be accused of having no guts.

But Hannah was also stubborn. If Gabby wanted to get Wood out of the clink, she could do it alone.

"I'll wait here," she said coolly, drumming her fingers on the steering wheel as she waited...and waited...and waited. Although she tried not to think about the outrageous story Gabby had told her, she kept replaying it over and over in her mind. She switched on the radio, hoping that music would distract her. It didn't.

Finally, Wood and Gabby emerged from the courthouse. Hannah's heart thumped madly in her chest at the sight of her husband. Something warm unfurled inside her, igniting an ember of desire that still smoldered from last night. When he saw her, their eyes met, and he smiled, as if he could read her thoughts.

There was no remorse on his or Gabby's face. In fact, they were both smiling as they walked toward the pickup. Hannah soon learned the reason why.

"It wasn't the forged-document thing at all. He got picked up for driving without a license," Gabby said cheerfully, when Wood flung open the door on the passenger side. She smiled gratefully at him as he gave her a boost up into the truck. "Red sure was surprised to see me. He hadn't even done the paperwork when I walked in. Lucky for us, I was able to convince him to let Wood off with a warning."

"Thanks again, Gabby. I don't know what I'd do without you." Wood gave her arm a gentle squeeze, then pulled the door shut, while Gabby blushed like a young schoolgirl.

Hannah caught a whiff of his aftershave, triggering all sorts of pleasant memories. Flustered, she started up the truck and backed it out of the parking space, ignoring the conversation going on between her aunt and her husband.

When they were halfway home and there still was no

mention of time travel or Madame Duvalee, Hannah as
sumed that Gabby had warned Wood not to bring up the
subject until they were back at the farm. She was right.

As soon as the three of them had their feet back on Davi
soil, it didn't take long for Gabby to discreetly disappear
leaving Hannah and Wood alone. They stood outside i
front of the house, acting like two strangers rather than a
husband and wife who had made passionate love throug
the night.

"We need to talk," he said soberly.

She nodded, swallowing with great difficulty.

"Everything Gabby told you is true. I know it sound
crazy—I still have trouble believing it myself. But, Hannah
one day it was September 9, 1876 and the next day it wa
September 11, 1998." He repeated the same story tha
Gabby had told her on the way to the courthouse. Whe
he had finished and she hadn't responded to any of it, h
asked, "Don't you have anything to say?"

"Yes, I do. Your game's over, Wood or Alfred or what
ever your real name is. You tried to scam us and it didn'
work, or did you forget that you signed the prenuptia
agreement?"

"You think this is some joke I'm playing on you?"

"Yes, and it's a cruel one. You hurt Gabby and whe
Jeremy finds out..."

"He'll understand why I didn't know a thing about bas
ketball," Wood interjected. "Or how to change the channe
on the TV. And why I asked to use the outdoor privy."

The image of him flushing the toilet repeatedly flashe
in Hannah's mind.

"Think about it, Hannah. I didn't understand half c
what you were saying and you saw what my clothes looke
like."

Bits and pieces of memory gave Hannah reason to su
pect that what he said could indeed be true. What if he ha

really come from another century? It would explain so many things...the blank stares, the odd phrases, the total unfamiliarity with anything motorized.

"And how do you explain this time travel?" she asked cynically.

"I can't. I suspect that it could have been lightning, since I saw a flash before it happened, and Jeremy tells me lightning hit that tree in the Nelson forty."

She dropped down onto the porch steps, uncertainty weakening her muscles. "Was that why you didn't want to come in from the storm? You wanted the lightning to take you back?"

He nodded grimly.

"And that's why you were so interested in history, isn't it?"

"Yes. I didn't lie when I said I wanted to find my sister."

"But you lied about so many things," she said, disappointment creeping into her voice. "Why did you pretend to be Alfred Dumler? If you had told us right from the start who you were and what had happened, we would have helped you."

"Have you forgotten that you tied me to the bed that first night I was here, even when you thought I was your invited guest?"

"Because you had marks on your neck and wrists—" she stopped suddenly. "Oh my God. Those were from a rope, weren't they? You said you had run into the wrong kind of folks." Fear widened her eyes. "Did someone try to hang you?"

She shuddered as the cold autumn wind sent a chill down her spine.

"You're cold." He took off his jacket and tried to slip it around her shoulders, but she shrugged away from him.

"I don't need your warmth."

"That's not what you said last night," he reminded her

And that, she acknowledged, was the problem. Last nigh' she had fallen in love with Wood Harris, and this mornin, she had discovered that it was all based on a lie. "I wan to pretend last night never happened." She buried her face in her hands.

"Don't say that." He sat down beside her and gently pulled her hands away from her face. "Hannah, look a me." When she lifted her chin and met his gaze he said "Last night did happen, and we both wanted it to happen I love you and I'm sorry I didn't tell you the truth. I wa going to last night, but I never expected we'd spend the entire night making love." He gave her a tiny smile tha still had the power to ignite the flame of desire in her.

She quickly looked away and jumped to her feet. "I should have never happened. You're a...a..." she traile off at a loss for words.

"Go on tell me, Hannah. What am I?" He, too, got t his feet. When she didn't answer he said, "A murderer? I that what you wanted to say?"

She didn't deny it. She couldn't because at this point sh honestly didn't know who Wood Harris was. "Why didn' you tell me the truth?" she asked shakily.

"Because you already thought I was crazy, and I coul imagine your reaction had I said, 'Oh, by the way, I trav eled across time from 1876 where a group of vigilante tried to hang me for two murders I didn't commit.'"

She gasped and shrank back from him.

"I would be dead right now if the time travel hadn' occurred." He reached inside his pocket and pulled out th newspaper clipping. "You might as well know the whol truth."

Hannah read every word of the article. She didn't war to believe any of it, yet she found herself asking, "Did yo kill George and Mary Nelson?"

He looked as if she had punched him in the stomach. "If you need to ask me that question, then last night must have been a mistake."

She clutched her arms to her waist. "What am I supposed to think? Since the day you arrived you've done nothing but lie to me."

"Last night was no lie on my part."

Hannah squeezed her eyes shut, not wanting to remember how good it had felt to be in his arms. "It only happened because we drank too much champagne."

"Then I believe I'm not the only one who was lied to," he said sadly, and started to walk away.

Hannah felt like one of the stalks of corn that had been mowed down by the combine. Only hours ago she had been on top of the world, ready to embrace a future filled with promise. Now she felt lied to and betrayed by a man she had thought she could trust. It made her angry, and the more she thought about it the angrier she became.

"Where are you going?" she called out to him as he climbed the steps of the house.

He paused and turned around. "Do you care?"

Hannah wanted to say yes. Every instinct inside her begged her to not let him walk out of her life, yet her pride stood in the way like a big old ugly weed, strangling her vocal chords.

"No."

"I didn't think so," he said quietly, then disappeared inside.

WOOD WAS IN THE LOFT packing up his few belongings when Gabby appeared, twisting her handkerchief as she entered the room.

"You're not leaving?"

He could hear the distress in her voice, and it tugged on

him emotionally. The last thing he wanted to do was hurt the woman who had been so kind to him.

"I have to go, Gabby. Hannah doesn't want me here." As difficult as it was, Wood knew it had to be said.

"That's not true, Wood. You know Hannah. She's as stubborn as they come, and her pride's hurt right now. But she'll get over it. She just needs a little time," Gabby assured him with her usual optimism.

Wood sighed. "I wish I could believe you, Gabby."

"Where will you go?"

"I'm not sure."

"You don't want to try to go back to 1876?"

"I'd be lying if I said I hadn't thought about it. If only I knew how to do it." He sighed. "Just before the lightning struck, there was this old woman who tied a pouch around my waist and poured sand in my hands. At first I thought it was the sand that might have sent me forward in time, but now I'm wondering if it wasn't something in that pouch. All I remember is that it had a terrible odor."

Gabby snapped her fingers. "I have something you may find of interest. Come with me."

She led Wood to her small library where bookshelves lined every wall. "By now you probably know this is where I spend most of my time." She motioned for him to sit down on the love seat. Then she pulled down a section of board that turned one of the bookcases into a writing desk.

She held up a thin journal bound in cloth. "Ah! Here it is."

She scooted in beside Wood, opening the pages of the book with extreme caution. "Remember when Jeremy was working on his family tree? Well, something I read back then came to mind today when you were talking about that pouch."

As if she were handling broken glass, Gabby carefully turned the fragile pages until she found what she was looking for. "Look, the date is smudged, but I'm pretty sure it says September 1876."

Wood examined the blurred handwriting and agreed.

"Shall I read it to you?" she asked.

"Please do."

She cleared her voice, then began. "They call me vile because I am different. Yes, I'm different. I know how to mix my herbs to do things people don't want to believe I can do, but today I was able to save a man from dying. I circled him with herbs."

An eerie sensation crept over Wood. "You think she was the old crone who ministered to me at the hanging?"

"They say she had mystical powers," Gabby said in a hushed tone, as if speaking too loudly might disturb the spirit of her deceased relative. "No one in the family talked about her very much. The story is that after her husband died, she was never the same up here." She raised a finger to her forehead.

Wood was not one to discount the possibility that a Davis had saved his life more than once. "If only I had that pouch," he said wistfully.

"But you don't have it, do you?"

He shook his head. "No. It must have fallen off during the time travel, but that doesn't mean it isn't here in 1998. It could be in the Nelson forty."

"And if you can't find it?"

He shrugged. "Then I stay in 1998 until fate decides otherwise. I still have to leave the farm, Gabby."

"Please don't go, Wood," she begged.

Wood pulled her frail body close to his and hugged her. "I'm going to miss you. Thank you for being such a sweet, caring lady."

"Can't you give Hannah a few days? I know she'll come around," Gabby asked, dabbing at the moisture in her eyes.

It was a tempting thought, but the harsh words that had

been said that morning had him saying, ''I'm sorry, Gabby, but Hannah's better off without me.''

THAT AFTERNOON storm clouds rolled in, darkening an already gray sky. Hannah thought it was appropriate. Her life was as unsettled as the atmosphere. Ever since her confrontation with Wood, she had fought the urge to go find him and tell him she was wrong. She did care where he went.

When thunder rumbled in the distance, Jeremy came running inside. ''I saw lightning.''

''Tell Gabby to make sure the windows are closed upstairs.''

Jeremy nodded and ran up the steps. It wasn't long before he bounced back down. ''Where's Wood?''

Hannah shrugged. ''You don't need to worry about Wood. He's an adult man who can take care of himself.''

''But he shouldn't be out in a storm. What if he gets zapped back?''

Suddenly Hannah remembered Wood telling her that he suspected lightning had been the vehicle that had taken him through time. It was the reason he had refused to come in from the storm that day he had been zapped by the fence.

''If he had been hit by lightning, wouldn't he be dead?'' Hannah asked, an uneasy feeling starting to claw at her stomach.

Jeremy shrugged. ''Wood says all he can remember is that he saw a bolt of lightning, then a bright light flashed in his eyes. It was so bright he thought he was dead—until he woke up in our cornfield.''

''That doesn't mean it struck him.''

''But I found him by that old oak that was split in two.''

Hannah mulled over Jeremy's words. Could Wood have been hit by lightning? It might explain why he had been knocked to the ground the day he touched the electric fence. Normally, contact with the fence resulted in a shock that had a person shuddering, yet with him, it had been much worse.

Just then Gabby came down the stairs.

"Do you know where Wood is?" Hannah asked, her uneasiness growing.

"He left. Told me he was going to the Nelson forty."

Before Gabby could say another word, Hannah had grabbed her rain jacket and was out the back door. "Hannah, wait!" Gabby called out, but she paid no attention.

She hopped in the pickup and jammed her keys into the ignition. "He wouldn't do such a crazy thing," she told herself. But what frightened her most of all was that she knew he would.

She headed for the Nelson forty, the rain coming down in blinding sheets, creating rivers of muddy water on the dirt road, forcing Hannah to reduce her speed. As the windshield wipers struggled to keep up with the driving rain, she talked to herself.

"Come on, help me get there. I have to get to him before it's too late."

As a bolt of lightning streaked across the clouds, Hannah's heart nearly stopped. "How could I have been so stupid!" she screamed aloud in frustration as the storm increased in intensity.

For Hannah knew she had been stupid. She loved Wood, and in her heart she knew he was not a man who could commit murder, yet she had accused him of just that. She had said so many things she wished she could now retract. Because she had been hurt. Hurt that he hadn't had the faith in her to tell her the truth from the start. And hurt that he had confided in Gabby, yet she, his wife, was the last to know.

Again thunder roared and Hannah cried out, "Oh, please, don't let him be gone! I can't lose him, not now."

By the time she reached the uncultivated field, she couldn't tell whether it was teardrops or rain falling on her cheeks. "Wood!" she called out repeatedly, running frantically toward the splintered oak.

And then she saw him—standing beneath an elm tree. He wasn't dead, and he was still here, on her farm. Relief sent the adrenaline rushing through her and she ran toward him. Within seconds a bright flash of lightning exploded before her. In an instant he had disappeared. "Wood, don't leave me!" she screamed in frustration.

Just as quickly a sharp crack warned her of danger. She looked up as the wind snapped a limb from what remained of the dead tree. Before she could react, the branch flew against Hannah's head. The last word she uttered as she was knocked to the ground was "Wood."

"Wood?" Hannah glanced down at her left hand. The gold band was still on her ring finger. It hadn't been a dream. "Oh, Wood," she whispered in longing.

"Do I hear sounds of life?"

A nurse with a stethoscope dangling around her neck and a blood pressure gauge in her hand entered the room.

"My head…" Hannah murmured, grimacing as she tried to move.

"Hurts pretty bad, eh?"

"I don't think I can get up."

"You're not supposed to. You've got a pretty nasty cut as well as a concussion."

"What happened?"

"I believe you got caught in the rain last night. Tree limb fell on your head. It doesn't surprise me. That was one nasty storm. The power was out in most of Filmore County." She set the blood pressure gauge down and reached for the medical chart at the foot of the bed. "Don't you remember the accident?"

Just like a photograph, the memory flashed in her mind. She closed her eyes, wanting to blot out the sight of Wood standing beneath the tree while the lightning flashed around him. In one brief flash of light she had lost him forever.

Tears streamed down her cheeks at the realization that he was gone. Forever. And she hadn't told him that she loved him, that she wanted him to be her husband. Forever. Only now that would never happen.

"There, now. It's not so bad. In a few days you'll be up and about again," the nurse said consolingly, patting her hand. "I do believe your family's in the waiting room. Been there all night is what I heard. They're worried about you. Would you like me to get them for you?"

Hannah mumbled something the nurse understood as consent.

A few minutes later, in marched Gabby and Jeremy, their faces lined with worry.

"Mom, are you all right?" Jeremy asked softly.

"You gave us quite a scare when you didn't wake up right away," Gabby added, her voice faltering. "You've been unconscious for almost a whole day."

Hannah reached out to take each of their hands and give them a squeeze. "My head hurts something awful, but I'm okay."

"You were lucky, Mom. You could have got hurt really bad."

"It was that tree I warned you about, Jeremy. I should have known better than to go near it."

"You mean the one that got Wood?" he asked.

So it was true. He was really gone. Again Hannah began to cry, this time sobbing so hard that the nurse asked Jeremy and Gabby to leave, saying in a quiet voice, "She needs a sedative for the pain."

HANNAH DIDN'T KNOW what pain medication she was given, but whatever it was, it produced the most wonderful dreams. Wood was at her bedside, holding her hand, kissing her knuckles and saying all sorts of sweet things. Like how she made his life complete. And how he would never ever leave her again.

"Time for dinner. We let you sleep through lunch, but you're going to have to eat this."

Hannah awoke to find a different nurse standing beside her, a tray of food in her hands.

"You must have been having a nice dream. You've been smiling ever since I entered the room," she said to Hannah as she set her tray down.

"Hmm. It was nice," Hannah said wistfully. "There was this man—" She stopped, afraid that she'd start to cry if she tried to talk about Wood.

"Did he have dark hair and brown eyes?"

"Umm-hmm."

"Good-looking?"

"Umm-hmm."

The nurse chuckled. "That was no dream. He's been here all day. I think he just went for a cup of coffee. Should I check?"

Hannah's heartbeat raced and her mouth went dry. The nurse slipped out the door. The next time it opened, Wood came through. In his hands was a small bunch of flowers.

"I've been waiting for you to wake up so I could bring you these." He walked over to the bed and sat down beside her.

"It wasn't a dream. You were really here." She reached out to touch his arm.

"Still am, if you want me." He smiled and stared at her with those gorgeous brown eyes that had the power to scramble her insides.

"I do want you," she said, a tear trickling down her cheek.

He wiped it away with his thumb. "Is that why you did something so foolish as to come looking for me in a lightning storm?"

"I had to stop you from getting killed," she said, a tiny hiccup accenting the word killed. "I've seen what you do in storms."

"I didn't go out to the Nelson forty in hopes of getting struck by lightning and carried back to 1876."

"But Gabby said..."

"That I had gone to the Nelson forty, and I had. To look for a pouch." He explained about the old crone who had comforted him right before the hanging, and how he and Gabby suspected Gabrielle Davis may have saved his life with her herbs. "I suppose we'll never know for sure if it was truly the herbs or the lightning. Actually it was Outlaw who found the pouch out at the Nelson forty, and I buried it. Then I cut down that monster of a tree that caused all of the problems."

"You don't want to go back to 1876?"

"Not when I have a beautiful wife who needs me." He put a finger beneath her chin. "Or was that the pain medication talking?"

Gingerly she wrapped her arms around him and kissed him. "I do need you and that scares me. It's part of the reason I said all those awful things to you. Plus I was being a bit stubborn," she admitted with a wry grin.

"Just a bit." He gave her another quick kiss. "You had a right to be hurt, Hannah. If I had been completely honest with you from the start, none of this would have happened."

She placed a fingertip to his lips. "Let's not talk about the past. I'd much rather discuss the future. Our future."

The last thing she saw before he kissed her were those dark brown eyes looking at her with a promise of love.

Epilogue

"What are these?" Hannah asked when she stepped into the kitchen and saw several brightly wrapped packages on the table.

"Your birthday presents," Jeremy answered.

"That tree limb took you out of here before we had a chance to celebrate." Wood led her over to the table.

"It's a good thing you didn't tell me these were waiting for me. Otherwise they never would have been able to keep me in that hospital as long as they did," she teased.

Not only were there presents, but cake and ice cream, too. It wasn't long before the doorbell rang. Hannah didn't miss the looks that passed between Gabby, Wood and Jeremy.

"Now I wonder who that could be? Another surprise?" Hannah inquired with a twinkle in her eye.

"You'd better get it, Mom," Jeremy advised, which only added to her suspicion that it was a floral delivery.

Only the man at the back door didn't have any flowers in his hands. "Can I help you?" Hannah asked the middle-aged man wearing a light blue leisure suit.

"I'm looking for Hannah."

Hannah smiled. "You found her. Come on in," she said with a curious glance toward the people seated at the table.

"He doesn't have any roses," Gabby whispered to Wood who shrugged his shoulders.

"What can I do for you, Mr—?" Hannah asked.

"Dumler. I'm Alfred, your mail-order groom."

There were four simultaneous gasps.

"You have a nice place here," Mr. Dumler said to Hannah, unaware of the effect his presence had on the people in the kitchen.

"I appreciate that you have good taste, Mr. Dumler, but I might as well tell you, I didn't place that ad in the magazine." Hannah pointed to her aunt. "She did."

"Does that mean you're not going to marry me?" he asked, in a voice that was as dull as the shineless shoes he wore.

Hannah walked over to Wood and planted a kiss on his mouth, then she turned to Alfred Dumler and said, "You're too late, Mr. Dumler. I've already found me a mail-order groom and I'm not sending him back."

The spring 1998 forecast calls for...

April 1998: **HERE COMES THE...BABY**
Pam McCutcheon
A front of morning sickness sets in with
temperatures rising at the onset of a sexy secret
dad. Highs: Too hot!

May 1998: **A BACHELOR FALLS**
Karen Toller Whittenburg
Heavy gusts of romance continue as a warming
trend turns friends to lovers just in time for one
friend's wedding...to someone else!

June 1998: **BRIDE TO BE...OR NOT
TO BE?** Debbi Rawlins
Expect a heat wave as the handsome hunk
building a bride's dream house sends soaring
temperatures through her fantasies.

Available wherever Harlequin books are sold.

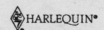

Take 4 bestselling love stories FREE

Plus get a FREE surprise gift!

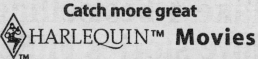

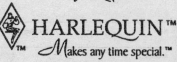

Welcome to *Love Inspired*™

A brand-new series of contemporary inspirational love stories.

Join men and women as they learn valuable lessons about facing the challenges of today's world and about life, love and faith.

Look for the following March 1998 Love Inspired™ titles:

CHILD OF HER HEART
by Irene Brand

A FATHER'S LOVE
by Cheryl Wolverton

WITH BABY IN MIND
by Arlene James

Available in retail outlets in February 1998.

LIFT YOUR SPIRITS AND GLADDEN YOUR HEART
with *Love Inspired!*™

Steeple
Hill™

LI398